The  Fall

Phillip Strang

BOOKS BY PHILLIP STRANG

Copyright Page

Dedication

For Elli and Tais who both had the perseverance to make me sit down and write.

Chapter 1

Angus Simmons, the host of a popular television programme, a house in Chelsea, a beautiful girlfriend and an expensive car in the garage, had it made – up until the moment he fell.

He had been thirty-nine years of age, a wiry physique in his teens, a natural athlete, graced with an irrepressible need for adventure and challenge, the ultimate belief in self.

At the age of eighteen, he had climbed the three tallest buildings in London, the first two with ropes and a partner, the third, and more difficult, solo and with no safety gear. His exploits had shot him to national attention.

Seven years later, he had made the first of three ascents of Mount Everest, and he was regarded as one of the leading mountaineers of his generation. On the last climb, six years after the first and leading a group of climbers, one had died of asphyxia, and another had fallen to his death on the descent back to Camp Four. Simmons was emotionally upset at the tragic waste of good men's lives. A subsequent inquiry exonerated him.

Detective Chief Inspector Isaac Cook had seen death before, but not a body that had fallen over eight hundred feet, hitting the building as it plummeted, before finally impacting on the roof of a parked truck.

Usually unemotional, he had to admit to surprise at seeing the man dead on the truck.

'And you were filming this?' Isaac Cook asked a film crew that stood to one side, separated from the body by crime scene tape and a couple of uniforms.

'We had permission,' an upset woman said.

'Tricia Warburton?'

'I was Angus's co-host,' the attractive and on-screen ebullient co-host of the weekly programme that showed obscure and unusual news stories from around the world, said.

'Permission from who?' Isaac asked. 'Climbing the Shard, London's tallest building isn't usually allowed, sensitive about the bad publicity when some fool falls off.'

'Not my area.'

'I assume you took advice, informed your legal team?'

'I followed procedure, not that it matters now, does it? Angus is dead.'

The woman was right, Isaac knew. The reason for the man being there, for his climb, and the situation's stupidity weren't important. It was that there was a suspicion as to why he fell.

Isaac could only imagine the panic at the television station: the fire-fighting, the pointing of fingers, a scapegoat to find.

'A friend of yours, Angus?' Isaac asked. 'Were you close?'

'My co-host, I've already told you that. We got on well enough, but we weren't dating, not lovers if that's what you're implying.'

'The truth's best in situations such as this,' Isaac said. He wasn't going to push the point.

'He fell, killed himself. Why ask these questions now?'

'For one good reason, and regardless of the stupidity of you and your television station's stunt, he didn't fall through losing his grip.'

'Then how?'

'Someone took a shot at him. Anyone you might know, enemies of his?'

Isaac felt that he was hard on the woman, but it was the early stage of an investigation, and quick action was essential. The person most likely to know some of the innermost secrets that everyone carries, and the dynamics of the programme that she had co-hosted was Tricia Warburton.

'Are you saying he was murdered?'

'Yes, elegant in its execution.'

'Elegant? That sounds as if you admire the person who did this,' Tricia said.

'Not admire, but it's original, and all because of a stunt. Good for ratings, was it?'

'It would have been. It was Angus's idea. The man was fearless.'

'And dead,' Isaac added. 'Whoever took the shot knew when he intended to climb.'

'Before I became a television presenter, I studied nursing. I didn't see a gunshot wound on the body.'

'You saw it?'

'What I could. Isn't it instinctive to check if the person's alive? Besides, it was surreal; none of us could comprehend what we had seen happen.'

Isaac had to concede the woman the point. In its immediacy, just after it has occurred, death often has an unexpected effect on people.

Out on the street, the crowds restrained by uniformed police officers, people staring out of office block windows, cameras with zoom lenses attempting to get a better view. After all, the death of Angus Simmons, the conqueror of Everest, the adventurer and generally acknowledged good guy, was big news.

'Considering the condition of the body, I wouldn't expect a gunshot to be visible. Simmons, a friend of yours?'

'An honest answer?' Tricia Warburton said.

'It's always the best,' Isaac said, 'and besides, the truth always comes out eventually.'

'The station intends, or they did, to get rid of either Angus or me. Another cost-cutting exercise; happens every few weeks. Not that it'll hit the back pockets of those in charge, a bunch of hypocritical money-grabbing bastards. Pardon my language, but that's how I see them.'

'Did Angus?'

'What do you think this stunt was about?'

'Simmons was making sure that it was you who received the literal kick up the arse out of the door.'

'Not that I can blame him, and if I could have climbed that damn building, I would have, but I'm just here as eye candy.'

'Did you hate Angus for what he was?'

'No, why should I? He was a decent enough man, never tried it on with me, not like those bastards who intend to kick me out. Besides, I don't need to. Angus and I were talking about forming our own production company, plenty of ideas. He was good at the stunts, a natural showman, and I'm good at logistics, putting the people in place, dealing with the finances, sweet-talking those who want to invest in two highly marketable commodities.'

'You and Angus, involved?'

Isaac's initial impressions of Tricia Warburton hadn't been favourable, but he found her astute as he spoke to her.

'Angus didn't fancy me, nor I, him.'

'I thought he was a man about town, squiring women, living with a model.'

'He was my friend, I'll admit to that, but I'm a one-man woman, not a floozy, and besides, behind the macho-man exterior, the women, the model as you say, Angus Simmons wasn't a lothario, quite the contrary.'

'Gay?'

'Bisexual. He concealed it well, probably didn't do anything about it, not good for the image.'

'Tormented?'

'We'd talk about it. He knew I was not available, not that he wanted me, felt comfortable in my confidence.'

'You're telling me now.'

'What else can I do, and besides, you said it yourself, the truth always comes out, and if he was gay or bisexual or asexual, pink or green, what does it matter? It's a liberated world, be what you want, do what you want, and what I want is for you to find out who killed him.'

'His death to be avenged?'

'Something like that.'

Isaac cast a glance over to the crime scene, saw his team and Gordon Windsor, the senior crime scene investigator. He needed to talk to them.

'What do you mean?' Isaac asked.

'The world's gone crazy, people killing people for no apparent reason. Angus, no reason to kill him other than his celebrity. I was his co-host; I could be a target.'

'I suggest you take care for the next few days.'

Tricia placed a hand on Isaac's shoulder. 'Take care of yourself as well. Who knows where this will end,' she said.

Tricia Warburton returned to her camera crew and picked up a microphone.

Isaac knew that she wouldn't take the care she should. There was a news story to film.

Chapter 2

Detective Inspector Larry Hill, DCI Isaac Cook's second in charge in Homicide, was standing close to the crime scene investigators. He was forty-five years of age, struggling with his weight, the result of overeating and alcohol, much to the chagrin of his wife.

Sergeant Wendy Gladstone, more years as a police officer than anyone else at the police station, worked through those who had seen Simmons fall. She was aware that some would have enjoyed the ghoulish entertainment, others would be traumatised, and increasingly in recent years, a dedicated group with their smartphones relaying the action to the four corners of the globe.

Isaac walked over to where Gordon Windsor, the senior CSI, was standing.

'Damn fool thing to do,' Windsor said.

Isaac had done foolish things in his youth, such as on a trip to Jamaica when he was sixteen. Jumping off the cliffs in Negril had seemed a good idea. However, he had hit the water at an angle, torn a muscle in his back and spent the last week of the holiday either in bed or taking it easy.

But now, he was older and wiser, a similar age to the dead man, and married to Jenny, as white as he was black, their son at the crawling stage.

'Falling was. Probably would have made it otherwise,' Isaac said.

'Even so, it doesn't alter the fact. The man was endangering public safety, making a spectacle of himself.

And what about her over there?' Windsor said, nodding his head in the direction of Tricia Warburton.

'I'm not sure what to make of her. Either she's putting on a show for the viewing public, or she's an emotional void. She'll need checking, but regardless, she was down at ground level, in clear view, no way she could have taken the shot. She reckoned the bullet hadn't penetrated.'

'She was right, hit him in the back, two vertebrae down from the neck. It could have been a ricochet off the building. If he hadn't been hanging onto the building, but somewhere more sensible, he would have been knocked over by the force, been in pain, but he would have recovered.'

'Can you graduate a bullet's trajectory and speed to ensure minimal damage, enough to cause the man to flinch, loosen his grip?'

'It's possible but seems pointless. I would need more advice before I could comment. Assuming the bullet's speed has reduced, then there's the wind deflecting its trajectory, and as a bullet slows, its straight line is deflected. We'd need the rifle first, get Forensics to conduct tests, but I reckon it was a lucky shot.'

***

Wendy Gladstone was the only one in Homicide at Challis Street Police Station who remembered Isaac as a uniformed police sergeant. Even back then, she had seen a uniqueness in the tall, black police officer, as had others. The London Metropolitan Police, aiming to be racially embracing, tolerant of all colours and creeds, had even featured him in promotions back in the early days. And then there had been his meteoric rise up through the ranks to an inspector and then to chief inspector, only to find his promotion opportunities now stagnating.

Commissioner Alwyn Davies, an unsmiling Welsh man, the head of the august police service, only two years in the position, did not like Chief Superintendent Richard Goddard, Isaac's mentor and senior. By default, Isaac was tarred with the same brush, and if Goddard couldn't progress, neither could he.

Sergeant Wendy Gladstone was unable to advance further due to her approaching retirement age, and Larry Hill, Isaac's detective inspector, was held back due to insufficient academic qualifications and an unwillingness to put in the necessary effort to acquire them.

Isaac had recognised Hill's attributes in a previous investigation, the reason he had brought him into Homicide. Larry Hill was a man-on-the-ground type of police officer, a breed who believed that on the street was where investigations were solved, not behind a computer screen or in an interminable meeting.

It was a view shared by Wendy, and in part, by Isaac. But Isaac had benefited from a university education; he saw that with technology and the dramatic leaps forward in forensics and pathology, crimes could be solved in the sanctity of an office.

Wendy preferred it out on the street, although her aching bones troubled her, not that she would ever complain, knowing that others in the police station were ready to pension her out of the force.

Bridget Halloran, Wendy's friend and Homicide's wizard with a computer, dealt with the department's general running and the ancillary staff.

'Where was the shot taken from?' Isaac asked Larry, who was standing in the street looking up at where the man had fallen from. Isaac, sartorially elegant, a made-to-measure navy suit, a white shirt, a matching tie; Larry, his clothes off the rack, and even though his wife had ironed his shirt that morning, it still had a faraway look, one of the collar points heading into space, his tie askew, the top button of his shirt undone, and his shoes a dull sheen compared to the chief inspector's mirror shine.

Isaac knew that Larry was on a slippery slope that would not end well. His wife, a good woman and loyal, was a social climber, always pressuring her husband to extend the mortgage, to place the children in a more expensive school, whereas he would have preferred a quieter life. He knew that some social climbers, those with aspirations of grandeur and fame, were up to the hilt in debt and that behind closed doors, when the designer clothes and the makeup were off, husbands and wives fought like cats and dogs.

Larry had tried to explain to his wife that a comfortable house, happy children and a loving environment were more critical than depreciating assets and shallow friends. Still, she wasn't having any of it.

'I've got uniforms checking high-rise buildings in the vicinity, looking for where the shot was fired,' Larry said.

'Keep me posted,' Isaac said as he walked over to his sergeant.

'Not a lot,' Wendy said. She had just finished talking to another witness.

'No one saw anything?'

'They saw him climbing, saw him fall, saw the mess on the ground, but no one saw the shot, not that you'd expect them to.'

'It may be best if you talk to the television crew, find out who had a grudge against him: discarded lovers, people who owed him money, others he had shafted.'

'All-round good guy, Angus Simmons?' Wendy said.

'No one's squeaky clean,' Isaac said. 'The man's got hidden depths to him, vices we don't know about. According to his co-host, he wasn't quite the macho man that he appeared to be.'

'If he wasn't, he kept it concealed.'

'It may not be accurate.'

'Tricia Warburton's not all she seems.'

'Observation or a personal opinion?'

'Too confident, full of herself, prick teaser if I was crude,' Wendy said.

Isaac disregarded her comments, aware that his sergeant had strong views, too quickly expressed some times. 'Any proof?' he said.

'Not yet, but she was here, egging the man on. She knows more than she's letting on.'

A commotion on the other side of the road, a woman shouting. Both Isaac and Wendy looked over, acknowledged the uniform who was manning the barrier. Isaac raised his hand, the uniform nodding in return. A woman dressed in a white blouse and a short skirt, wearing stiletto heels, rushed forward.

'Are you in charge?' she said to Isaac.

'I'm the senior investigating officer, that's correct, Detective Chief Inspector Cook. And you are?'

Isaac playing by the book, Wendy knew. Everyone knew who Maddox Timberley was: Page 3 girl, centrefold in most men's magazines, the object of many a young man's lust, many an older one who should have known better.

'Maddox Timberley. It's Angus, isn't it?'

'Did you know he was going to do this?'

'He told me, said it'd be good for the ratings, good publicity for the both of us. He's dead, isn't he?'

'I'm afraid he is,' Isaac said. 'This must come as a shock to you.'

Wendy expected the woman to break down in tears; Isaac didn't. To him, there was a hardness in her, similar to Tricia Warburton.

'It is. Angus, he never puts a foot wrong, done this before, even climbed Mount Everest. Can you believe that?'

'We're aware of his history,' Isaac said. 'How did you find out?'

'It's on the news. Tricia's live on the television.'

Wendy was aware of Maddox and her reputation, only too willing to strip off for a photo if the price was right.

'You don't like her?' Wendy asked.

'Angus did, thought she was alright, fancied her probably.'

'Did you mind?'

'Not much. I've got a flight this evening, the Bahamas, a photo shoot.'

'You'll need to cancel it,' Isaac said.

'I can't. The penalties if I don't go, my reputation.'

'Miss Timberley, Angus Simmons, your boyfriend, the man you were living with, has been murdered. You're a person of interest,' Wendy said.

'Murdered, Angus, no way. Everyone loved him,' Maddox Timberley said, her composure starting to slip, the realisation of the situation. 'He was good to me, never hit me, nothing like that.'

'A lady's man?' Isaac asked.

'Are you inferring he wasn't?'

'His masculinity has been questioned.'

'These comments that he was bisexual or gay, that's all they were. The media always portrays me like a tart, makes up stories, screwing whoever, but the majority's a lie. I grew up in a good Christian family, parents who loved each other, loved their children.'

'Unusual name, Maddox.'

'Freda Sidebottom from Rotherham doesn't sound so good.'

'That's your original name?' Wendy asked.

Maddox's suppressed emotions were released as she spoke of her family and where she had come from. Wendy grabbed the woman as she went weak at the knees, the tears starting to flow, the shock of the reality washing over her.

Isaac cast a glance in Tricia Warburton's direction, saw that her cameraman had his lens trained on them, the woman talking into her microphone. He may have misjudged Maddox Timberley; he still wasn't sure about Tricia Warburton.

Chapter 3

Angus Simmons's sexual proclivities were important, but not as much as where the shot had originated.

'No more painful than a severe bee sting,' the pathologist said at the autopsy, 'enough to cause an instinctive reaction to put a hand on the area, to flick away.'

Enough to cause a lapse of concentration and death, Isaac knew.

Maddox, the deceased's girlfriend, her manner more like Freda Sidebottom than the persona of Maddox Timberley, sat soulfully in the interview room at Challis Street. It was a charmless room; the walls painted beige, the ceiling white. A camera was mounted high in one corner of the room, a metal cage around it, and there was a small table with four chairs, two to each side. The recording equipment controls and a digital clock were secured to the table, the recorder in an adjacent room.

Maddox Timberley, not a suspect presently as her alibi was firm. She had no firearms experience, and even if she had, it would have taken a competent marksman, someone with training, to execute the shot.

'It came as a shock,' Maddox said. She held a cup of coffee in her right hand. To her side, a lawyer, but not needed, not yet, Isaac thought, but then, he had been misled before by a pretty face and an easy manner. He thought back to it: early in his career, a Swedish au pair he was dating at the time who had killed not just one man but several, her behaviour resulting from a troubled childhood and sociopathic tendencies.

'When the cameras were off; when Angus wasn't performing for the camera, what was he like?' Isaac asked.

'He was studious, and the feats that he accomplished, the challenges he accepted or took on, were well thought out. He planned meticulously, never took a chance, and he told me that climbing the Shard wasn't that difficult, only looked so from the ground.'

'And you believed him?'

'I trusted him.'

'Loved him?' Wendy, an incurable romantic, asked, not only for the sugary-sweet sentiment but also to judge the relationship's strength. She knew that her DCI would focus on the reality, but if Maddox Timberley was to be absolved of any collaboration in the death, her feelings towards Angus Simmons were important.

'I was very fond of him.'

'An honest answer,' Wendy said, realising that a gushing, overly-emphasised proclamation of undying love would not have been sincere, not from a person whose history of former lovers was well known.

'We had been together for nearly two years, and Angus wasn't a man to commit, not to me, not to any woman.'

'Why did you stay with him?' Isaac asked.

'Because I could be myself, no need to pretend with Angus, nor he with me.'

'Compatible?'

'A dull, boring couple at home, content to lounge around in our pyjamas, to read a book, to watch a mushy romance on the television.'

'Loving?' Wendy asked.

'If by that you mean that we were at each other like rabbits, the answer is no. I believe I explained that before.'

'You said he was placid,' Isaac reminded Maddox.

'He was always buying me flowers, remembering our anniversaries, the little things that happened in our relationship, but a lover he was not.'

'Did that concern you?'

'When every hot-blooded male over the age of fifteen wanted to jump me, no. I've already told you that in public, I'm Maddox Timberley, but at home with my parents and then with Angus, I was the gap-toothed skinny rake my parents had raised, the person that Angus liked.'

'The gap's gone,' Wendy said.

'I enjoy the limelight, the same as he did. Both of us seduced by fame and fortune, the lifestyle that came with it, and if pouring myself into a skintight dress, too short for decency, is the cost, then so be it. Angus was the same, and climbing buildings when he no longer wanted to was the price he paid.'

'Are you saying he had trepidation?'

'Never with his ability. Climbing buildings was irresponsible, something he did when he was younger and sillier, but not at his age. You see, Angus was socially responsible, more interested in the environment, social discourse, politics eventually.'

'Then why climb?'

'He hadn't wanted to climb that building. Pointless, he said, but the programme's ratings were plummeting and Tricia, she was desperate to hang on to her job. Her job was on the line, and he did it as a favour for her.'

'Does she know this?'

'Maybe, maybe not. You'd have to ask her.'

'Tricia told us there was a plan afoot to get rid of one of the programme's hosts, to run with just the one.

If he had succeeded in bringing the focus onto him, he would have taken the job, not her.'

'Or if the ratings improved, they would have kept the two.'

'And now, the ratings will be through the roof, and there's no contest as to who is to be the host. A motive?' Isaac conjectured.

'Angus intended to leave next year anyway, bigger fish to fry.'

'Another programme?'

'A few more mountains to climb, a book to write, politics if he could get an endorsement. He only did it for Tricia, no one else.'

'Does Tricia know this?'

'It's unlikely. Too dumb to figure it out.'

'Then why do it?'

'That's Angus, loyal to those he respects, those he trusts.'

'Misplaced?'

'No. Angus could see goodness in her. I couldn't, but then, he was a better judge of character than I am.'

'We judge you to be decent,' Wendy said. 'Are we wrong, as dumb as Tricia?'

'Another five or six years, when the surgeons can't maintain my figure or my face, then Maddox Timberley will fade away. And as I wither, possibly write a racy book on life in the fast lane, men I've known, kinks and all.'

'Married to Angus?'

'We had talked about it, but not with him.'

'Why?' Isaac asked.

'I want children, and with Angus, that wasn't possible. He didn't want to be responsible for bringing a child into the world. He felt that the world was in turmoil, and the future was bleak. Not that he was morbid about it, saw himself as a realist. Even if I could have talked him around, it wasn't my right to do.'

***

At the murder scene, the usual traffic flow had resumed, the only signs the crime scene tape, a couple of uniforms and no parking down the side of the street where Simmons had fallen.

Gordon Windsor's report showed where Angus Simmons had lost his grip, the chalk marks with his fingerprints visible, smudged when the bullet had struck. And as one of those who had ascended the building commented afterwards, apart from the spectacle of someone climbing free, it was not as dangerous as it looked.

Two days had passed since the incident. Two days of conjecture, discussion, meetings with Maddox and Tricia and the production crew, attending the autopsy, ensuring the next of kin were informed: a mother in Scotland, a father in London, neither of whom had been surprised at their son's death.

'He was always going to die young,' Angus's mother said. 'As a child, climbing a tree or scurrying around. Even in the middle of winter, swimming in the loch, getting a cold, the flu, pneumonia once. We nearly lost him that time.'

'How old was he?' Wendy asked the woman on Zoom, a video call without the need to travel.

'Pneumonia, ten years of age.'

Thankfully, Wendy hadn't had to inform the woman of her son's death; a police inspector, close to where she lived, had been assigned the job. The mother, an avid reader with no interest in television and only a small radio in her cottage, hadn't received the news from the media.

She had taken it well, stoically, according to DI Cameron.

And now, on the video conference, Angus's mother sat upright, looked straight into her iPhone. She spoke with a Scottish accent.

'When was the last time you saw him?' Wendy asked.

'Three months ago. He was up here for a week, his usual self.'

'Swimming in the loch?'

'Every day. Angus never failed to challenge himself, always one accident or another. It was always a broken leg, a broken arm, a twisted ankle, and then he fell while climbing once, an outcrop not far from here. He fell twenty feet, landed in a swampy marsh, in hospital for a couple of weeks.'

'Schooling?'

'He never had much time for it, not that he was dumb, far from it, but it bored him. He was a difficult child, unlike me, unlike his father.'

'His father?'

'A decent man, more suited to the city than me. We met at university, lived together for a few years, and then when Angus was on the way, we got married, did the right thing by the child, attempted to make a go of a flagging relationship, more for Angus than us. I took Angus, went back to the house I had grown up in as a child, and we lived there. I still do, even after Angus took off.'

'Took off? Were you in agreement?'

'Angus had things to do. I was exceptionally proud of what he achieved, but he was a star that shone too bright. His death, tragic as it is, was not unexpected.'

'He didn't fall of his own accord,' Wendy said.

'Angus upsets people.'

'How and why?'

'I don't mean maliciously, but he created envy and jealously. People were intimidated by his optimism, his willingness to tackle challenges that others deemed impossible. People lost face because of him, and Mike Hampton ended up blaming him for what happened in South America.'

'I've heard of the name,' Wendy said.

'Not that I give it much credence, but Hampton hated Angus because of what had happened.'

'Enough for Hampton to take revenge?'

'I wouldn't know.'

'When was this?'

'I suggest you talk to Mike Hampton. I only know Angus's version, even though he thought he was blameless for what had happened.'

'Were they friends?'

'Angus never had many friends; Mike would have been his only one. A loner even as a child, not with his face in a book or staying in the house, but out on the moors, sometimes disappearing for days on end.'

'You worried?'

'Yes, dreadfully, but that was Angus, and then after a few days, there he would be sitting down at the kitchen table, cleaning a rabbit that he'd caught, expecting me to put it in the oven for him.'

'Which you did.'

'I was resigned to Angus's fate. I knew that one day he wouldn't come home, and now, he hasn't. My anguish and sorrow are behind me; emotions deadened by his lifestyle.'

'Yet, you loved him as only a mother could.'

'He was a remarkable child and an even more remarkable adult, and I hoped that one day he would stop, but I never expected it.'

'Maddox Timberley?' Wendy asked.

'She came up here with him once. I liked her, and so did Angus, thought that he might be settling down.'

'She has a reputation.'

'So had Angus, but he was a quiet boy, kept to himself, never troubled anyone, other than his poor mother who worried about him. Maddox was fine by me, never judge a book by its cover, and up here, two weeks she spent about six months ago, she fitted right in, took off the high heels and the makeup, helped me around the house, even cleaned a rabbit for him. He liked her a lot.'

'Love?'

'Not Angus, not as you'd understand. He was solitary, not emotional, no hugs and kisses for his mother.'

'We're told that his libido wasn't high.' Wendy wasn't sure how to phrase the question to the mother.

'It wasn't a passionate romance. Angus preferred physical challenges, and Maddox, away from the spotlight, wore a pair of old jeans and a torn shirt. Good family values, that was Maddox, not like what we had shown Angus. His father's a decent man, bit of a bastard though, can't keep his hands where they should be.'

'Women?'

'Meet with him, judge for yourself. Maddox never met him; Angus wouldn't have risked it.'

'He would have made a play?'

'Not his father, but he would have been looking. That's why I brought Angus up here, away from him. Needn't have worried though; Angus was never going to be like his father.'

Chapter 4

A construction worker found the site where the shot had been taken. Larry Hill was out at the scene within the hour, the twenty-first floor of a new residential high-rise construction.

'Blows up here sometimes,' the foreman, a tall, well-built man with a Liverpudlian accent, said.

With no windows, the wind howled through, safety barriers in place to prevent a mishap; sufficient according to the site foreman and its safety officer, not enough for Larry.

'The day of the murder?' Larry asked.

'Not sure we'd know. We had an industrial dispute, the place locked up tight.'

'Security?'

'Hardly. They don't like to waste money, and besides, what's to steal? Concrete and rebar, not something you can put in a backpack, sell down the pub.'

'If the place is shut up tight, how did the shooter get up here?'

'If it were us, we'd climb the stairs or use the construction elevator.'

'He wasn't you, and the elevator wouldn't have been working.'

'Then, if he wasn't hiding up here from the day before, and that's unlikely, not many places to hide and it's perishing cold at night, he came up the stairs.'

'Twenty-one floors?'

'We do it on most days.'

'I wouldn't,' Larry said, although the construction elevator attached to the side of the building had been dusty and hesitant, and it had groaned as it rose from the ground below.

'Too many cooked breakfasts from what I can see, Inspector. You'd have a heart attack before the tenth floor.'

Usually, Larry knew, people were careful in what they said to a police officer, a degree of respect for the law, an unwillingness to tempt providence, leave themselves open to suspicion, even if they hadn't done anything wrong. However, men who had hard physical jobs acquired a toughness and took no such care. These were beer-swilling men, men who swore profusely, shouted at each other, fought on occasion.

Larry, still not used to the exposed surroundings, leant up against a concrete wall.

'You're right,' Larry said. 'Fond of a beer as well.'

'Spend a day with us. We'll soon get the flab off you. Stuff that dieting nonsense.'

'I might take you up on that,' Larry said, knowing that he wouldn't. He was a sedentary man, the energy slowly draining from his body, yet up high, away from the pollution down below, the cold, biting air entering his lungs, he had to admit to feeling better.

"He would have had to be fit,' Larry said.

'It depends how long he was here before he took the shot,' the foreman said. 'He would have been exhausted, and even us, we're puffing if we walk up, okay after a couple of minutes, but you…'

'A heart attack,' Larry interjected.

'Almost. Army training, I know about weapons,' the foreman said as he looked at the rifle mount that had been left behind.

To the rear of the men, the sound of an approaching elevator, the crime scene investigators arriving, the site closed for the day.

Kitted up, the CSIs went to work, a further safety barrier installed by the site foreman at Gordon Windsor's request.

Time was of the essence as the weather was inclement, storm clouds rolling in. It was sheer luck that only two days had passed since someone had lain on the dusty concrete floor and taken the shot, the site protected from the harshest winds by a small rise from the floor, the base of an expansive yet so far open window, the glass not installed. However, the rain would soak the immediate area, making investigation difficult.

'Not sure we'll gain too much here,' Windsor said. 'A clear sign that whoever it was used gloves, and judging by the mount, he knew what he was doing.'

'Professional?' Larry asked.

'Competent,' the reply. 'Either an enthusiastic sports shooter or ex-military.'

'Not ex-military,' the foreman said.

'How can you be sure?' Windsor asked.

'Did my bit for Queen and country, served overseas, saw action.'

'Admirable,' Windsor said. 'Why not military?'

'One floor down, there's glass in some of the window frames, less wind turbulence, a better place for a sniper.'

'Yet, the shot was successful,' Larry said.

'But where, on the shoulder?'

'The upper body.'

'It's a difficult shot; the best position was down below. At least, the shot would have been fired from a more stable position, increase the percentage of success,

25

and if you want to distract someone, don't go for the shoulder, go for the lower back. Simmons was an experienced climber; he must have encountered birds flying out from a crevice in a rock, put his hand on a spider, even a snake. Nerves of steel, balls the size of an elephant, that man.'

'You admired him?'

'Who didn't?'

The foreman was right on two counts, Larry realised. Angus Simmons was a person universally admired, someone who would not easily be distracted by a bullet slamming into him, or in this instance, impacting his upper body. His focus on the climb, the same as someone in the middle of a battle, not registering an injury, continuing to fight.

'Was it murder?'

'Murder as a result of a criminal act, taking a shot at Simmons.'

'I was trained that if I took the shot, the target was taken down, not winged. You don't leave it to chance.'

'Nothing much to be gained from here,' Windsor said. 'From what we can tell, a man of medium height, size nine boots. Forensics will conduct tests, see if they can give you more, but I doubt it. Still, we'll be here for the rest of the day, try and trace the boots back down the stairs, and you can get Bridget Halloran to check CCTV cameras in the area, see if you can pick up the person, but that's a long shot, busy on the street.'

***

Charles Simmons, Angus's father, was dressed in a suit when Isaac and Wendy visited him at his home. An imperious-looking man, Wendy instinctively didn't warm to him. However, as the senior investigating officer, Isaac chose not to form impressions of a person until their actions and what they said allowed it.

'Angus was always headstrong, individualistic, not given to discipline or following the consensus,' Charles Simmons said. 'You've spoken to his mother?'

'We have. She's said more or less the same,' Isaac said. 'She also expressed an opinion that she wasn't surprised at his untimely death.'

'I've not seen her for over thirteen years, and we don't agree on much, but she's right. Not that the police should be surprised either. After all, climbing buildings when there's an elevator doesn't make a lot of sense, nor does climbing mountains just because they're there.'

'You sound as if you disapproved,' Wendy said.

'On the contrary. We get one shot at life, no reason to waste it, only to get hit by a bus outside your front door. Too many people are stagnating these days, bleeding the social services, contributing nothing. To hell with the lot of them, a blight on civilised society.'

'Your views are not conventional,' Isaac said.

'Aren't they? The world is in a mess, and it's up to a select few to right it. Too much pussyfooting around, a government committed to pandering to every fringe group, desperate for their vote.'

'Did your views impact your son? Did your wife agree with your stance?'

'My ex-wife would disagree. Granted, she believed it was up to the individual to stand up for themselves, to be counted, make their mark, and not burden society. But, for me, I'm more extreme, a believer in affirmative action.'

'Your son?'

'He was the most balanced and courageous individual a person could be proud to know, and he was my son. I believe that explains my position.'

'And now he's dead, and neither you nor your ex-wife shows the expected emotional response.'

'If that means we're not breaking down in tears, barely able to stand up or to function, then that is a failing of those observing. Our son was stoic, unemotional, impervious to fear or outright demonstrations of affection or hate or loathing.'

'Mr Simmons, do you loathe?'

'I will express my views. This world is going downhill fast, and changes are afoot, an eventual battle for society.'

They were the words of an educated man, Isaac knew, but they were not what the majority would agree with. Charles Simmons was a radical, ready to instigate change if he could, but that was not what was important. The death of his son was.

'Who would have wanted your son dead?' Isaac asked.

'The world is full of malcontents. Try Mike Hampton.'

'Your ex-wife mentioned his name. We've not interviewed him yet.'

'I suggest you do. His hatred of Angus was pathological.'

Simmons took a seat, removed a small flask from inside his jacket and took a sip of what Isaac assumed to be whisky. 'Purely medicinal,' he said.

'Mike Hampton?' Isaac reminded him.

'Hampton's luck changed. The two were climbing in Patagonia, a technically challenging ascent. Hampton fell, broke his back, paralysed from the waist down. He lives in Kent, a small cottage, drafting endless diatribes about mountaineering and whatever else, including how Angus had destroyed his life.'

'Unhinged?'

'Mentally, I'm sure he is. However, you can't blame him in some ways. An active outdoorsman, similar to Angus, and then a vegetable.'

'Not totally,' Wendy said.

'It was to him, would have been to Angus. Angus died doing what he enjoyed best, living life to the fullest. He couldn't have handled incapacitation. Die if you have to, best to do it in full control of your faculties. Go out on a high.'

The reaction of the parents troubled Homicide.

However, despite an apparent lack of sensitivity, both parents were peripheral to the investigation. Mike Hampton was not.

Chapter 5

'I hated the man, glad he's dead.' Mike Hampton, confined to a wheelchair, bearded and ear ringed, was not sparing in his appraisal of the man he blamed for his current condition.

'Your position is clear,' Isaac said, staggered by the intensity of Hampton's venom.

After all, he and Larry had only just met the man, having made the trip down from London to Kent.

'So that you know, I didn't kill him. How could I, stuck in this goddamn chair day and night, barely able to feed myself?'

However, Hampton's misfortune on a mountain in South America was not the pressing issue; it was Simmons's subsequent death.

'We're not accusing you, Mr Hampton,' Isaac said. 'Apart from your dislike of the man, the general opinion is that Angus Simmons was well-liked.'

'Maybe by others, but not me,' Hampton said, grabbing hold of a bottle of water and taking a long drink.

'Your wife?'

'She let you in the door, not that she's here every night, got herself a fancy man.'

'Did your accident render you incapable?'

'That's about the only part of me that works, but she wants to party. She told me the night before we left for South America that she and Simmons were involved. She said it to rile me, to get me to divorce her, but she knows what she'll get.'

'What will that be?' Isaac asked.

'We had a prenup, clear that my money was sacrosanct, and her only entitlement was what she earned, a portion of the increased value of our assets.'

'Mr Hampton, pardon my being blunt, but you don't appear to be financially sound, not enough assets for her to worry about.'

'You can be as blunt as you like. It's not much this place, but it's functional, and Kate thought that once she had her claws into me, I'd indulge her whims, dig into the money I've got invested.'

'Are you saying her marriage to you was mercenary?'

'We had a few good years, and then this,' Hampton said, looking down at his withered legs.

'Her attitude changed?'

'Over time, and before I broke my back, we drifted apart. I can't say that I helped, but what was the point? Angus and me, we were like brothers.'

"You fell. Tell us about it.'

"It was Patagonia, down the bottom of South America. Mountaineers, we're never finished. After you've climbed Everest, the Matterhorn and the Eiger in the Alps, a few more in the Himalayas, then you're challenged to look for more difficult climbs. Patagonia's got plenty of technically challenging climbs, not the highest summits, though. Cerro Torre, part of a four-mountain chain in the Southern Patagonian Ice Field, is not that high but was regarded as the world's most formidable mountain, with constant high winds, a mushroom of rime ice overhanging at the top. Some reckon the ice isn't part of the mountain, so it's not the summit, and they get up to it, claim they've conquered the mountain, but not Angus and me. After all, we had climbed the other three

31

peaks in the chain; we weren't going to accept a compromise.

'I was leading, just below the ice overhead. The wind was intense, the temperature was dropping fast, snow clouds coming in. Only a handful of climbers have made it to the top, but we were determined. Angus slipped, hanging in mid-air, held by a bolt rammed into the mountain during a previous attempt. I'm trying to get down to him; Angus is struggling, his judgement impaired. The bolt weakens, gives way, puts his weight onto me. I can't hold him, not for long. It's up to him; we're compromised, and it's either him or me, but Angus, he claimed afterwards that he was confused, disoriented, made a mistake, but I don't believe it. After dangling for what seemed an eternity, probably no more than twenty seconds, I can't hold on.'

'You could have cut his rope.'

'It's not the movies up there. It's a real life-and-death situation; people don't make magnanimous gestures, dramatic music in the background. I wasn't going to condemn my friend. It was up to him to do what I would have.'

'Would you?'

'I would have, but Angus – all those years of friendship, the trust we had placed in each other when climbing, and his courage failed him. He chose his life over mine.'

'You fell?'

'We both fell, only there was a ledge thirty feet below. He managed to land on fresh snow; it winded him, but he was out of danger, a safe place to descend from.'

'And you?'

'I caught the ledge at an angle. Angus managed to hold on to me, but I couldn't move, in agony, screaming for him to let me go, to plummet to my death.'

'An unusual reaction,' Isaac said.

'The only reaction. I was incapacitated, beyond help. It's a decision that an experienced climber must be prepared to make.'

'What happened?'

'Angus propped me up against a rock overhang, secured me to the mountain with bolts and rope and left me, promising to be back within eight hours.'

'Was he?'

'The weather set in, but he made it back in fifteen. I was stretchered down, then airlifted to a hospital, spent six weeks in traction, then flown back to England.'

'Angus saved your life.'

'It was his life that was forfeit, not mine. He failed us both on that mountain.'

'The mountaineering community?'

'They lauded him for what he had done, but they never knew the truth.'

'You didn't tell them?'

'Regardless of the truth, Angus had condemned me to purgatory. I hate him, always will, but I didn't kill him. I should have on that mountain, but I couldn't have done it, and I certainly couldn't have taken a shot at him.'

***

It seemed to Isaac and Larry as they drove back to London that Hampton's hatred of Angus Simmons was ill-founded. On a mountain, the wind strong enough to blow you off, the temperature well below zero and getting colder, was not the place to undertake a detailed analysis of how a person should or should not behave. And besides, nothing that had occurred hadn't been detailed by Angus Simmons after their return to England. The slipping, the hanging from a rope, the tragic fall and the breaking of Hampton's back – all recorded in detail.

According to Simmons, there had been a tragic set of circumstances, and the decisions made, based on years of climbing together, had been correct. Hampton's blaming Simmons after the accident and making that invective public led to him becoming ostracised by his mountaineering peers.

If Hampton had a jaundiced view on life, it was clear that his wife, Kate, didn't. One day after the visit to her husband. Wendy and Larry sat down with her at a restaurant in Knightsbridge. Larry, always ready for a good meal, ordered a steak, and Wendy, more conscious of the calories, ordered fish, the same as Kate Hampton, an attractive woman in her early forties.

'Mrs Hampton,' Larry said, 'thanks for meeting with us.'

'Please, call me Kate.'

'Kate,' Larry said, 'your husband was a great friend of Angus Simmons.'

'He was. Did he mention about my having an affair with Angus?'

Wendy was taken aback by the woman bringing up the subject, assuming that she and Larry would have to tease around the subject.

'He inferred it,' Larry said. 'It could be that his current situation may cause him to say things that he doesn't believe, a need to get a reaction, to be noticed and listened to.'

'Sympathy, that's what you mean. When we met, a wonderful man, so alive, full of dynamism, optimistic without equal, and then, that accident. It not only destroyed him, but it destroyed me as well.'

'You realise that our interest in your husband and your relationship with him is because of Angus Simmons's death.'

'I do. Mike and I will resolve our issues, although Angus won't. He was a good man; someone, my husband, had loved.'

'Loved?' Wendy said.

'As a brother. Two men able to judge each other's mood, what the other was thinking, an ideal attribute when mountaineering. Mike used to say, "the man's got my back; I've got his". They had great success up until that incident.

'I was against them going; too much in one year. They had climbed K2 in the Himalayas, and then they were off to Patagonia. They were pushing the envelope, too many mountains, too much success. We all need a rude awakening at times to give us a sense of reality, but the two of them, lauded from pillar to post, endorsements for this and that, plenty of money, not that Mike ever needed it.'

'Your husband alluded to that, that he didn't care for money or assets.'

'Angus didn't come from money, not as much as Mike's anyway. Mike's parents in the north of England, successful in business, made sure their son could follow his dreams.'

'We researched it, found that neither he nor Angus used their own money, not if they could, sponsors once that had made their mark, friends in the early days or on a shoestring.'

'You've met Mike, formed an opinion, probably not favourable. Regardless, he never was into showing off,

35

no designer clothes, expensive motor cars, big houses. He could have afforded it all.'

'Embarrassed?'

'Of his wealth, yes. Mountaineering, his great passion, is to do with struggle, forcing the body and the mind to tackle extremes. He didn't want to be a champagne climber.'

'Did Angus know this?'

'He did, not that he ever betrayed Mike's confidence. Mike changed after he came back, and sure, once or twice after he came home, we slept together, but his heart wasn't in it. He had become depressive, too sorry for himself. After that, he and I went our separate ways, led our own lives. It's a pretence, but what can I do?'

'He said you wouldn't leave on account of the money.'

'I don't leave because I'd prefer it to be the way it was, not that he'd believe it.'

'Since you and he stopped sleeping together, what have you done?' Larry asked.

'A person doesn't live by bread alone; I find myself the occasional man, no emotional involvement. Mike knows, I'm sure he does, but what can I do?'

Wendy understood the dilemma: an aura of all-pervading negativity would eventually suck the life out of any in the immediate vicinity.

'Angus, one of these men?'

'Never. I'd meet with him occasionally. Angus was concerned for Mike, always wanted to help, blamed himself for what had happened.'

'I thought no blame was attached to him.'

'None was, but you always wonder after the event. A tragedy had occurred; the instinctive reaction is to look for a reason, to justify it, but Angus had done the right thing. Two men trapped in an impossible situation with no ideal solution, only the reality that someone was likely to be injured or killed. It could easily have been Angus, but it wasn't. I wish Mike would understand, and then he and I could continue as before.'

Chapter 6

The only person who professed genuine hatred of the dead man was Mike Hampton, and he wouldn't have been capable of taking the shot.

As Homicide's senior investigating officer, Isaac Cook surfed the internet, checked out the backgrounds of both men, their climbing exploits, the picture of the two of them on the top of Mount Everest, a Union Jack strung from one to the other. The greatest of friends, men who trusted each other with their lives, cognisant of the risks, able to mentally compartmentalise them, knowing that if there was a problem up high on a mountain, it was about teamwork and self-sacrifice if needed. Yet, Hampton maintained a pathological hatred of Simmons. It concerned Isaac more than it should. To him, there was something amiss in the animosity, a missing piece of the jigsaw, but if there was, did it matter?

Putting Hampton to one side, the team refocussed on Simmons's father. He was a wealthy man, but none of it had been forthcoming to his son.

'I used to see my son from time to time,' Simmons, an eccentricity about him, said. His house, more of a museum than a home, the lights dimmed, the curtains closed, the smell of leather and wood. To one side of the front door, a full set of armour.

'Japanese,' Simmons said. 'I'm a collector, war paraphernalia, weapons, that sort of thing.'

He spoke casually, a throwaway line as if he collected matchboxes or stamps. Isaac, not an expert on ancient weapons of war, knew one thing, reinforced as they entered a room at the rear of the house, two large swords crossed and mounted above the fireplace – that what was in the place was worth millions of pounds.

Another suit of armour in the room, English this time.

'Genuine?' Larry asked.

'Everything in this house is,' Simmons replied. He was impressed by Isaac, tall, black, a proud bearing, elegantly dressed. His reply to Larry was casual and disparaging, not pleased to be questioned by a person who should have recognised quality but didn't.

Another time, Isaac would have gladly spent an afternoon at the house, going from one item to another, quizzing Simmons about where he had obtained each piece, its history, construction method, and its significance.

'Angus met a tragic fate,' Isaac said as he sat down in a plush chair. He thought it to be from the nineteenth century, Napoleon the Third.

'My son was a unique individual, a man who lived life to the fullest. I can't say that I'm pleased he died, but if you challenge yourself, take risks, no doubt alienates people, then sometimes it comes back to bite. My ex-wife, Angus's mother, raised him well. I did what I could, but it wasn't that much, not as much as I would have liked.'

'Why's that?'

'We weren't destined to be together for long. I'm too impatient, irascible, whereas my ex-wife is more easy-going. There's nothing wrong with either, but hardly the requisite for a long and happy marriage, and we didn't want Angus to be the meat in the sandwich. My wife took Angus up to Scotland, gave him the upbringing that he needed. I stayed here, made money, and ensured he had the best education he was willing to accept and all the

39

opportunities he wanted. Neither of us agreed with mollycoddling the boy: too much of that in society these days. What he achieved, he achieved through tenacity, the right attitude. We made a man out of him.'

'He's dead,' Larry said, not as diplomatically as he should.

'If by your tone, you believe that I should show more remorse, Inspector, then you are sadly mistaken. The Simmonses do not show weakness; a proud tradition of military service, stiff upper lip.'

'I'm sure Inspector Hill didn't mean to offend,' Isaac said, 'but this is a murder enquiry. If it had been a climbing accident, we wouldn't be here, nor would we have spoken to your ex-wife, but this is different, one that is proving to be frustrating.'

'I can understand your concern,' Simmons said. 'However, in my defence, life is finite. If life has been abruptly terminated, the reason why is immaterial. He risked his life on many occasions, somehow always came back intact from wherever. Murder or a genuine mishap, the reason is unimportant. It may be for you. It's not to me.'

'Will you mourn him?'

'Behind closed doors, Chief Inspector. Not here with you and your inspector, not in public.'

'Our problem is that we've only found one person who disliked him,' Isaac said.

'Hampton knew the risks. There was no reason to have blamed Angus. It shows a weakness of character on the man's part. Don't consider him a suspect.'

'Due to his disability?'

'Not that it would help, but that's not what I meant. Hampton hasn't enough nerve to do it.'

'You're ex-military?' Larry asked, choosing his words carefully.'

'I am. That's why the interest in historical war memorabilia.'

'An impressive collection,' Isaac said.

'It is. Cost a fortune, but that's not the point.'

'We believe your son had a cavalier approach to money.'

'An admirable trait garnered from his mother, approved of by me. If you do what gives you the greatest satisfaction, then money will never be an issue. This collection that you see. I never considered the cost, only the joy of these items, not caring at the time, but now, worth a fortune, not that I'd ever part with them.'

'Your wealth? This house? Where did it come from?'

'In part, inheritance from my father, and after that, trade.'

'What type of trade?'

'It's not relevant, as you've already said, considering you're here about the death of my son.'

'Possibly not, but we need an angle as to why someone would go to the extreme of killing your son.'

'Are you sure that it's murder? It could have been a warning.'

'A warning about what? Is there something we don't know about? Although it's murder, the intention was obvious.'

'Angus and Hampton's wife, you've been told?'

'Hampton's wife has denied it; her husband believes it to be true.'

'It was. He came here once with her, spent the night upstairs.'

'You knew?'

'It was supposedly a domestic argument, Hampton and his wife, and Angus, the Good Samaritan, was consoling her.'

'More consoling than she needed?'

'He spent the night with her, came down the next day, looked as though he hadn't slept, not much anyway, and she wasn't much better.'

'Was this before or after Hampton fell, broke his back?'

'After, I believe. I can't be sure, and it was only the one time I saw her here.'

'Why here? Why not a hotel or his place?'

'Maybe it was before he fell. Hampton, if he had suspected, might have been looking for his wife. Mike Hampton didn't know about this address. If it was before the man fell, then Angus was pushing his luck.'

'Do you have any ideas on why someone would target Angus?'

'Apart from Hampton, not really, but then again, Angus didn't grow up with me. I was there for him, but we weren't close, and he never took me into his confidence. Surprised he brought the woman back here that night, pleased he did. Showed that he was comfortable with me, not the ogre that he believed.'

'Your wife telling your son tales when he was a child?'

'To some extent, but that was fine. Angus was an exuberant child, hyperactive. Down here in London wasn't conducive to his well-being; in Scotland with his mother was. He grew out of the hyper stage, but still exuberant, pushing the envelope. If it hadn't been mountaineering, it would have been something else, possibly criminal, probably stupid.'

'Does crime run in the family?'

'It depends what your political leanings are. There's an ancestor, picked the wrong side during the English Civil War in the seventeenth century, sided with the Royalists, lost his head for that error of judgement.'

'You would have chosen the other side?'

'I doubt it, although I would have been more careful. If you're losing, you sue for peace or make a strategic withdrawal. Standing up in the main square professing your devotion to the king and his successors is not the most discreet.'

'Your business, you never mentioned what it was before,' Larry said.

'Trade, nothing more. I would suggest you focus on my son, not me. And now, gentlemen, I wish you a good day. If you wish to talk further, please telephone and make an appointment.'

***

Tricia Warburton, by association, was tainted with scandal and intrigue. She had been close to Angus, having co-hosted their weekly programme with the man. She had already been interviewed; her alibi was solid as she had been reporting Angus's ascent, and she had denied any romantic involvement.

It was midday, a café not far from Tricia Warburton's house. Wendy Gladstone assigned the task of getting behind the attractive exterior, the celebrity persona, and the makeup that Wendy thought excessive.

'I told the police that Angus was a colleague, not a love interest,' Tricia said as she drank her coffee, careful not to spill any onto her clothes, to wipe her lips with a small handkerchief after every sip.

'You've said that before, and we're not forming a judgement, only getting to the truth. It's the same with every murder investigation, a need to conceal the truth, a fear of what might be found, other lovers suspicious. Do you, Tricia, have a lover?'

'Blunt, aren't you? Why would I answer a question like that? And if I did, it's personal.'

'I'll take that as a yes. We don't have time for beating around the bush. Angus was killed for a reason, although it could have been only intended as a warning. The most logical explanation is a distraught lover, statistically the most likely, although it could be something else. Fame through association, someone with mental issues could garner celebrity status by killing the celebrity. That's happened before.'

'I know, John Lennon.'

'Would you, if you and Angus had had a few too many alcoholic beverages one night, have ended up in bed with him?'

'You mean a one-night stand?'

'Exactly.'

Tricia Warburton looked over at the waitress, raised her hand, pointed at the two cups on the table. 'You'll have another?' she said to Wendy.

'Avoiding the question?' Wendy's reply.

'I'm just not sure how to respond. Is this important?'

'It is.'

'Yes, I would have been interested. I'm not that innocent, a bit of a tart in my teens, made men out of a few boys, but not these days, slowed down a lot.'

'We've all been there,' Wendy said. 'A farmer's son, didn't know what hit him.'

'That might be alright for you, but for me, media fodder.'

'Is your celebrity that important?'

'My career's not over, not by a long way, and if there's a scandal, it stays around forever. Why these women send naked photos to their boyfriends, I'll never know. One way or the other, they always end up on social media.'

'You wouldn't do that?'

'I'm not saying I wouldn't if there was no risk, but I can't afford it. I can tell you the truth. I don't want to be damned, and believe me, I'll be labelled a slut by those that don't like me, a hussy even by those that do.'

'You've not answered the question.'

'It was soon after we started working together, an assignment up north. Angus intended to swim the length of Loch Ness, a charity gig with another twenty swimmers. Angus wasn't into a relay of swimmers; he wanted to complete the distance solo, harder than the Channel as the water temperature is around five degrees centigrade year-round.'

'Did he succeed?'

'He came close, but the cold got to him. In the end, we didn't focus on him, only on the others.'

'He's got time on his hands, pent-up energy, disappointment.'

'All three. It's late at night, the two of us in the hotel bar. We're downing whisky, Angus talking about his life, me about a failed romance. One thing led to another, and then the next morning, I wake up, and there he is in my bed.'

'Are you saying you don't remember what happened?'

'I remember.'

'What else?'

'Nothing more, only that social media would make it sleazy and dirty, the two hosts of a popular programme screwing on the shores of Loch Ness, frightening the monster. The only monsters that night were Angus and me, and neither of us would have scared anyone, that drunk we were.'

Chapter 7

Charles Simmons identified his son's body; Angus Simmons's mother preferred to stay in Scotland for the time being. Meanwhile, the investigation continued, albeit slowly. Initially, a flurry of media interest, but soon the public's interest in Simmons waned, replaced by another murder somewhere, a war elsewhere, by the general flotsam, celebrities getting married, getting divorced, some going to jail.

A person who had never watched much television, not even as a youth, Chief Inspector Isaac Cook sat in his office, his laptop open, staring disinterestedly at the screen. There was a report to prepare, a budgetary estimate to give to the chief superintendent, Richard Goddard, up there on the top floor; hallowed ground some of the cynical jokers in Challis Street would say, but never Isaac.

To him, Goddard was a good man, dedicated to the police force and justice, a hard taskmaster at times, defensive of his people. The two men had known each other for a long time and had formed a friendship outside of the office, but inside Challis Street, no favours were shown.

'Any ideas?' Larry said as he put his head around Isaac's door.

'Perplexed,' Isaac's reply. 'Why would someone want to kill Simmons? Apart from Hampton, everyone else admired him.'

'Not everyone's been honest that we've spoken to, or there are others we don't know about yet.'

'Former lovers?'

'Bridget's compiling a list, checking women photographed with him.'

'Are there many?'

'Not a lot find. Most times, Simmons kept his private life just that, private.'

'What about Tricia Warburton? I reckon she could be a hard woman,' Isaac said.

'Her alibi's firm. Other than that, some men, one she lived with for a year, broke up two months ago.'

'Have you contacted the last one, the one who moved out?'

'It was her that moved back to a place in Bayswater. Since then, she's been single, no man in her life.'

'She's a celebrity of sorts; the newspapers and the magazines always find them another romance, whether it's true or not. Who are they showing her with?' Isaac asked.

'Not my area, celebrities and their love lives. And besides, she may be all smiles and teeth on the television, but she's got a degree in English from Oxford University,' Larry said. 'She's very smart, careful to conceal it, no doubt uses it when the time is right.'

'We've seen her on camera, interviewed her. She appeared the same whether a camera's in her face or not.'

Isaac did not feel comfortable with the situation. The manner of Simmons's death was so bizarre as to stretch credulity. Why would anyone go to such trouble to cause the man to fall, knowing there was a probability that he would have hung on, or the shot could have missed?

'Wendy met with her, got an admission that she had had a one-night stand with Simmons. That must count for something,' Larry said.

'Sleeping with the man after a night of heavy drinking doesn't mean she was fond of him.'

'Are you suspicious of her, instinct telling you there's more to the woman than what we see?'

'Lack of anything better. Any success with where the shot was fired from?'

'A competent shot, a man of medium height, fit enough to have walked up twenty-one floors carrying a rifle mount and a rifle with telescopic sights.'

'Fingerprints?'

'Not on the mount.'

'Why leave it? If the rifle's taken, then why not the mount?' Isaac asked.

'It's easier to trace a weapon back to its owner.'

'A rifle would need a firearm certificate, assuming it was registered.'

'Murderers don't usually worry about technicalities, not if they're serious.'

'Which means you're leaning towards a gifted amateur.'

'Supposition, and what about the father? Devious?'

'Almost certainly. Ex-military, personal inheritance, trade. Qualifications for a position in espionage or dodgy trade deals on behalf of the government, easy to make enemies.'

'Even if that's so, why would it impact the son?' Larry queried.

Two men put forward possibilities, restating what was known, speculating on what was not, formulating a plan to move forward, an integral part of policing, accomplished by the cohesive, functioning group of individuals he had formed in Homicide. Isaac was confident of a new avenue of enquiry.

'We can't answer that. Unless we have a motive, we've got nothing. Pressure Tricia Warburton, try to break through the veneer. The woman's skilled at adopting a persona. Her parents might open up, childhood friends, any issues with the law, rebellious teen, drugs, protesting in the street, that sort of thing.'

'In court when she was fifteen, marijuana, and then two years later on probation for knocking off a policeman's helmet while under the influence.'

'Drugs?'

'Alcohol. Youthful high jinks, a period of stupidity, flirted with Bolshevism at university, but she still got her degree.'

'Lovers?'

'A child at twenty-one, the father unknown. The child's twelve now, a private school.'

'The father?'

'There's no name on the birth certificate, and besides, it's before Angus's time, nothing to do with him.'

'Even so, find out more about her, but not from the woman herself.'

***

The news that the programme Angus Simmons and Tricia Warburton had co-hosted was to be cancelled, did not come as a shock to the pundits who followed such matters.

Tricia Warburton was the first person Homicide contacted after the announcement.

'The bastards,' Tricia said as she sat in Challis Street.

'What's behind it?' Isaac asked.

'The bastards,' Tricia repeated, the makeup askew, wearing a pair of jeans ripped at the knee, a blouse that was stained, her hair going in all directions.

'Did you drive here?' Wendy asked.

'I did.'

'You'll not be driving home. You're drunk.'

'Just a couple.'

'A couple of dozen. Hand over your car keys. We'll make sure you get home safely. Drunk in charge of a vehicle won't make your day any better.'

'It can't get any worse.'

'Miss Warburton, it can,' Isaac said. He didn't feel inclined to be as agreeable as Wendy. What he needed was the truth, the reason behind her sacking. He intended to get it.

Wendy put out her hand, receiving in return a set of keys. 'Thanks,' she said. 'No problems, not now. How about black coffee?'

'I could do with vodka, not coffee. Those bastards.'

'Those bastards terminated your contract and your crew without a warning and an explanation. The most they said was a mealy-mouthed statement that due to financial restraints and the recent death, the man irreplaceable according to them, they had decided to break with Miss Warburton and her team. There's more, but most of it is thanking you for your valued service, the usual jargon when you get shafted.'

Isaac chose 'shafted' over 'terminated'. It was a subtle attempt to show that he sympathised with the woman, empathic even, as he had been sidelined in the past, pushed to another department for no other reason than a commissioner who wanted his own man in charge of Homicide. For Isaac, the woman might be innocent of all sins, but for now, she was guilty of an error of judgement, an indiscretion or possibly a crime.

'No more alcohol, Tricia,' Wendy said. 'You need sobering up, and what's happened to you brings the focus onto you, what you know, what they suspected.'

Wendy made a phone call. Five minutes later, Bridget entered the room. She carried a coffee for Tricia, as well as a plate of sandwiches. 'I thought your visitor might be hungry,' she said.

'Not for me,' Tricia said as she picked up one of the sandwiches. Her behaviour, alcohol aside, was erratic.

Isaac bade his time as the coffee was drunk, the sandwiches eaten, and Tricia had taken time out to freshen up. Eventually, all three were ready, Tricia looking better than before, her hair brushed, lipstick applied.

'Tricia, let's go through the reason they terminated you, not this nonsense about financial constraints.'

'They believe that Angus and I were pulling a stunt, that he was meant to pretend to fall, regain his grip and complete the climb.'

'Is that it?' Wendy asked.

'Not totally.'

'The truth is always the best,' Isaac said.

'The same as honesty is always the best policy. Well, let me tell you, it isn't, never was, never will be.'

'What do you mean? Was it a stunt gone wrong?'

'Angus knew what he was doing. He could have been up that building in half the time. And if he had, he wouldn't have been shot.'

'Who else knew this?'

'The film crew, no one else.'

'Does senior management believe that someone passed on that information to the person who shot Angus?'

'They don't believe; they know it.'

'Proof?'

'Condemned at the altar of public opinion; pronounced guilty by social media, a pariah in the newspapers, my career over.'

'That's not what I asked,' Isaac said.

'Talk to them, but they'll tell you what I'm about to. They received an email, anonymous as they always are. Slagged me off, called me a conniving bitch, an adulterer, a murderer, and the crew with me, in collaboration.'

'They took it seriously?'

'Conspiracy theories don't need proof, just enough people to believe the nonsense.'

'You had a substantial following on Facebook,' Wendy said.

'I did. It served me well, raised my profile, but the public is fickle. By this time next week, my following, apart from the determined, the neurotic and those with their marriage proposals, will be gone, and no one, regardless of whether you find the murderer or not, will retract their condemnation. I'll be forgotten, a nobody.'

'Hardly a nobody,' Wendy said. 'Does other people's opinion matter that much?'

'To me, it does.'

Isaac knew that Tricia Warburton was right, having had an experience of television and the viewing public in the past: another murder investigation, the suspected murder of a leading lady.

He remembered the woman long after the case was closed, her eventual death resulting from a hit and run, the investigation swept under the carpet, a file long buried in the police vaults.

'Did you see the email?' Wendy asked.

'I saw a printout.'

'Do you know who it's from?'

'Anonymous. I thought I was clear about that.'

'You were,' Isaac said. 'Could it be the actions not of a disgruntled fan, but someone astute, recognising gains to be made?'

'It doesn't matter, not to me. My career is over.'

Isaac felt like giving the woman a shake. Her state of mind, the creeping negativity, dramatically changed from her previous optimism.

'Emails can be traced back to the source,' Wendy said.

'I don't have it. You'll need to talk to those who shafted me.' The bitterness remained.

'I'll give you a lift home,' Wendy said. 'I'll get someone to follow with your car. Tomorrow will be better.'

Chapter 8

Allan Baxter's death, a person that both Simmons and Hampton had climbed with, made the evening news. An avalanche earlier in the season than expected had buried him under a hundred feet of snow.

Maddox Timberley, who had met Baxter, had been asked for comment, the closest person to the late Angus Simmons. A wonderful man, well respected and well-liked, especially by Angus, she had said.

Wendy met with the woman later that day, received a different opinion.

'Angus didn't care for Allan, thought him a difficult man to work with, as well as he took chances sometimes. Not that I'd say that, would I?'

Wendy understood the woman's sensitivity. Nobody wanted to hear evil of a person after their death, except Hampton, but he was a man embittered by circumstance, a man condemned to loneliness and derision.

'We're no nearer to solving what happened on the building,' Wendy said. 'Not sure if we can trust Tricia Warburton, not certain if Angus wasn't taking a risk.'

'What do you mean?' Maddox said.

'Ratings, all-important as you know. Not everybody would have approved of Angus climbing that building.'

'Once Angus had decided, there would be no changing his mind, not that I mean he would be reckless. A meticulous planner, that was Angus, and as for what happened to Baxter, it wouldn't have happened to him.'

'He was in a similar position in Patagonia, climbing with Hampton.'

'It's not the same. If he had known about the possibility of an avalanche, Allan Baxter could have chosen to take the risk. If it had been Angus and there was an adverse report, he wouldn't have gone, and climbing buildings for ratings, knowing there was an inherent risk, would have been unconscionable to him.'

Wendy thought that Angus's girlfriend was naïve. Simmons had enjoyed the limelight, the fame, the best seat in a restaurant, even the paparazzi snapping a shot of him and Maddox by the side of a swimming pool.

Even though he had complained about the incident, it hadn't harmed his career, nor Maddox's, a photo shoot of her on a Caribbean beach one week later.

'Maddox, you've met Mike Hampton?' Wendy asked.

'The accident was before my time, but Angus used to speak about him.'

'Fondly?'

'Always. It upset Angus that Mike was that way, and I know that he tried to make friends with him, even went out to his house once, got as far as the front door.'

'You were there?'

'I went down with Angus. At the door, a woman, not Hampton's wife; Angus knew her, someone else, unpleasant.'

'Did she introduce herself?'

'If you mean, did she announce who she was, extend a hand in friendship?'

'That would be the usual approach.'

'She was offensive, started shouting at Angus, blaming him for her brother's accident.'

'Describe her?'

'Rough, tattoos up both arms, her hair shaved close to the scalp, butch.'

'Did Angus know her?'

'Upset him, the sister's manner, but as he said on the drive back to London, the black sheep of the family, trouble with the law, in jail a couple of times.'

'Then why was she there? We've found no record of her, not with her brother or with Angus.'

'With Mike the way he is now, I would have thought that was fairly obvious,' Maddox said. 'The man's found an ally, another blackened heart.'

'Hampton's wife never mentioned the sister,' Wendy said. 'How long ago since you went there?'

'Three months, no more. You don't think…'

'I think nothing, not yet, but we'll need to check out this woman, find out why we haven't heard about her before.'

***

Isaac and Larry were at the television station at eight in the morning, security easing them through after a glance at their warrant cards. From outside, the building had looked austere, a style of post-war modernism, redbrick, metal-framed windows. Inside, the walls knocked out, the building transformed into modern and fresh-looking, contemporary art on the walls.

'Chief Inspector Cook, Inspector Hill, pleased to meet you,' a young woman said. 'We're expecting you. If you'd be so kind as to follow me. I'm Alison Glassop'.

The woman glided them through a maze of corridors and into an elevator. She was public relations excellence without a blemish or a hair out of place, pearly-white teeth, the perfect complexion and poise.

A boardroom at the top of the building, a view out over the city, a group of people standing, beaming smiles, hands extended. It was not what Isaac and Larry wanted. However, it showed the senior executives' intent, their need to smother the negativity the station had attracted after Angus had died, the public relations disaster that had ensued after removing Tricia Warburton and the people she had worked with.

'This is Bob Babbage,' a gnome of a man, barely to Isaac's shoulder, a pointed nose, downcast eyes, said. Isaac didn't need to be told that the man making the introduction was Jerome Jaden, the chief executive officer and majority stockholder.

'Bob's our company lawyer,' Jaden said. 'He deals with any legal issues we have.'

Unsaid, but Isaac knew he was there to stop Homicide from asking embarrassing questions, to prevent any of those in the boardroom saying anything prejudicial. Alison Glassop was the personable front of the company, Babbage was the hard-nose, not there for popularity or corporate conscience.

Isaac shook Babbage's hand, as did Larry. He was, Isaac knew, the main adversary in the room.

Jaden moved along the line. A woman in her forties, elegantly dressed in jacket and trousers, carrying more weight than she should, her hair cut short, her appearance perfect. 'I'm Karen Majors, head of sales. It's a tragedy, losing Angus like that,' she said.

Babbage's ears pricked as the woman spoke, ready to pounce if she digressed.

Isaac imagined that the group had been versed in what could be said, what couldn't: contrition, sympathy for the deceased, keep to the reason that Warburton and Simmons's people were removed, breezed over with corporate jargon, executive decision, financial necessity, failing ratings. Babbage would have trained them well, annoying some, pleasing others, but as with a political party, unity when in public, dissension when not.

'We never met him, but we've met his co-host on a few occasions, as well as his girlfriend,' Isaac said.

'If we discuss these items formally in sequence at the table, it would be more constructive,' Babbage, attempting to maintain a casual manner, but failing, said.

'It's murder, Mr Babbage. Our discussions here today will be of our choosing,' Isaac said.

'Last but not least, our head of programming, Tom Taylor,' Jaden said, attempting to defuse the tension.

The man looked to be no older than thirty, the new broom brought in to sweep out the old. 'Pleased to meet you,' he said.

To Larry, Taylor was the male counterpart of Alison Glassop, pearly-white teeth, perpetual smile, shallow.

'It was you that sacked Tricia Warburton?' Larry said.

'Terminated, a corporate decision.'

'Yes, that's understood. But it was you that told her?'

Babbage was on his feet, hovering close, his eyes darting from person to person.

'Tom's just taken over the position,' Jaden said. 'Unfortunately, we had to let go of the previous head of programming. A sad loss, but it was his time.'

'First Tricia Warburton and then her crew, and now we hear that the previous head of programming has left the company. We'll need to interview him,' Isaac said.

'That can be arranged.'

Both police officers knew it would be, but only if the man had been versed in what to say.

If the company wasn't responsible for a man's death, they were playing a dangerous game, which could backfire in their face. Attempting to protect the television company's image in the face of a homicide investigation was not a wise move.

In Isaac's view, anything less than total honesty raised suspicion and indicated probable deception. Jaden, a man with a long history of television and radio company ownership, should have known that, but Babbage probably didn't. And removing the head of programming at the same time as Tricia Warburton was suspicious.

The meeting commenced with Isaac and Larry on one side of the large table, Babbage, Majors and Taylor on the other. Jerome Jaden sat at the head, his chair superior to the others', a sure sign of powerplay, mine's bigger than yours. Alison Glassop fussed around, a beaming smile, ensuring everyone had a cup of tea or a coffee, spending longer attending to Tom Taylor, a clear sign of more than a professional relationship.

'Mr Jaden,' Isaac said, once Alison had left the room, 'Angus Simmons's death is murder. Who and why remains a mystery, a mystery that hopefully, we can clear up today.'

'Tragic,' Jaden's reply.

'I believe that's been said enough already.'

Apart from Babbage, the sweet-talking charm offensive from those at the TV station had finished. Isaac knew there was a hard-nosed businessman behind Jaden's façade, only interested in financial gain, not the viewing public or those who worked for him.

'Very true.' Jaden conceded the point.

'Simmons fell due to a bullet to his upper back, although it did not impact with great force. Anything less, and he might have held on, but as we know, he didn't.'

'Are you suggesting suicide?' Taylor asked.

'Are you?' Larry replied.

'No,' Taylor said, a nervous stutter.

'Now that's been cleared up,' Isaac said. 'We've been told that it was planned for one of the co-hosts to go. Correct?' Isaac said.

'I can confirm,' Jaden said. 'It's not only us; other stations are doing the same. Advertising revenue is down.'

'Signalling the eventual demise of television broadcasting as you would understand it.'

'Change is inevitable. We are taking action, and besides, nothing is certain. There will always be a market for television. But of immediate concern is revenue, the lifeblood of this organisation. Karen's done a sterling job, but she can't work miracles. And as for this reduction of hosts, that is not a correct statement.'

'I should have said one host if the ratings stabilised or reduced, two hosts if they increased, and from what you've said, that means more adventurous stunts, more risk, the probability that someone would do something stupid, which Simmons did. A sense of regret?'

'No, why should there be? We didn't condone or approve of what Angus did, and, I should say, with Tricia's approval. All we said was that the ratings needed to improve, the advertising revenue to increase.'

'Was that the responsibility of Angus and Tricia? Advertising revenue, ratings?'

'It was. Angus had experience from his mountaineering exploits, knew how to get sponsors, and Tricia had worked in radio before. They weren't asked to collect the money, only to ensure that the programme brought in the viewers and improved the ratings. And they had done a decent job, but the odds were against them, no doubt the reason Angus attempted that damn stupid climb. No different from when he and Hampton climbed that mountain.'

'A mistake? You knew about it?' Isaac asked.

'It was before he worked for us. Not that we knew at the time, but we had to research Angus. We needed to check out if he was responsible, of good character. And we needed to get insurance for him, cover our backs if anything went wrong.'

'Mr Jaden means professional diligence,' Babbage said, miffed that the 'cover our backs' comment had got through.

'I understand,' Isaac said. 'Corporate responsibility, all-important. What did you find?'

'Angus Simmons wasn't a risk-taker. Sure, he took on challenges which to us looked foolhardy, but he was a meticulous planner, well regarded in mountaineering circles. He was a good choice for a co-host.'

'Tricia Warburton?'

'Fine by us,' Karen Majors said. 'I knew her from before, a magazine we both worked for. Attractive, personable, strong work ethic.'

'Sexy, as well,' Jaden said.

Isaac looked over at Babbage, waited for him to react to the sexist comment. The man sat mute.

'What Mr Jaden means,' Karen said, 'is that Tricia was easy on the eye, and for television, she was ideal. Angus had rugged masculinity.'

'This fart-arsing around, pretending that we're something we aren't, is pointless,' Jaden said. 'The police are here to see us as we are.' Looking over at the lawyer,

'Bob, sorry, we can't play this game. Karen thought Tricia was a bitch and Tom fancied her, although he's getting it off with Alison now.'

Isaac was pleased. Jerome Jaden was known to be a man with a quick temper, a fondness for crudity, and a bluntness in dealing with his staff and competitors.

'Let me point out that I didn't dislike Tricia,' Karen said.

'Not a bitch?' Isaac asked.

The conversations were getting interesting. It was what Isaac liked: plain-speaking, unchecked emotions.

'She was a bitch, tried to take my job at a magazine where we both worked. I dealt with her there. To be honest, I like the woman, but all's fair in love and war. We would go out for a drink occasionally, call each other outrageous names, have a laugh about it.'

'She's upset about being removed from the station,' Isaac said.

'Tricia? Upset? It's hardly likely. She received severance pay, a hefty bonus to go, no bad publicity or talking out of turn.'

'It's a public relations debacle for you,' Isaac said.

'Chief Inspector,' Jaden said, 'you don't seem to understand. There's no such thing as bad publicity, only how you deal with it.'

'Are you saying you knew beforehand of what she was likely to say?'

'Do you want to go down this road?' Babbage said to Jaden. 'What you say here will become part of a criminal investigation.'

'I know what I'm saying. Bob, sit back, let me deal with this.'

'In your own time,' Isaac said.

'Jim Breslaw, the head of programming before we gave Tom the job, wasn't in favour of getting rid of Tricia. That's why I let him go.'

'We still need to interview him.'

'As you wish, not that he can help you, too stuck in his ways, remembers the good old days, the time before social media and YouTube. Anyway, here's how it goes. Simmons is dead, intentional or otherwise, murder or an accident; none of that matters to us here. Sure, we can pretend to be sorry, even believe it, but business is business, and the show must go on. I'm sure you've heard that adage.'

'I have.'

'Good. Angus is dead, and logically we should be throwing our support behind Tricia, bolstering her, promoting her heavily as the new look, but we aren't. Instead, we sack her and all her people, make them feel as though they've been dealt a savage blow, which they have.'

'It doesn't make sense.'

'Not to you. Simmons is dead, Tricia's out on her ear, the social media is going wild, the other television stations are crucifying us. But he who laughs last laughs longest.'

'How?'

'You still don't get it. Give it a couple of weeks, wait until the heat has died down, and then resurrect Tricia, her programme, the staff she wants, an increased budget, and she can travel the world, looking for the bizarre, the most interesting, the stories that will pull in the viewers.'

'The damage's done?'

'The viewing public, I don't think so. They'll complain, then applaud. In the meantime, Karen's out there, bringing in the advertising revenue. It's a brilliant plan.'

'If you say so. And what about Tom, your head of programming?'

'We'll bring in a high-flyer, put Tom alongside him, let him learn the ropes. Tom's capable, just a little wet behind the ears. A couple of years, he'll be able to take over the job.'

'Alison Glassop?'

'That's up to Tom.'

Taylor just smiled.

'Does Tricia know about this?' Larry asked.

'She does now. We kept her in the dark for a couple of days, let her blow off steam. But now, she's got a contract in front of her. She'll fight us for more, but Bob will hold firm, give in slowly.'

'I don't like it,' Isaac said.

'Chief Inspector, you deal with facts; we create illusions. I don't expect you to like it, but none of us had anything to do with Simmons's death. That's all that you need to know,' Jaden said.

Chapter 9

Isaac instinctively distrusted Jaden, and if the man had made a statement that wasn't true, it did not bode well. However, Isaac believed the man more than he did Tricia Warburton's denial. Jerome Jaden was smart, many years in the business, known as a straight shooter. He wouldn't have risked raising the ire of the police.

Larry met Tricia this time, the friendly female banter with Wendy not working the last time. Either Wendy was losing her touch, or Tricia was more circumspect, more devious than first thought.

The inspector and the celebrity met: one of them in his forties and going to seed, the other in her thirties, svelte, jogging every day, her hair coiffured, her tan embellished every week.

Larry chose one of his favourite pubs, upmarket enough for the lovely Tricia.

In the dim light of the pub, the woman was more attractive than the first time he had met her, and she was beguiling.

'Inspector, why are we here?' Tricia said. 'Is this to discuss Angus's death, or is it something more?'

She was making him feel uncomfortable as if she was doing it on purpose. Larry didn't like it. 'A drink?' he said.

'A glass of wine for me.'

Larry left the table and went over to the bar to place an order.

'Is that her off the television?' the barman said.

Larry took out his warrant card, showed it. 'Give me a white wine for the lady, a pint of beer for me.'

'No need to have worried about me,' the barman said as he pulled the beer. 'See them here all the time.'

'See who?'

'The rich and the famous. Some are pleasant, leave a decent tip, some are miserable sods, heads up their arse, deem the plebs not worthy to lick their boots. What's that one like?' The barman cocked his head in Tricia's direction.

'So far, she's delightful. Never know, not truly, not when you're a police officer.'

'Too friendly, you don't trust them; difficult, you're suspicious.'

'That's it.'

'Did she have anything to do with him that fell off that building?'

Larry felt that cordiality had gone far enough. He picked up the drinks and returned to his seat.

'Plenty to say?' Tricia asked.

'Fount of knowledge.'

'Him or barmen in general?'

'They don't miss much, only too willing to talk if the money's right or the conversation is convivial.'

Larry clinked glasses with Tricia and took a sip of his beer.

'He eyed me up and down, wondered what you were doing here with me, whether we were an item?'

'Something along those lines.'

'They assume that I'm an easy lay, sleeping around with whoever.'

'Do they?' Larry said although he knew pub conversation, not averse to taking part in it sometimes. And yes, Tricia Warburton would be regarded in that light, even more so given that her co-host had fallen to his death under mysterious circumstances, speculation about her and Angus Simmons.

'You know they do, more so now. You must have heard it, a man like you, out and about, delving into humanity's cesspit.'

'Sergeant Gladstone reckoned you had been coy with her.'

'Wendy never bought me a drink.'

'Tricia, if you're trying to make me feel embarrassed, you're succeeding. But if you're trying to be smart, it'll backfire on you. There's nothing to be gained by any attempt at subterfuge and deception.'

'I don't think I was any more than open with you.'

In front of a camera, you may be excellent, but I'm the expert here; this is my game, not yours.'

Tricia took a drink from her glass, put it down on the table. 'I'm not sure if you just ticked me off or if you were joking,' she said.

'I don't joke, not when there's a murder. Hiding facts because you believe they would prejudice you will not work, cannot work.'

'Did you know that actresses were regarded as no more than prostitutes, liberal with their favours, selling their bodies for gain?'

'I've never understood why,' Larry said. 'That's what he thought, the barman.'

'During the eighteenth century, actresses' and prostitutes' social standing was targeted by moral reformers and satirical authors. The moral reformer targeted actresses for criticism as their actions and speech on stage were considered immodest. The satirical author was interested in publishing any related scandal that surrounded the actresses.'

'That's not the view today.'

'Isn't it? I'm not an actress, but I'm in the public eye. Your friend at the bar, he's typical, reckons I'm easy, and I'll have you twisted around my little finger in an instant.'

'You're denigrating yourself,' Larry said. 'I don't share his views.'

'You're a police officer. You've seen the dregs of society, the wanton licentiousness of some, the perversions of others, but that barman – he's seen nothing, been nowhere, experienced nothing. I'm guilty by association, convicted by the social media warriors, seduced, at least in their minds, by him and his ilk.'

'Why are you telling me this?'

'I know how it appears, that Jerome Jaden had planned it and that I was a party to it.'

'Your contract?'

'Precisely. And believe me, once it's general knowledge, the pundits will be out there in the ether, saying that Angus's death was planned to get the ratings and that my contract was in the bag before he died, that I was screwing Jerome all along.'

'Are you certain?'

'Of course I am. How much of what they splash on a magazine's front cover about people such as me is true?'

'I don't take notice of it.'

'You don't, but others do. The perception of the actress, or in my case the television host, as a prostitute, is alive and well. I'm about to be lambasted.'

'It's happened before?'

'You know it has. You would have checked my background, found old boyfriends, where I'd gone to school.'

'I did. What are you going to do?'

'What I've done in the past. I'm going to ride it out, take the flak, the slurs, the innuendos, even smile at the cameras.'

'If you're lying…'

'I'm not. Once my contract is signed, Karen Majors goes into overdrive, drumming up advertising revenue. The station's promotions team starts getting me onto the early-morning chat shows, putting me on every other radio station throughout the country, and Angus not even cold in his grave.'

'Abhorrent as it may be, you embrace it,' Larry said.

'It's seductive, the same as alcohol is to a drunk.'

'I know the feeling.'

'You'd be a good-looking man if you lost some weight, looked after yourself,' Tricia said.

***

The appearance of Gwyneth Simmons at Challis Street on a wet and rainy day had not been expected. After all, it had been she, stoic in Scotland, who had said that she would not come to London until her son's body had been released for burial.

'It was time,' Angus's mother said. She looked unfashionable and old, dressed in a heavy coat that had seen better days, the sleeve cuffs frayed, the collar askew and on her head, a yellow plastic hood. She was dry, if not warm.

Wendy brought a heater over to where she sat, and Bridget gave her a hot drink.

'Time for what?' Wendy asked once the woman had removed the hood, taken off the coat and placed them to one side of her.

'The truth.'

Not wishing to proceed without either her DCI or her DI, Wendy messaged both.

Larry arrived first, realised the implication of the woman's presence, phoned Isaac and told him to get to the office pronto, no time to lose.

Jenny, Isaac's wife, looked over at her husband, saw him bouncing their son on his lap. She was happy, content with her lot in life, a loving husband, a healthy child. However, she knew the look on her husband's face after receiving the phone call. He was champing at the bit, desperate to get to the station.

Jenny took their son from Isaac, kissed him on the cheek, and said, 'Go.'

Isaac responded with a kiss for his wife and another gurgle for the baby, wriggling its toes as he left, eliciting a smile in return. Soon, the child would be walking, and then, the first day of school. Life was passing him by, and he hadn't made superintendent, and the bills were coming in, the cost of living increasing, and he was feeling the financial pinch.

Even so, as he sat in his car and turned the ignition, he had to agree that life was good and he was a lucky man.

At Challis Street, aware their senior investigating officer was on his way, Homicide waited. The peripheral staff, the evidence collators, the administrators, the others, who slackened marginally when the boss wasn't in the office, upped their game, moved around more, filed their reports, sending them to Bridget, who would prioritise and then present them to Isaac daily.

Twenty minutes later, Isaac sat down with Larry and Gwyneth Simmons. The room was cold for Isaac, adequate for Angus's mother, who had come from a bracing Scottish climate.

'The truth?' Isaac said. 'Is this what we are here for?'

'Yes, the truth of what happened on Cerro Torre,' Gwyneth Simmons said. 'Everyone that is if you exclude Mike Hampton believes it to have been an unfortunate accident, a life-and-death situation, a split-second decision needed, played out in a dangerous environment. But Angus told me the truth.'

'Which is?'

'Mike Hampton was having trouble with his wife. She had told him that she was involved with Angus, but it wasn't true. It was another man that she was seeing.'

'He accused your son?'

'Mike told Angus that he would see him dead for what he had done.'

'They patched it up in South America, my son and Mike, and that it was his wife making up stories. She's like that. Have you met her?'

'I have,' Isaac said.

'Did you form an opinion?'

'I wasn't looking to form an opinion, only to establish facts.'

'Kate met Mike at a function in London, an awards ceremony. She was there with someone else, no idea who it was. Mike used to be a bon vivant, a lover of life and women, and Kate was his type of woman. He took her from whoever she had come with.'

'That doesn't paint a good picture of her,' Larry said.

'You never met Mike before his accident; I had. Kate became a wedge between the two men. Angus used to say that mountaineering was thirty per cent skill, seventy per cent determination. He disagreed with gifted amateurs paying for someone to nursemaid them up the highest mountains. He felt it was a distraction, so did Mike, and then there's Kate in Mike's ear, causing confusion, dissension between the two men, taking plenty, giving little.'

'The mysterious lover?' Isaac asked. 'Was there one?'

'It wasn't Angus.'

'Then who?'

'Angus never told anyone, only me. He knew I would never reveal who it was, but now that my son is dead, I must tell you.'

'Please do.'

'Justin Skinner, another mountaineer, climbed Everest one year after Angus and Mike climbed it that first time. He's as hard as nails, a brilliant climber, a sharp businessman. If you want to climb Everest and you've got enough money, he'll take you, not so sure if you'll get back.'

'What does that mean?'

'On his last, two of his group perished.'

'Any repercussions?'

'For Justin, none. On the mountain, up high, you're a dead man walking. Every climber knows it, accepts the risk. Six died last year on the mountain, their bodies still up there. Did you know that if a person is beyond the point of no return, still breathing, but semiconscious or unable to stand, incapable of getting down before nightfall, they're declared dead, left up there alive?'

73

'I've read about it,' Isaac said. 'No option from what I know.'

'There isn't. Kate Hampton was sleeping with Skinner when Mike was overseas. He was the one keen on bringing Mike on board to take paying clients up Everest, his wife primed while she was in bed with Skinner, whispering in her husband's ear later.'

'Is that it?' Isaac said.

'No. On Cerro Torre, close to the summit, Mike starts up again about his wife and Angus. Angus wasn't prepared, and on a mountain, the focus is moving one foot in front of the other. It's not the place to discuss who's sleeping with who.

'It was Mike who lunged at Angus, made him lose his grip, held up only by Mike and a climbing anchor. Mike would have been responsible for Angus's death, not that he probably intended that result, but it got out of hand. Angus managed to hold on, Mike fell, broke his back.'

'Angus could have left him,' Larry said.

'Not Angus. He's a purist, believed in the camaraderie of mountaineers. He secured Mike and went for help. He saved his life.'

Chapter 10

The one unassailable certainty in the investigation –
someone was lying. Larry had his money on Simmons's
mother; Wendy was more inclined to Kate Hampton.

Isaac reserved his judgement until more was
known about Skinner, another mountaineering legend,
one of only three hundred and forty-four who had
completed the ascent of the seven summits, the tallest
mountain on each continent: Kilimanjaro in Africa,
conquerable by a fit individual, Elbrus in the Caucasus
Mountains of Europe, Aconcagua in South America,
Vinson in Antarctica, Denali in Alaska, and then Everest
in the Himalayas. Carstensz in Indonesia, although
technically not in Australia, made the seventh, as its
tectonic plate allowed its inclusion. On the Australian
mainland, Mount Kosciusko was no more than a Sunday
afternoon climb up a gravel path.

Mike Hampton had completed six, and Angus
Simmons had ascended five, not considering Kilimanjaro
as a worthy inclusion.

At the television station, an air of benign
introspection.

'A public relations disaster, this constant negativity
over Simmons's death,' Jaden said.

On the receiving end of his anger, Karen Majors,
the head of sales, the person who was there to generate
advertising revenue, but wasn't. She didn't speak, not
because she wasn't capable of holding her own in a
conversation, but because it was her job on the line.

Given a chance, she'd shift the blame, find a scapegoat: Tom Taylor would do.

After all, she'd been opposed to his appointment. The only thing that had been in his favour was that he was sleeping with Alison Glassop, the perpetually smiling female, a favoured niece of Jaden's.

Another person present, the wily Bob Babbage, a capable orator, able to twist the truth, or a non-truth if it suited. He was keeping quiet, letting Jaden rant on, taking in what was being said, ready with a defence when needed.

Tom Taylor kept glancing over at Alison, looking for moral support.

'And how do you explain this headline?' Jaden continued.

'It was Jim Breslaw's idea,' Karen Majors said, judging it time to pass the buck.

'No use to me, is it? The man's gone, paid off. We, or should I say you, need to do something.'

'We ride it out,' Babbage said. 'It's a glitch, not only us, all the other television stations are feeling the pinch, and advertising revenues are down across the board.'

Tom Taylor looked out of the window, nothing to say, nothing that would make any sense. Alison moved alongside him, gave him a nudge, a subtle wakeup call.

Taylor opened his mouth, knowing that he had to say something, but no words emanated.

'Say it, Tom,' Jaden said.

Red in the face, wishing a hole in the floor would open up and swallow him, Taylor cleared his throat; better to say something than nothing, to be shot down in flames if that was to happen, go back to administration, an accounts clerk if it was to be.

'We weren't responsible for him making the climb, regardless of what the newspapers are saying,' Taylor said, hesitantly at first, but as he spoke, he became more confident, more fluid in his delivery.

'Yes,' Jaden asked. 'So, what are you suggesting?'

'We can't alter public opinion, but we can mould its perception. Bob's right, revenue's down, that's a fact, which means we need a bigger slice of the pie.'

'Spouting from a textbook doesn't get us anywhere,' Jaden said. He could see himself in Taylor at a similar age, unsure, tongue-tied.

'Maybe it doesn't, but Karen saying it was Jim Breslaw's fault is a good idea.'

Karen Majors looked over at Tom, gave a small smile, realised that Taylor, behind the greenness and the face of youth, had the makings of a shrewd operator, someone to watch, to cultivate.

'We infer that Breslaw was aware of Simmons's foolhardy attempt and that he had approved it without seeking authorisation,' Taylor continued.

'But he had,' Babbage said.

'Had he? Is it recorded?'

'You weren't there, but Karen was, so was Jerome.'

'I don't remember,' Karen said. She did, but she knew where Taylor was taking the discussion.

'I was distracted,' Jaden said. 'I can remember him bringing it up, but I believe we categorically forbade it, thought it was a crazy idea, climbing without permission, no insurance.'

Babbage, who had been there and knew the truth, concurred with the majority. 'That's it,' he said. 'Jim Breslaw disobeyed orders. A court-martial offence.'

'His actions were treasonous, placed us in a quandary.'

From a corner of the room, a whisper of a voice. 'If I may speak,' a bespectacled woman said. 'You asked me to attend.'

'Yes, that's correct, Helen,' Jaden said. 'You were going to give us a rundown on our financial status.'

Helen Moxon stood up. She was even shorter than Jerome Jaden, a rotund insignificant woman who most people at the station avoided, a smell of cats, a desk in a dark corner of the building.

'I asked Helen to conduct a financial analysis of the current situation,' Jaden said. 'When you're ready, Helen.'

The woman passed around a sheet of paper to each of those present. 'I've kept it short,' she said. 'If needed, I can detail it, put up a PowerPoint presentation.'

'Short is fine.'

'Very well, Mr Jaden.' As a lowly-paid functionary, a junior accountant in the company, over-familiarity was not appropriate.

Helen commenced. 'Advertising revenue is down by fifteen per cent this quarter. That's nearly thirty per cent down from the same period last year, although the station has reduced expenditure by eight per cent this year.'

'Which means?' Tom Taylor asked.

'Mr Jaden's seen the detailed figures, but in simple terms we are, on an adjusted monthly basis, running in the red, to the amount of eight per cent each month.'

'The conclusion?' Karen Majors asked.

'Six months, unless one of two things happens.'

'Which are?' Tom asked.

'I should think that's damn obvious,' Jaden said. 'I asked Helen to give the facts, not a convoluted spreadsheet with more columns than there are letters in the alphabet. What she prepared is based on advertising revenue, operating costs, money in the bank.'

'And best and worst projections,' Helen said.

'Thanks, Helen. If you could leave us, that would be appreciated.'

The woman left the room as silently as she had come.

'To answer your question,' Jaden continued, coming back to Tom's earlier question, 'we either reduce costs or increase advertising revenue. The banks are not going to help us, not this time.'

'We could go under,' Babbage said.

'If we do, you can all forget your performance bonuses, your stock options, severance pay.'

Babbage had been prepared for such an ultimatum; he had made plans to leave before the final curtain came down, but foregoing severance pay and stock options weren't on his agenda. 'We need to save the station,' he said.

'Can I speak again?' Taylor said. 'My idea of what we should do.'

'The floor's yours,' Jaden said.

Tom Taylor stood up, Alison squeezing his left hand as he rose, unseen by the others, although Karen Majors had picked up a discreet glance between the two. He moved to the end of the table, the side diametrically opposite Jerome Jaden. Full of confidence now, the aphrodisiacal power of importance. 'We crucify Jim Breslaw, heap all the blame on him.'

'Even if it's not true,' Babbage said.

'It's survival of the fittest, not the most honest nor the saintliest, and certainly not of those who care for the truth.'

'He's right,' Jaden said.

Karen Majors was not without compassion for Jim Breslaw, a man who had dealt with programming for twenty-three years, through the halcyon period when viewer numbers increased each year, and advertising revenue rose exponentially. Then, the drop as social media, streaming video and fake news took off.

'We lay the blame on him, tell the world that Jim had done everything to protect his job, not concerned for anyone's safety, only his generous salary, willing to take down the station, to sack who he could, to place the blame wherever.'

'And we sacked him once we found out, only to discover that he had approved Simmons climbing that building, Tricia Warburton believing that we agreed to it,' Jaden said.

'Jerome, you're right. As I said, crucify Jim Breslaw, a press conference, reveal that Tricia Warburton is coming back on board, a revamped format, guest stars, and travelling the world. Beef her up, a tight skirt, low-cut top.'

'She'll not go for it,' Karen Majors said. 'She's not that stupid, nor is she a tart.'

'I never said she was. And besides, that was always the plan. I'm just saying to up the rhetoric, to lay it on thicker, to push harder. Pay her what she wants, put it in her contract that she's to act accordingly, get the male viewers excited, the women envious, press releases about her past life, her lovers, current romances, make up a few.'

'How much is this going to cost?' Jaden asked.

'Plenty. Get Helen on the job, run the numbers. It's either make or break.'

'Don't forget that someone killed Simmons,' Babbage said. 'The police will still be sniffing around.'

'Let them. Denigrate Breslaw whenever possible. Any good with a gun, Breslaw?'

'An amateur shot,' Jaden said.

'All the better.'

'And how do you expect to lay the blame on Jim?' Karen Majors asked.

'Social media. If you can't beat it, use it. There must be companies out there that will post anything anywhere.'

'In this country?'

'No idea. It's social media; they can be anywhere. Feed them what we want, let them run with it, and you, Karen, work your arse off, grab all the revenue we want, screw the other stations.'

'Can this work?' Babbage asked.

'It can and will,' Jaden said. 'Tom, you can take control of this. Is that okay with you?'

'It is if I can have Alison to help.'

'You can have Alison any way you like,' Jaden said, the smiling Alison blushing.

***

A flaming head of red hair, a bushy beard, a moustache covering his upper lip, Justin Skinner looked every part a mountain man.

Taller than Isaac, broad-shouldered and muscular, Skinner shook Isaac's hand firmly, a bear-like grip, and then Larry, patting him on the chest. 'Could do with a bit of exercise,' he said. 'Your chief inspector, he's looking fit, fit enough for rock climbing. How about it, DCI Cook, interested?'

'Not now, I'm not,' Isaac said. Skinner's repartee wasn't unexpected. After all, they were standing in a draughty barn in Snowdonia in northern Wales, the headquarters of Skinner's training centre for budding rock climbers and mountaineers.

'You should. Good for the spirit; make a man out of you or a woman if you're female. You're here about Angus, I suppose.'

'We are,' Larry said. 'A few questions.'

'If I was sleeping with the lovely Kate Hampton?'

'That's one,' Isaac said.

A young woman in climbing boots, wearing an overlarge woollen jumper and a pair of faded jeans, passed over three mugs. 'Hot chocolate, just the thing for a day like this,' she said.

'Thanks, Rachel,' Justin said. 'I was telling the chief inspector he'd make a good climber.'

'A good something else as well,' the woman said, winking at Isaac as she left.

'Good sort is Rachel. She climbed Everest, first attempt. Not many do, makes the rest of us look like amateurs.'

'She's only a slip of a girl,' Larry said.

'Tougher than she looks. We've got a thing going, not sure how long it'll last. Rachel's a free spirit, takes her climbing seriously, not much else.'

'There's a style about you, not what we associate with climbers,' Isaac said.

'You mean my easy-going nature?'

'Angus Simmons was a serious-minded individual, although Mike Hampton, we couldn't form an opinion about.'

'Hampton was always that way, a glass half empty outlook on life, although Kate reckoned, he had another side to him, not that I ever saw it. Angus was a serious individual, ambitious and determined, but me, I'm a natural showman, a big mouth.'

'When you're climbing?'

'A singular focus, getting up to the top, staying safe, getting down again.'

'Hampton didn't?'

'Accidents happen, mistakes are made. You can't be that precise, and if you waited until the risk was negated to zero, you'd never go. If you go up Mount Everest, you must be prepared to die, to let loose if you make it back, to party on once you get back to Kathmandu. Have you been there?'

'Neither of us have,' Isaac said.

'You should go; a great place.'

Isaac and Larry hadn't driven since four in the morning just to chat with Justin Skinner, no matter how interesting and entertaining the man was. It was still a murder investigation, and Skinner had become a suspect due to Gwyneth Simmons's statement.

'Kate Hampton?' Isaac said, reminding Skinner that he had brought up the woman's name.

'It can't be much fun for her, stuck with Mike,' Skinner said.

'According to information we received, she's finding her fun somewhere else.'

'Not from me, not unless I'm down south.'

'And if you are?'

'There's no harm done. What's good for one is good for the other.'

'Mike Hampton?'

'Not sure if he's capable, not after that fall, stuck in that wheelchair all day. If it was me…'

'A high cliff, propel yourself over the side?'

'Not me. It's all to do with mental willpower, force the challenge, take on the impossible. He could still climb, not the same as before, but small challenges, each one more difficult than before, and he could abseil, use his arm muscles.'

'Kate Hampton?'

'Why not? No harm done, and Mike, he doesn't know.'

'A regular occurrence?'

'Once every few weeks. She tells him she's off to see a friend for a long weekend, tells Mike it's a female.'

'He doesn't realise?'

'That's up to him. I can't give him sympathy, and as far as I'm concerned, he's a nobody, blaming Simmons the way he did.'

'Is it possible that Mike Hampton attempted to kill Angus on Cerro Torre?'

'Not on the mountain. I told you, once you're climbing, it's a different mindset.'

'Hampton thought Angus was having an affair with Kate before they went to Patagonia. Was it you?'

'It could have been, but then I wouldn't know if she had anyone else. Angus wasn't much of a lover, so I've been told, but Kate liked him.'

'Who told you about Simmons's lovemaking?'

'Kate. I've not thought about it before, but she was double-dipping, Angus and me, even Mike.'

'Does that upset you?'

'Should it?'

'Rachel?'

'She's a whirlwind, that one, serious about climbing, lost a husband in the Alps, there when he fell, heard him scream.'

'Her reaction?'

'On the mountain, professional. Down on the ground, inconsolable, took her a year before she climbed again. She'll not get emotionally involved, too hard on the soul, seeing someone you love die.'

'Have you?'

'Not me. Life's a ball, enjoy it, don't get stuck with a nine-to-five existence,' Skinner said.

Likeable as Justin Skinner was, neither Isaac and Larry wanted his life. Isaac had Jenny and their son; Larry had his wife, and even though her social-climbing could be irritating, he still loved her.

Chapter 11

Charles Simmons met with his former wife, a woman he had once loved intensely, the mother of his only child. The meeting was tense: unspoken sorrow, unresolved issues, forgotten love.

'You're looking well, Charles,' Gwyneth Simmons said. She had dressed for the occasion, remembering that the man she had once loved was a stickler for appearance, always dressing for dinner, no sitting around a kitchen table of a night, a bottle of wine on the table, a couple of plastic cups, a pizza from a shop around the corner.

Gwyneth had grown up in the Highlands, a subsistence farmer for a father, a mother who taught at a local school. She had loved them, yet abhorred their indifferent attitude to the world outside of the valley where they lived.

It was her father who was the more intractable, a legacy of his father returning home from the trenches, from the Battle of the Somme, missing not only his lust for life but also one arm and the use of one eye, blinded by a mortar.

The grandfather, bitter about life, had married his childhood sweetheart, a rosy-faced highland lass, seventeen years of age, who had borne him two children, one of whom was Gwyneth's father, the other child dying in a German prisoner of war camp in 1943.

The McLoughlins, Gwyneth's maiden name, were a hardy bunch but mostly unsuccessful. Her father barely made a profit from his farm, relying in no small part on the meagre stipend of his wife, Gwyneth's mother. And then, her mother was dead, before her time, a reason never disclosed, not to the child, thirteen years of age at the time.

What happened to her father, Gwyneth never knew, for after the age of fourteen, fostered to a second cousin of her mother's, she never saw him again.

As for Charles, life had treated him better. Incurious as a child, spoilt as he had been, then a good education, an apprenticeship with his father, soon rising through the company.

At the age of twenty-six, he had struck out on his own, purchased a half share in an agency mainly selling land and farms, some in Scotland, which is where he had met Gwyneth, two years younger than him, working on reception at the hotel where he was staying.

They were married within two months, living back in London one week later, and unbeknown to either, a child on the way.

At first, Gwyneth, the dutiful wife, eager to please, took care to dress well, went to the hairdresser's, bought only the best clothes, ensured that her husband's meal was on the table when he came in. But over time and with a child, the effort required to look after one outweighed the other. And then, Charles Simmons, a demanding man, strayed, returning one night reeking of perfume, his collar marked with lipstick.

Distraught, an inviolate trust broken, she had moved into another room in the house for two months, leaving Charles one night after the two had discussed the situation and returning to Scotland, back to her parents' neglected home. In time, and with money from Charles, she renovated the house, built on an extension with two more bedrooms, a bathroom with hot water and a shower. She had the electricity connected, no longer reliant on an old diesel generator that was out of order more than it was in.

Angus Simmons had the outdoor life during holidays and weekends, a school in Edinburgh during the week.

Neither wishing to remarry, the parents occasionally met to discuss his upbringing and to attend school events. After Angus left school, forsaking university for challenges other than academic, his parents met less often, the reason so many years had passed since they had last seen each other.

'I'm sorry about Angus,' Charles said.

'We always knew that his life would be short,' Gwyneth said.

'What a life, so many adventures, places he went, things he did, challenges conquered.'

In a rush of emotions, the two embraced, tears streaming down their cheeks.

'I miss him.'

'No more than I,' Gwyneth said. 'Who could have done such a wicked thing?'

The two hugged, long and lingering, remembering a past life, their son who was no more.

'We always knew, didn't we?' Charles said.

'But murder?'

'Some people embrace life, yet burn too soon. Angus was always to meet his fate, and it should have been on that mountain when Hampton fell.'

'Do you know the story? That Mike believed Kate was having an affair with Angus when all along it was Justin Skinner.'

'That snake,' Charles replied. 'What did she see in him?'

'Life.'

'What does that mean?'

'Mike Hampton was Angus's friend, a great mountaineer, a lousy human being.'

'The same as me, is that what you're saying?'

Charles Simmons had been an unfaithful philanderer. A man who saw no wrong in what he did, giving scant regard to the woman he married, the child he had produced, preferring the company of others – a successful man, liked by many, charismatic, a charmer, his conscience unscathed.

'It's what men do,' Charles had said when Gwyneth took him to task. It wasn't, not as far as she was concerned. Then, to rub salt into the wound, three weeks after she had left for Scotland, a phone call from one of her so-called friends saying that she was moving in with him.

Gwyneth reflected that Angus, removed from his father's wayward influence, had grown up to be a better person, a girlfriend at school, a few other relationships and then Maddox Timberley, a woman she liked.

It had been Angus's twentieth birthday, a small affair at a pub. Gwyneth had arrived with an older sister of hers, a matronly woman, given to church work and singing the praise of the Lord, the pub anathema to her. Still, she had relented and come, only drinking orange juice, looking with disdain at her sister quaffing champagne.

Gwyneth's lapse was due to Angus's friend, a long-haired blond boy of nineteen, their hands touching under the table.

She had suspected that her son found attraction in either sex, noncommittal in her distaste. After all, she was a libertarian, believing in the individual's right to follow whatever course they chose in life as long as no other person was offended or hurt. However, it upset her to see Angus with another male, realising that her values, open and free with others, didn't embrace her son, a young man who had pursued manly activities all of his short life, not men, and not in that pub, and not in front of her sister.

'A lousy human being? No, you were never that,' Gwyneth said. 'Frustrating, a bad liar, an even worse husband, but you did your duty, made sure I was secure and that our son was educated, a good grounding at school.'

'Could we?' Charles asked.

'Get together again? An interesting thought. Not that I'm averse, but no, not now, not at our time of life, and not with our son dead, his murderer still out there.'

'But we know who it is?'

'Do we? I've thought about it, the reaction when Angus won that award. Justin Skinner thought it should have been him, and Mike Hampton was seething.'

'He always seethed, nothing unusual there.'

'It was around the time Skinner started messing around with Kate, but with him, water runs off a duck's back. I wouldn't have been surprised if he blamed Angus, Kate going along with it.'

'I never liked her, a look about her,' Charles said. Even though the relationship between him and his wife had ended a long time ago, he had to admit that it was good to see her, to talk to each other the way they had when they were young: the plans they had, the number of children they wanted, where to live, where to love. And then he had fouled it up, all for a night of passion with a work colleague, a woman not worthy to stand in his wife's shade.

The next day he returned, guilty as charged, feeling the sorrow within him, knowing that he had crossed the line from forgiven to condemned. And then, Gwyneth and their child at the railway station; a long and lingering kiss, like two lovers parting for a couple of days, but each knowing that it was forever. And here she was, talking to him again, the way it had once been, but not of plans for the future, of love, but murder and hatred and disloyal wives and false friends.

'Why Kate married Mike, I'll never know,' Gwyneth said. 'Sure, he was the hero type, but he was always grumpy. Not like Angus, but then we always suspected, even from a young age. Not that it mattered, not that much, but it seemed apparent that he would never marry, and then he met Maddox.'

'Do you think he would have married her?'

'He might have. Maddox was keen.'

'Have you spoken to her?' Charles asked.

'Not since it happened. I want to see her, to say how sorry we are.'

'And to try to find out who killed Angus. It has to be either Justin or Mike.'

'But how? Most of the time, Justin's up in north Wales and Mike's hardly agile. Anyway, Mike's angry, not violent.'

'He was supposedly in Patagonia.'

'Angus said he was,' Gwyneth said, an emotion sweeping over her, a possible doubt.'

'Are you sure that Angus told you the truth?'

'I have to,' Gwyneth said as she put her arms around Charles. Whatever the truth, she needed someone to be with her. 'I'll stay here with you if that's all right.'

'That's fine. Welcome home,' Charles said.

***

Emulating the phoenix, a legendary bird rising from its funeral pyre, renewed and youthful, Tricia Warburton's resurrection was no less dramatic.

It was seven o'clock in the evening, and for Isaac an early night away from the office, a promise to Jenny to spend time with the baby, 'bonding' she called it.

The rest of the team were still in the office, processing paperwork, writing reports, taking the opportunity to sit down quietly and mull over the murder investigation. However, for Larry Hill, after a busy day out at the crime scene, following up with shooting clubs, checking who of those known to the investigation might have had an interest in shooting, his mulling consisted of closing his eyes and falling asleep.

Wendy Gladstone, also tired but not having the benefit of a couple of beers for lunch, was awake but sore, arthritis troubling her again. She sat with Bridget Halloran, looking over her shoulder as Bridget typed at the keyboard.

'Any luck with car registration numbers close to where the shot was taken?' Wendy asked.

'Needle in a haystack, better to find the weapon,' Bridget said.

Two minutes after Jaden came on the television screen, Isaac's phone call woke Larry. 'Put on the television, Jaden's channel,' he said.

'We're excited, ecstatic even, that Tricia is back with us in an exciting new format, a programme that will elate you, our friends,' Jaden said. To one side, Tricia Warburton, even more provocatively dressed, her bosoms proud, the makeup thicker than ever.

Jenny, who had watched with Isaac, thought the woman looked tarty in a classy way. 'She's sold out if what you said about her is true.'

'She admitted the clothes and the breasts were for the viewing public, but she's ambitious.'

'I can see why you like her,' a nudge in Isaac's ribs.

'Purely professional,' Isaac said jokingly. He still appreciated a pretty woman, and the woman on the television was undoubtedly that.

It was Tricia's turn to speak. She was not as upbeat as Jaden, more subdued, reflecting on past events. Coached by Karen Majors and the ever-smiling Alison, who was, as Jaden had said at the meeting six days earlier, giving herself to Tom Taylor any way he wanted.

'Pathos,' Karen had said. 'Show plaintiveness, a sadness about Angus Simmons. Don't overdo it, don't dampen the mood of the press conference, but humility goes a long way.'

Coached almost as much as an American president delivering a state of the nation address, Tricia spoke. She spoke of her fondness for Angus Simmons, his heroic character, his taming of Mount Everest, his commitment to the programme they had co-hosted, to the television station and the leadership of Jerome Jaden. The last statement a pencilled-in addition from the man himself.

'Nice touch,' Jaden had said, 'shows that we're a team dedicated to our viewers and each other.'

Bob Babbage, the company lawyer, careful to ensure that the wording of Tricia's speech didn't cross over the line from honest and heartfelt to probably criminal, had to cover his mouth with a hand at Jaden's comment. Too many years with the man had long since destroyed any belief in Jaden's interest in others; he knew him to be a money-grabbing bastard who'd shaft Tricia at the first hurdle if he could, ratings or no ratings. Even so, Babbage would stay for the foreseeable future, see which way the ratings went, whether Jaden could achieve what others thought impossible, work a miracle.

'We're in production,' Tricia continued, 'and our excitement is high, bringing you stories from around the world, giving me the chance to experience different cultures, diverse opinions. To show men and woman achieving great things; the family of man, or should I say persons, united as never before by what we'll be bringing to you.'

Jaden took the microphone from Tricia who took the opportunity to pull down her dress.

There were more speeches, Karen Major putting in a none too subtle plug for her sales department. Tom Taylor wet behind the ears, but learning fast, giving a rundown on the exciting and innovative programming, a touch of the new with the old, streamlining as needed, expanding as required, cognisant of the viewers. It was clichéd but effective; Alison was watching from one side, proud of her man, loving towards him and of him. She was anxious to move on from public relations, to host a programme, Tricia's if she faulted or became too demanding, more than willing to dress the same as Tricia, to do whatever was necessary. To her, Tom Taylor was in the bag, and he was making a go of it; he'd do for now, but one step backwards, and she'd re-evaluate.

A voice from the back of the room.

'Jerome, Ashley Otway, *The Sun* newspaper.'

'Yes, Ashley,' Jaden replied. He smiled but knew that the conference was about to go south if he didn't nip it in the bud.

'We're excited to hear of Tricia's new programme.' Ashley Otway knew that a gentle wind up was better than going full blast at Jaden.

'Thank you, Ashley, for your remarks,' Jaden replied, hoping to head the woman off, to wrap up the press conference, to get out of the room.

'I've not finished. Jim Breslaw, removed at short notice, Tom Taylor, brought in soon after. A good decision?'

'I believe so. Jim served us for many years, did a great job, made mistakes at the end, but times change, people's viewing habits are not the same as before. New ideas, innovation, someone who understands the younger generation, a person savvy with social media. That's what Tom's brought with him. He's integral, a force for change, positive change, he told us when we offered him the job. He'll not let us down, I'm sure of it.'

'The police believe that Angus Simmons was murdered. Doesn't that concern you more than this hoo-ha we've seen here today. And isn't Jim Breslaw implicated, the man who would have approved that stunt, now thrown to the wolves?'

'Ashley,' Jaden said, a broad smile on his face, 'Jim was in error, not us. And besides, this is a police matter, let us not forget. I can't speak about what happened, nor can anyone else here today.'

'But…'

'Ladies and gentlemen, it's good of you to come, to join with us in this celebration, to wish Tricia all the best, knowing that she has our full support,' Jaden said. He wasn't about to let a petty-minded, mealy-mouthed reporter destroy the press conference.

Jaden left the room abruptly, the others following soon after.

In the next room, away from the dispersing crowd, Jaden grabbed hold of Babbage by the collar. 'You bastard. You're our lawyer. I told you to make sure there were no dumb questions.'

'I did, paid her off not to act dumb. No one else asked.'

'Then what happened?'

'Her newspaper. It's not only the television stations that are struggling; it's the newspapers as well. She's protecting her job, taking a backhander from us.'

'Deal with her,' Jaden said. 'Offer her a job, bribe her more, but make sure she doesn't write it up.'

'Jim Breslaw?'

'Make sure he doesn't talk, not about Simmons or us.'

'He'll want money,' Babbage said.

'Don't tell me, just make sure Breslaw keeps his mouth shut. Simple enough, even for you, or do we have to get rid of you, give the job to Taylor?'

Babbage, not sure what to say, nervously replied, 'He hasn't got the time or the legal qualifications, what with programming and keeping Alison entertained.'

Jerome Jaden, his anger vented, said, 'You're right, Bob. The man's busy. Just deal with that damn Ashley whatshername, make sure Breslaw doesn't talk.'

Chapter 12

A bizarre press conference, Isaac had thought, initially full of positivity, not forsaking that one of their media stars had died recently. Degenerating into verbal fisticuffs with a determined reporter and concluding with Jerome Jaden walking off stage and out of the door, Homicide met at six the next morning, prompt.

'It didn't go according to plan,' Larry said.

'They must have paid Tricia Warburton plenty,' Wendy's comment.

'Bridget, what do you reckon?' Isaac asked, the woman holding three folders in her hand.

'Selling herself, not that I minded either way.'

'Cheapened herself?'

'If she's smart, it might be a good move, but I wouldn't be sure. You've met Jaden; a decent man?'

'An entrepreneur, been in the business a long time,' Isaac said. 'Any dirt on him?'

'He's not made himself popular, put a few competitors out of business.'

'Is there any more?'

'Heads of sales tend not to last long. He keeps his lawyers close, takes action easily, protects his base.'

'All in the file?' Wendy asked.

'It is,' Bridget said. 'I've added more details on Jim Breslaw, included Ashley Otway. Jim Breslaw, you know about. The whiz-kid, Tom Taylor, was given the position soon after.'

'Whiz-kid?' Larry said.

'You know what I mean. Young, smart-arse, thinks he knows it all.'

'Research or a personal opinion?'

'A bit of both,' Bridget said. 'Taylor left school, good results, a degree in media management; did well again, won a prize one year for best student. He's no dummy, but no real-world experience. More than likely Jaden's stooge, not like Breslaw, who had been around forever, almost back to black and white television, the epilogue at the end of programming for the day, the national anthem as the television channel turned to black.'

'Prehistoric,' Isaac said.

'It seems that way, although it was only 1967 when colour kicked off. Breslaw became involved in the eighties, did well, but then the world moved on. Breslaw, fifty-nine, not so good with computers and the youth today, started to lose market share.'

'Market share, or was it across the board?'

'Across the board; fifty minutes less viewing per day on average across the population since 2010. Significant if you're generating revenue. Jerome Jaden's haemorrhaging money, not got enough to pay for Tricia Warburton to fly around the world, bringing you the stories you want, not if it's unsuccessful. The man's taking a gamble, and Breslaw, if he'd still been there, would have told him so.'

'Ashley Otway?'

'Entertainments reporter. Interviews celebrities, endures their piffle, makes out she's interested,' Bridget said.

'What else?' Larry asked. 'She seemed to be on to something last night.'

'Thirty-seven years of age, single, a political reporter, up and coming, spoilt her copybook, asked questions where she shouldn't have.'

'Such as?' Isaac said.

'Do you remember a couple of years back, Members of Parliament cheating on their expenses, claiming their primary residence in London as a second home, only used when parliament is sitting?'

'I do; a couple of ministers forced to resign.'

'There was another one, more senior, a house in Richmond, close enough to be a daily commute to the Houses of Parliament, a small two-storey terrace. He claimed it as a second residence.'

'Was it?'

'He failed to mention that he had a mistress in there, Spanish, from Madrid, taught dancing in the area, whirled him around the bedroom of a night. Otway found out about his monkeying around, a bit on the side, asked him the question one night over a glass of wine.'

'Why wine? Why at night?'

'The man's sharp, aware that Otway was on to him, thought that wine and a late-night seduction were one way out. He was a powerful man, still is, and Otway's ambitious. The man had the ear of the prime minister, could ensure that she got the first question when he was willing to answer questions, not that he is that often.'

'How do you know all this?' Larry asked.

'Don't ask,' Bridget replied.

Bridget's accomplishments with computers and hacking were legendary, not only in Homicide but also throughout the Challis Street Police Station, even in Scotland Yard. Careful how she went about it, only revealing what was needed for an investigation, Isaac knew that one thing she wouldn't do was reveal names or addresses unless relevant.

'As you were saying,' Isaac said.

'This minister thought Otway would be a fine addition to his stable, unable to believe that she wasn't having any of it. He couldn't deny that he had a mistress, Otway already having spoken to the woman in a supermarket close to the love nest. The next day, after she rejected the minister, he made a few phone calls, and Otway's given an ultimatum: entertainments or get on your bike.'

'The verbal or literal bicycle?'

'Verbal. If she applied anywhere else, doors would be locked. This unnamed man wasn't the only one cheating the system, and men of influence, newspaper owners, television station proprietors and others are all into one thing or another. The minister's vice was women, still is.'

'The Spanish mistress?'

'Still dancing the Flamenco with the minister, another love nest, a different address, but the expenses scandal continues.'

'And if she continues to pursue Jaden?'

'Jaden's not got the political clout, hardly likely to stop her pursuing a cause.'

'She's meant to be bringing light and frivolity to the newspaper, not investigative journalism,' Larry said.

'What she's doing is not important,' Isaac said. 'What she knows, or suspects, is. Talk to her, find out if she'll talk, or if she's determined to keep it to herself.'

'She'll want a scoop from us if she agrees,' Larry said.

'Give her first bite of the cherry, assuming it's not prejudicial to the investigation. Run anything she writes past me first, let Chief Superintendent Goddard know, let our legal department peruse it.'

'Seems a lot to check.'

'If Otway's willing to take on a government minister, she's no pushover. Kid gloves with her until we're comfortable.'

'It would be best if you meet with her,' Wendy said. 'She's educated, more than DI Hill and me.'

'Wendy's right,' Larry said. 'She's all yours. Practise your dance steps.'

In Homicide, occasional humour never went amiss, always an excellent way to defuse the tension, the morbidness of dealing with death. Isaac took it in his stride, felt no offence, no need to tell his inspector off for his impertinence.

'I can barely put one foot in front of the other,' Isaac said. 'It might be best if you and Wendy meet with Breslaw as soon as possible. Now that Otway's mentioned him, she's sure to meet with him, and Jaden's not going to be far behind.'

***

'If you're here to ask stupid questions, to look for an angle, you're wasting your time. I'm beyond all that, enjoying my retirement.'

Neither Larry nor Wendy was prepared for Jim Breslaw's outburst. After all, he had been cordial when he opened the door of his modest semi-detached house in North London and had welcomed them in, ensuring that Wendy had the best seat in the room and that Larry was comfortable.

Jim Breslaw was slim, with drooping shoulders, a weather-beaten look, a full head of hair. Wendy could tell that he had used a hair dye, although she couldn't see the point. Her husband had gone through the getting old stage, the need to exercise daily, comb his hair forward and let it grow longer. She had told him off for the folly, that with age comes wisdom, and a distinguished older man is more attractive than someone who can't accept the inevitable.

Wendy's husband had had her; Jim Breslaw had no one, his wife having passed away at forty-six, a brain embolism.

'Retirement suit you?' Larry asked.

'I thought I was good for another five years, but Jerome had other ideas. Something to do with a new team, dynamic, fresh ideas, innovative this and that, whatever twaddle he could come up with.'

'Your opinion of Jerome Jaden?'

'After what he did to me?'

'Before would be more appropriate,' Larry said, shifting on his seat to let a cat find its place alongside him.

'Jerome's a bastard, in the nicest possible way.'

'I've never met a nice bastard,' Wendy said.

'You've led a sheltered life. Jerome Jaden would sell his mother if there were an advantage,' Breslaw said.

'Selling your mother?'

'Figuratively, that's what I mean. He was a shoot from the hip man, made decisions on the fly, thought about them afterwards, rescinded them later if there was a better option.'

'He wasn't a details man?'

'Instinctive, a good judge of what the people wanted, who was best suited to work for him, their job description.'

'You admired him?'

'Greatly, still do, even after he showed me the way out.'

'Instinctive or stupid?'

'Jerome knew what was going to happen after Angus pulled that stunt.'

'You mean after someone shot him.'

Larry got up from his seat, the cat exercising its right to more room on the chair, sticking its claws into his leg.

'Sorry about that,' Breslaw said. 'They think they own the place.'

'Are you fond of cats, Mr Breslaw?' Wendy asked. She was comfortable, and no cat was going to oust her from where she was seated.

'I can't stand the damn things, but they were the wife's. The last thing she said to me before she died was for me to promise to look after her pets. She knew I would have found homes for them. Seven years this November since she passed on, and to be honest, the cats have been company.'

'You and your wife, close?'

'As close as any married couple could be after twenty-five years together. I was upset for a while, but she hadn't been a well woman, even before the embolism, too much weight, a dicky heart.'

'Did work become your obsession afterwards?'

'Not so you'd notice. What did Jaden say?'

'That you went back to the halcyon days when advertising revenue and viewers were easy to attract. That it was a lot easier back then, words to that effect.'

'He's right. I'll not dispute that, although he might not have told you that television isn't going to last, not indefinitely. Oh, sure, they can streamline the company, get rid of the old warhorses, the dinosaurs as Tom Taylor would say, smart-arsed little brat, but there's only so far you can go.'

'You're not a fan of Tom Taylor?'

Breslaw moved from where he had been standing and moved closer to the window. 'I have a passion for gardening,' he said.

Larry looked over at Wendy, lifted his eyebrows, a sign that he didn't know what Breslaw was talking about or why he had changed the subject.

'Tom Taylor?' Wendy repeated.

'The weather's not been that good lately, too dry for the vegetables, better for growing flowers, not that I'm much bothered with them, although I've got a rose bush that's doing well. Rosemary, she used to like flowers, not that she was a gardener, preferred to be indoors most of the time. A great knitter, always a jumper at Christmas, and then, she had the cats, not that they're all still alive. I don't replace them. I let them fade away, the same as me.'

'Mr Breslaw,' Wendy shouted, 'you're digressing.'

'We were talking about Tom Taylor, and now you're going on about the garden and your wife,' Larry said.

'Maudlin, that's all. I'd still prefer to be at the station, keeping myself busy. I feel as though I've been thrown on the scrapheap,' Breslaw said. 'The modern generation think they know better than their elders, disrespectful too.'

'Was he?'

'He was after my job, always sucking up to Jaden, sweet-talking with Karen Majors, kissing and canoodling with Alison.'

'I thought they were discreet in the office,' Wendy said.

'Maybe they were, but she's related to Jerome, favourite niece, something like that.'

To Wendy, who had experienced her husband's illness and demise, Jim Breslaw showed early-stage senility, which seemed illogical, given that until two weeks before, he had been Jaden's head of programming. A person doesn't degenerate that quickly.

'Take us back to the day you left the station,' Larry said.

Breslaw's strange behaviour confused them, but it wasn't why they were there.

'Two days after Simmons fell, Jerome calls me into his office. Karen Majors and Babbage are there, both looking contrite, not that Babbage would be.'

'Why?'

'Bob Babbage, hard-nosed, a rationalist. If, as we now know, I was about to get the ceremonial kick out of the door, he wouldn't have been sorry.'

'No emotion?'

'Babbage is what he is. I was a pain in the rear end, always wanting more money for programming. It's a tight market, and most of the programmes we purchase, especially if they're good, are expensive. Basic economics and he knew it, but the margins are not there.'

'Jerome Jaden, known in the industry as a man who could drive a deal.'

'Jerome came up through the good years, the same as I did. It was a lot easier back then, but now, I struggled, so did Jerome. Neither of us could come up with an angle to maintain ratings, and Karen Majors, she's not on top of her game.'

'We've not heard any comments about her,' Wendy said.

'And you won't, not yet. The industry is in flux, and Karen's as good as any other, but she can't do much about it.'

'Tom Taylor?'

'Not sure, and that's an honest answer. He's temporary, looks the part, the fresh new look, catering to a younger audience. I didn't go much for him, not personally, but who knows, he may pull a rabbit out of a hat.'

'He'll survive?'

'Young, attractive, a charmer, he will, one way or the other.'

'Alison Glassop, any part in all of this?'

'Apart from her being Jerome's niece or is it grand-niece, I'm not sure which, not that it matters much. She was keen on Tom, not that she can be blamed for that, but whether she's a conniving little bitch or a sweet young thing, I'd not know. She didn't bother me, and she did pretty the place up.'

'That sounds sexist,' Wendy said.

'It wasn't meant that way. You asked me for an honest opinion; I gave it.'

'The climb? Did you approve it?' Larry asked.

Focus lost, Breslaw was once again looking out of the window. 'Looks like rain,' he said. 'Saves me watering it later on.'

'Mr Breslaw, the flowers can wait; we can't,' Wendy said.

'Yes, yes, you're right. I'm sorry, don't know what came over me.'

Senility or a nervous breakdown, the trauma of the last weeks affecting Breslaw's mental state, Wendy couldn't be sure.

'The climb?' Larry said once more.

'I'm meant to take the blame.'

'Who asked you to take the blame?'

'It was in my severance package, not that it's written down. They want me to be the scapegoat, but I won't be.'

'Who would have wanted Simmons dead? Who at the station?'

'Tricia Warburton, she wanted him out, but taking a shot at him, not her.'

'Then who?'

'Jerome liked her, keen to keep her on, but the others wanted Simmons.'

'Jerome Jaden gets what he wants?'

'Once, he might have, but times have changed.'

'He's the owner,' Wendy said.

'The majority shareholder, answerable to the executive, to other shareholders. He has a lot of power, but it isn't absolute.'

'Who did you prefer to stay on, to host the programme?'

'Simmons. A remarkable man.'

'But not a pretty face.'

'He never was, but still remarkable. I wanted the programme to be more focussed on outstanding sporting and cultural achievements.'

'Jaden?'

'He wanted scantily-clad bimbos, frivolous happenings around the world.'

'Which format would have best served the station?'

'Sporting and cultural achievements, more credibility, significant, more reputable.'

'Financially?'

'Celebrities up to mischief.'

107

'And you wouldn't have agreed?'

'I wouldn't have resigned. It's academic, though. I was shown the door. Do you know, they even changed the lock on my office door?'

'Who gave Angus Simmons permission?'

'Nobody, probably. Simmons, if he had decided, nobody would have stopped him.'

'Did you know before he climbed?'

'I only needed to know when they would have a programme for me to schedule in.'

'And if you'd seen him climbing?'

'If he had reached the top, I would have shown it.'

'Even if it was illegal?'

'Even.'

'It was irresponsible, dangerous, gives young people crazy ideas.'

Jim Breslaw was back at the window. 'There's a break in the clouds. I might need to water the garden after all,' he said.

'A wasted trip,' Larry said on the drive back to the office.

'Was it?'

'Who knows. Time will tell.'

***

'Enemies in high places, it seems you're good at that, Ashley,' Isaac said.

'No more than you. I'm told that the Met's Commissioner Davies doesn't think much of you.'

'Touché. Anyway, it's good to see you. How long has it been?'

'Since you stood me up? Eight years, give or take a few months.'

Isaac hadn't mentioned in the office that before Wendy had come into Homicide, before Larry, before Isaac had married, he and Ashley Otway had been out together a couple of times.

Isaac wasn't sure why he hadn't told the team. It had been during his first murder investigation, back then inspector, not chief inspector, and Ashley had been a police reporter for another newspaper.

Since then, the two had drifted apart, nothing unusual, as both were ambitious, neither looking for undying love, only a good time.

Back then, Isaac was a few pounds slimmer, jogging regularly. Ashley had been cute with a pert nose and blue eyes, and as he studied her now, the light streaming into the room from behind her, he saw that time had aged her slightly and that she bore an uncanny resemblance to Jenny.

A waterfront restaurant at Camden Lock, a glass of wine each, a menu to peruse; it was almost like old times, the two of them, even if it hadn't lasted long, enjoying each other's company. And then, Isaac remembering, she had gone overseas, a promotion to a political reporter, following a trade delegation led by Gabriel Doveton, the minister of trade, a junket out to the Middle East, a chance for those on the trip to get drunk, strike a few deals and declare it a success. The only fly in the ointment was the diligent Ashley, revealing that bribes had been paid at the highest level in one country, an eighty-million-pound contract awarded on the back of them.

Hushed up, as they often are, a copy of the Official Secrets Act thrust under Ashley's nose and a retraction by the newspaper.

'No one believes retractions,' the newspaper's editor had told her in the confidence of his office. 'In future,' he'd added, 'run it past me, check with our legal beavers. Don't want to get on the wrong side of those in power, even if they're on the fiddle, do we?'

Ashley continued to follow the rules, to expose when there was something to reveal, running it past her masters, modifying the story, an inflexion here, another word there. If the name was likely to cause trouble, an anonymous source quoted, to bin the story if the legal team said so.

With a degree in journalism and left-wing beliefs, Ashley, young and idealistic, had seethed on more than one occasion. Still, with time, the rough edges smoothed, the extreme ideology tempered, she adopted a change in tactics.

Still determined, still believing that journalism was about truth and justice, she carefully acquired her moles: people who would, out of idealism or a need for money, slip her news of happenings behind the scenes in the Palace of Westminster, the Houses of Parliament.

She came to know about those who were fiddling their expenses, incompetent, and others only in it for the money and prestige. And the most heinous was rewarded with a peerage, kicked up to the House of Lords if they kept their mouths shut.

Eventually, sickened by the hypocrisy and in a fit of despair, she had written the article about the minister and his Spanish mistress; the editor and the legal team, no longer as diligent as before, not checking all the copy that she submitted.

It had caused a political storm, the opposition shouting at the prime minister to remove his minister, to set an example. Ashley Otway was moved to entertainments, more out of political expediency than for what she had written.

The editor congratulated her, and the minister resigned – to concentrate on serving his electorate, to spend more time with his family. And then, nine months later, after the storm had blown over, he was back on the front bench, a more senior ministry to run.

The newspaper continued to publish articles on government corruption. But without their best investigative reporter, now confined to interviewing boy bands and ill-mannered movie stars, they weren't as incisive as before.

'Why did you take on Jerome Jaden?' Isaac asked.

Ashley took a sip of wine. 'It's murder, not celebrities or reality stars dragged out from under a rock somewhere. They're unimportant, but Simmons was an impressive individual, worthy of more respect, and there's Jaden, up on that platform, preaching about a new world dawning with Tricia Warburton leading the singing.'

'You don't like her?'

'I've nothing against her. It's not her per se. Ambition's not a crime.'

'On the back of murder, it could be,' Isaac said. He had liked Ashley before, still did. But then, he had liked a lot of women in his time, almost married one or two. Yet always a reason he hadn't, the reason why he had chosen Jenny, why she had chosen him.

'You're after the dirt?'

'We know some of it, nothing criminal, not yet. You have a reputation for getting under people's skin. Have you found anything?'

'Apart from that fiasco the other day?'

'Yes.'

'I'm not about to indulge in gossip.'

'You're aiming to get your old job back?'

Ashley put her cutlery down, looked across the table at Isaac. 'I am,' she said. 'One way or the other.'

'You could join the police force, put your investigating skills to good use. Sixty-five thousand pounds a year for a chief inspector.'

'Isaac, you may be able to get by on that, but I can't. Multiply that by two, and I might be interested.'

'So might I,' Isaac said.

Ignoring Isaac's flippancy, Ashley continued, 'I've not got anything. I was dangling the bait, seeing if I could get a nibble.'

'Did you?'

'Jaden brushed me off, treated me as a junior.'

'A hit to your ego?'

'You're trying to rile me. It's not going to work. Get me another glass of wine, assuming your sixty-five thousand can afford it, and I'll tell you what I know.'

'Expenses,' Isaac said, and the two of them laughed.

Ashley drank from her second glass of wine; Isaac sipped at his first. Around them, the diners were coming and going, while outside, the weather looked gloomier by the minute.

A waiter came over. 'Dessert?' he said.

Isaac flashed his warrant card. He knew the waiter was trying to hurry them up, get them out, and lay the table for the next diners.

Taking the hint, the waiter said nothing, only moved away. Ashley caught his eye. 'Ice cream, a glass of cognac.'

'I didn't know you were a drinker,' Isaac said.

'I'm not, but you're on expenses. No point holding back.'

Isaac couldn't remember her as a drinker back when they had dated, but then she had been idealistic, conscious of her figure, uncorrupted by life. She had changed, more than he had. If his memory was correct, he preferred the younger Ashley to the woman sitting across from him.

'What do you know?' Isaac asked after she had her ice cream and cognac.

'Not sure it's going to help your enquiries, but Bob Babbage has another job offer, just in case.'

'Seems logical, protecting himself if the new programme doesn't work out.'

'It won't.'

'How can you be so certain?'

'It may be everything that Jaden says, and Tricia a surprise to all of us if she makes a good job of it, the ratings shoot up, and it's a spectacular success. But it won't make a difference, not in the long run, not even in the short.'

'Why?'

'When was the last time you watched television?'

'I never did, not even as a child.'

'You're the exception. It's to do with the numbers. Fewer viewers, less advertising revenue, more money spent on promoting the programmes. Television stations are passé, the same as newspapers. Either they find a way to make a profit, or they're dead in the water, and Jaden knows this, the last throw of the dice for a desperate man.'

'How do you know this?'

'A little sniffing around, contacts of mine.'

'Tom Taylor?'

'Smart, fancies himself and anything in a skirt. He's currently squiring Jaden's niece, and he's got another on the side, not that she'd know about it. Pretty little thing, not much between the ears, although that's not where his interest in her lies. No different to you in that respect.'

Isaac remembered their last conversation before they broke up, a phone call late at night, her accusing him of playing the field, sleeping with her friend. Much to his chagrin, she had been right. In his twenties, a young man, athletic, strong and muscular, attractive to women, he had misbehaved, the prerogative of youth.

And now, he had changed, changed for the better, but had she? He wasn't so sure, but whether she had or not, it didn't concern him. The past was where it belonged; the present was better.

'This other woman? Important?'

'Taylor's got no power, too young to tie his shoelaces, let alone put one over on Jaden. The sweet Alison may be in love, but she's not that bright, and if Jaden finds out that her boyfriend is putting it about, he'll be for the chop.'

'Babbage, any dirt on him?'

'Not that I've heard. He's a bastard, but then lawyers are.'

'What about you, married, living with someone?' Isaac asked.

'No one serious. Don't say you still fancy me?'

'My days of chasing wanton females are over.'

'And I was wanton?'

'Ashley, you were, and you know it.'

'It was fun. Not like now, not with murder and Jerome Jaden, newspaper editors and sleazy politicians.'

'Welcome to the human race, warts and all,' Isaac said.

Chapter 13

Kate Hampton's increasingly close involvement with some of the investigation's key players warranted her being called into Challis Street Police Station. Distinctly irritated, angry that the focus was on her, she sat in the interview room, a sullen look on her face.

'Mrs Hampton,' Isaac said, 'we need to know the relationship between you and your husband.'

'Is this important? Neither of us was there when Angus died, and my husband's hardly Mr Action Man.'

'We're not accusing,' Wendy said. 'Just trying to get to the truth, to find out who would have had a motive, nothing more.'

'Well, it wasn't me.'

'We've not said it was. There's no need for hostility,' Isaac said.

'Very well, what do you want? I don't have all day.'

'Where do you have to be, that's so important?' Wendy asked.

'I don't see that it's any of your business, so why should I tell you?'

'Mrs Hampton, this attitude of yours is counter-productive and raises suspicion,' Isaac said.

'We have reason to believe that your husband's accusation that Angus Simmons was having an affair with you at the time of his accident was incorrect,' Wendy said.

'I've already stated that.'

'And that,' Wendy continued, 'you were sleeping with Justin Skinner.'

'Who said this? Justin? I wouldn't be surprised if it were, but I wouldn't.'

'Wouldn't you? Why not?' Isaac said.

Kate Hampton was fidgeting on her seat, rubbing her right forearm with her left hand. Her body language was not right, and her eyes were moving around the room, not looking directly across the table.

'Because I wouldn't. Isn't that good enough?'

'Unfortunately, it's not. If your husband believed it was Angus you were sleeping with, that would explain your husband's behaviour in Patagonia, the reason he quarrelled with Simmons. Your lies could have resulted in your husband's infirmity and Angus Simmons's death. How do you plead? Guilty?'

'Very well. I might have inferred I was having an affair with Angus, although in my defence, Mike was being a bastard, accusing me of this and that. He's a possessive man, insanely jealous.'

'Did you know this when you married him?'

'To some extent, but then after the honeymoon, after the period where you can't keep your hands off each other, he changed. Wanted to know where I was going, who I was seeing, whether it was serious.'

'Was it?'

'No. A night out with some friends, female, by the way, and there he would be on my return, checking on how many drinks I'd had, who I'd met, what we'd spoken about, ad infinitum. After he had vented his spleen, he'd come on all amorous, expecting me to reciprocate.'

'Did you?'

'Stifling, more like a prison. No, I didn't. It's better now, our relationship, sad to say. There's not much he can do, and he's in a permanent state of self-pity, blaming everyone else for his woes.'

'No physical contact, you and your husband?' Isaac asked.

'Not for a long time. Even before he left, we were sleeping in separate beds, him believing it was because I had a lover somewhere.'

'Did you?'

'Not out of choice, out of necessity. I was in my early thirties, and I didn't sign up for celibacy.'

'If there was no love at home, you looked elsewhere?'

'Not look. I still believed in marriage, and I had loved Mike, but he had killed it in me. You can't understand how I was suffocating, not that I'm making excuses for my behaviour.'

'Angus, your lover?'

'It was the day before Mike was to leave for Patagonia. We'd had a blazing row, him obsessing about this and that, driving me to despair. I was ready to move out of the house, but he was off for six weeks, a chance for both of us to cool down.'

'I would have thought the mental preparation would have rendered your husband more tranquil, less demanding, less suspicious,' Isaac said, willing to concede that the woman's story was plausible.

'Six weeks away, time to condition the mind, to go through the climb step by step, double-checking, triple-checking the equipment. That's when the mental discipline came in, not in England, and not with me. He was looking for a farewell roll in the hay, but I wasn't having any of it. Not that I can blame him, but he was being a prick. Apologies for my language, but there you are.'

'You came up with this lame story about Angus?'

'I was angry. I was wrong. I knew that as soon as I said it.'

'Why did you?'

'I knew how much Mike and Angus loved each other. They were brothers in spirit, inseparable as climbers, the perfect team. It was spiteful, but what could I do? I was at my wits' end.'

'Justin Skinner?'

'If I had mentioned Justin's name, Mike wouldn't have believed me. But Angus, that had the impact. He was mortally wounded, the ultimate betrayal. And that's what he took to Patagonia.'

'We believe that your husband attempted to kill Angus Simmons in South America,' Isaac said. 'Is this possible?'

'You'd need to ask a psychoanalyst, but he might have. Betrayal by a loved one, or in this case two, is a stronger emotion than hate, or I would have thought it was.'

'How do you feel about yourself now?' Wendy asked.

'The same as I did when I first heard about the accident, sick to the stomach.'

'Justin Skinner?' Isaac asked one more time.

'I disliked Justin from the first time I met him, an arrogant man who cared for no one, using people, discarding them when it suited. He's the worst kind of human being.'

'Your husband knew of your dislike?'

'He didn't see Justin in quite the same way. There's a bond amongst elite climbers, a trust that exists, but Mike knew of Justin's foibles.'

'Were you having an affair with him?'

119

'An affair infers emotion, and I wasn't bringing that to the relationship. We had got together at an awards ceremony. Mike didn't go, not sure why. Anyway, Justin's there; I'm there. We're both staying the night in the hotel on the same floor, two rooms apart. One thing led to another, and we ended up in bed together.'

'You've slept with him since?' Wendy asked.

'I felt dirty the next morning, spent forever in the shower trying to scrub Justin from me, to rid myself of his smell, of what I'd done. Justin said it was foolish, just harmless fun, two lonely people, a night of passion. I told you what a bastard he was, and he was that morning.'

'Yet, you continued the relationship.'

'Maybe I shouldn't have, but then Mike comes home from Patagonia, and after a couple of months, I meet with Justin. The disgust lessens with time, and no one ever knew.'

'You're meeting him today, the reason you're anxious to get out of here.'

'Yes, every few weeks. It's sex, not love, nothing more.'

'Mike's sister?'

'A terrible woman, fond of Mike, hated me.'

'Any reason, the hate?'

'I married her brother.'

'Does she know about Justin Skinner, what happened in Patagonia, on that mountain?'

'I doubt it. Deb's not the brightest, slow on the uptake. She believes what she believes.'

'Is Mike fond of her?'

'It's a complex relationship. We never spoke about it. Talk to her, but don't expect much, and I doubt if it'll help your investigation,' Kate said.

'The truth always does, and you, Mrs Hampton, have lied,' Isaac said. 'I hope you've told us the truth today. I don't want us to meet again at this police station.'

'I slept with Angus once. It was before I met Mike. My husband knew about it, and, as I said, a long time ago.'

'Are you sure your husband was fine with that?'

'Who knows what goes on in the twisted mind.'

The interview concluded. Those present went to their respective corners: Kate Hampton to a hotel in Hammersmith, Wendy to visit Deborah Hampton, Isaac to his office, another report to prepare.

***

Maddox Timberley had encountered Hampton's sister at Hampton's house. Her opinion had been unfavourable, like Kate Hampton's.

Wendy and Larry drove the one hundred and twenty miles to Dorset, to visit Hampton's sister. Motorway conditions for most of the way, but eventually ending up on a narrow country lane which petered out into a muddy track, their car slipping and sliding. Finally, they drew up at a rustic farmhouse.

Larry had never had a craving for country life; he was a city boy, born and bred in London, the smell of diesel and cigarettes more enticing than manure and wet grass.

Wendy took a deep breath, sampled the smells and the animals in the field, a gaggle of geese announcing their arrival, a dog sitting on the porch, not willing to move, wagging its tail.

'Don't worry about Buster; he won't hurt,' a woman who had come out of the house said.

'I grew up in Yorkshire, a place just like this,' Wendy said. 'It takes me back.'

'You're the police?'

'We are. Inspector Larry Hill, Sergeant Wendy Gladstone.'

'I'm Deb. You'd better come in, get the weight off your feet. I'll make us all a cup of tea, coffee if you prefer.'

'Tea will be fine,' Larry said.

The two officers looked at the woman who had just turned her back on them and walked into the farmhouse.

'Not what we expected,' Wendy said.

'The description's accurate.'

A voice from inside. 'Come on, haven't got all day.'

Inside the house, the smell of burning wood from the fire and bacon from the kitchen.

'Long drive? Bacon and eggs okay for you? Sausages, home-grown, or their provider was. Sent the animal to the slaughterhouse last week.'

Deborah Hampton had grown up in the north, the child of a successful businessman and his lay preacher wife, as far removed from a farm as could be imagined. Wendy, who had grown up on a farm, was used to eating the livestock, willing to slaughter when needed.

'That'll be great,' Larry said.

'Likewise,' Wendy said.

'You're here about Angus?'

'We need to speak with you. So far, we've been drawing blanks. No motive.'

'You've spoken to Kate?'

'We have.'

'Angus's piece of skirt?' Deb said.

'She said you were impolite to her.'

Buster wandered in and sat in front of the fire. He looked old.

'I've had the dog for close to ten years, inherited him from the previous owners. He's meant to be outside doing what sheepdogs do, but he's earned his rest. A good dog in his day, but the back legs are going, not sure how much longer he's got.'

'He still looks good,' Wendy said, although she said it more out of politeness than truth. The dog was indeed old, greying around the muzzle, its breathing laboured.

'Buster will join us for breakfast,' Deb Hampton said. 'Loves bacon.'

'Why country life?' Larry asked.

'No doubt you've got a few more questions for me. Such as, how come a demure city girl, the product of northern affluence, is covered in tattoos, a shaven head, wearing men's clothing.'

'We do,' Wendy said.

'Formal or informal?' Deb said.

'Breakfast?'

'Stay where you are. I'll bring it over. No, I meant the interview. No doubt Kate's told you what a bitch I am, not too bright.'

'Words to that effect.'

'She puts it about, does Kate. Not that I was a slouch in my day, but then who wasn't?'

Saddled with a large plate each, both Wendy and Larry curtailed their questioning, instead focussing on their breakfast.

'We'll go in the other room when you're finished,' Deb said. 'Buster's manners are not so good after a good feed; the air tends to get a bit whiffy with him.'

Silence reigned for a while. To Larry, condemned to eating muesli and yoghurt for breakfast seven days a week, Deb Hampton's country fare was a breath of heaven.

'I've not eaten so well since I lived in the country, up north,' Wendy said.

Buster took his position by the fire, spread himself out, yawned and promptly fell asleep. Larry, who had driven on the way down, could have joined the dog. The tired eyes from driving, cooked breakfast and a warm fire – seductive and inviting.

Wendy nudged Larry, his eyes drooping. 'Inspector, we've got a job to do.'

Larry sat on a chair in the other room, more of an alcove, not as solid a structure as the main house, and distinctly colder.

'We'd like to record the interview if that's acceptable,' Wendy said.

'Fine by me, no secrets to hide,' Deb said.

'Deb, are you close to your brother?'

'I am.'

'Yet, the two of you are opposites.'

'You're judging me by my appearance, by Mike's current situation.'

'I'm not trying to, but it's hard not to form conclusions that others might.'

'Others don't concern me.'

'Before we start, maybe you could give us a brief encapsulation of your and your brother's lives,' Larry said, the coldness and the breeze coming through a gap in the timberwork keeping him awake.

'We grew up in the north, a small town not far from Newcastle. Our father was a successful businessman, fingers in many pies, nothing illegal. Our mother, a farmer's daughter, had met our father at a church function. Our mother was religious; our father wasn't, just that church gatherings were a good place to meet with the opposite sex. More innocent times back then, no social media, no online dating sites, meet up, make love and then move on.'

'A generous term for what they are,' Wendy said.

'Very well, I would have said screwing, but I wasn't sure if I should. My language isn't that good, swear like a trooper.'

'Don't change on our account,' Larry said. 'We've heard it all before, plus words you wouldn't even know.'

'I'll still try to maintain my best behaviour,' Deb said.

'Your parents?'

'Our father died five years back, a heavy smoker all his life, got to him in the end. Our mother died a few years earlier, both taken before their time. She had grown up during a difficult time in the north. Two bad years and the small farms were feeling the pinch, too many people going hungry. Even when our father met her, she was frail, and even later, when they were married, and in a good house, her health didn't improve. She always came down with an illness before any of us. Eventually, pneumonia got to her. A blessed relief in some ways, as she was suffering, could barely walk.'

'You didn't grow up on a farm?'

'We used to visit my grandparents when we were young, and I always loved it there. Out on the farm, there was a sense of freedom. Our father was a stickler for discipline, minding your Ps and Qs. Laughing didn't come often.

'I was rebellious from puberty. Mike was determined to be out of the house; a job in an office working for our father would have driven him mad.'

'You both left?'

'Mike, at sixteen, a stint in the army, fought overseas. He never returned, went to university on his return, and climbed at the weekends and holidays. You know his story from then on. Google it if you don't.'

'What about you?' Wendy asked.

'Rebellious, not so much against my parents, never hated them, nothing like that, but my father's going on about finding myself a decent man and settling down. One day, I'm sitting in a café, not far from the house. A group of bikers come in. I'm sitting there, young and innocent. We get talking, and soon after, I'm on the back of one of the bikes, a biker's moll, tattoos, all the antics they get up to.'

'Bonnie and Clyde?'

'I wasn't Bonnie, and the man I latched onto wasn't a Clyde, nothing gay about him. He was rough, swore, got into fights, but treated me better than the other men treated their women.'

'Your parents?'

'I'd phone them occasionally, never let on what I was getting up to, but I was having a blast, cruising the highway, getting drunk out of my mind, screwing around, and then there were the tattoos. Eventually, I got my own bike, ditched the man, shaved my hair.'

'And bought a farm,' Larry said.

'In time, I grew out of the lifestyle, but I couldn't go back to my parents, not even if I conformed, which I had no intention of doing. I like shocking people.'

'You shocked Maddox Timberley, Angus's girlfriend.'

'I've no time for people like her, sticking their nose in the air, thinking that just because they've got a boob job and straight teeth, they're better than me.'

'You realise that your appearance is disarming,' Larry said.

'I do. Kate, you do want to know about her?'

'We do.'

'Kate never liked me, not that I worried. I kept out of the way, although I had met her down here at the farm.'

'Polite to each other?'

'For Mike's sake. Not sure what he said about me to her, but I'm sure it was complimentary, even if he acknowledged my shortcomings. We're very close, always were, always will be. In time, the two of them are married, and I received an invite to the marital home, not that it excited me that much, but Mike's my brother, and she's his wife. We get along well enough, talking about this and that, my lifestyle, my running with bikers, the shaven head, the tattoos. Kate's a bit of a prude, old-fashioned ideas, not that it stopped her screwing Justin Skinner or sucking up to Angus.'

'You knew Angus?'

'Best friend of Mike, how couldn't I? I liked him back then, although he wasn't what he seemed.'

'Bisexual?' Larry said.

'Not that. Who cares, not these days, but as I said, Kate's a prude. She cared, not that it stopped her sleeping with Angus on one occasion.'

'Some people believe Simmons to be innocent of all crimes.'

'Some might, but I'm not one of them. When I was younger, I fancied Angus, that's before I found motorbikes.'

'You have somebody?' Wendy asked.

'Jock lives a couple of miles from here, has a farm, not as good as this; not too smart either, but he's fun. Once a week, sometimes twice, he'll come over here, or I'll go over there. No talk of love or marriage, none of that.'

'You were married?'

'A biker's wedding, vow to love and honour, to make myself available, to be traded for whatever.'

'Were you?'

'No, but they have strange ideas about fidelity. Most of the time trying to be anarchistic, to make sense of a crazy world, making a complete hash of it.'

'Yet, you stayed?'

'I'd been educated, good family values. I could see it for what it was, but I enjoyed the lifestyle for a few years, no intention of staying forever.'

'The tattoos?'

'They're there now, nothing I can do about it, not that I want to, and as for the shaven head, get down here during the winter, mucking out stables, giving the animals their feed, wading through knee-deep mud to rescue a newly-born lamb, and you'll realise the nonsense of what's important. Put that Maddox down here, and she'd be in tears for a week, dead within two. Vapid, brainless, flat as a pancake without a couple of plastic bags shoved up her front.'

'Silicone implants,' Wendy corrected the woman.

'I know what they're called. A fancy name, charge twice the price to have them put in than they're worth, three times to take them out.'

Deb got up from her chair, rushed into the other room. She came back a few minutes later.

'I had to let the dog out; incontinent, never know when he's going to leave a calling card on the carpet. One day, sooner than later, I'll have to do the right thing by him; not today, not tomorrow, never if I could.'

'You're fond of the animal?' Larry asked.

'You know what they say – if you want a friend, get a dog.'

'We do,' Wendy said.

'I've not had much success with friends, let you down, but not with Buster. He's always there for me, rain or shine. You can't say that about people.'

Bitter, almost as if she was feeling sorry for herself. Larry noticed the signs, not sure if there was more behind that exterior: a vulnerability, a history of abuse, events recessed in the depths of her mind.

'Mike's your brother; you're close. Doesn't that make him a friend?'

'I love the man dearly, but when he was making a name for himself, he was arrogant, and now, damaged goods after Angus let him fall. He's a miserable so-and-so. One I could deal with, tell him to shut up and act normal, and the other, I can't take, or only in short doses.'

'Don't you think Kate feels the same way?'

'I'm not begrudging her finding another man, not now. Mike's abrogated his responsibility. He used to be the more positive of the two of us, but now, sitting there, blaming everyone, especially Angus, what's the point?'

'You've forgiven Simmons?'

'No, but life goes on. If Jock weren't such a dolt, I'd marry him and have a couple of kids, unsure if I can. No point complaining.'

'Medical?' Wendy asked.

'Self-induced. Not that I mean a dodgy backyard abortion. A biker's moll, and sometimes the men can be rough, see a woman as no more than a piece of meat.'

'The man you were with?'

'Died, duelling with another biker, me as the prize. He came around a corner too fast, skidded on oil and slammed straight into a tree. It took them two hours to peel him off.'

'The other man won?'

'By default. I wasn't too keen on being traded in the first place. The next day, after I had smashed a fist into the other man, I shaved my hair, got myself a motorbike, told the gang they could either accept me as I was or they could shove it.'

'What did they do?'

'They accepted me after I had gone through their rite of passage, initiation into the tribe, silly and childish.'

'What did you do?' Larry asked.

'Don't ask,' Deb said. 'You don't want to know.'

Larry did, but he wasn't willing to pursue it.

'I rode that bike for two years, getting tattoos and speeding tickets along the way. Then one day, I pulled up at the side of the road, saw the sign for this place. I drove down the track, stopped at the front door, got off my bike, scared the people living here witless and asked how much.'

'What did they say?'

'After they figured that I wasn't stuffing around, they gave me a price. Three weeks later, I moved in. I gave them cash, my parents' inheritance. Mike wasn't the only one with money.'

'Could Mike have killed Angus?' Larry asked.

'In his condition, not a chance.'

'Deborah Hampton?' Larry asked.

'It needs to be asked,' Wendy said. 'Could you have killed Simmons?'

'When I first heard about the accident, but not now. I'd have Mike down here if he weren't such a pain; the fresh air would do him good. He could feed the chickens, help out around the place, but he won't come.'

'We believe that Angus wasn't having an affair with Kate when they went to Patagonia. We've got that from two sources now, but that Kate, in anger, mentioned Angus, knowing that Mike would be distraught that his wife was cheating with his best friend.'

'If that's true, it doesn't affect the outcome. Mike's sitting in that miserable house while she's out doing whatever and whoever, and Angus is dead.'

'We need to understand the background to solve the murder,' Wendy said.

'Talk to Justin Skinner. He's handy with a gun.'

'You've been?'

'Mike had. Kate's a bitch, but she's no murderer. I could be, but Angus wasn't worth the effort,' Deb said.

Chapter 14

After meeting with the police, the one night in the hotel had stretched into two, a friend covering for her if Mike phoned, not that he would, Kate Hampton knew that much.

She had loved Mike back when they first met. A man with determination, an easy manner about him, considerate.

It was Mike who she still preferred, although since the accident, even before, he had been burdensome, impossible at times, and Justin Skinner had become an irresistible diversion.

The truth of the accident she didn't know, only that she had never known Angus to be angry, whereas Mike blew hot and cold, forgot soon after, but she had told him she was sleeping with his best friend.

It was her fault that Angus had died and why Mike was unable to fend for himself, the reason why she had spent two nights in a hotel room in Hammersmith with a man who would maltreat her, a man who would be unfaithful and uncaring.

Even when her husband was away climbing, he'd attempt to phone once a day.

As Skinner slept, Kate Hampton dressed, picked up her handbag and the travelling case she had come with, and left the room, closing the door quietly.

She felt dirty, the dirt that comes from sin. She knew that Justin Skinner, once he saw her gone, would continue to pursue her.

To make it work with Mike, Skinner's persistence couldn't be tolerated, a diversion that she didn't want to or couldn't deal with.

Confused, she got into her car and headed west. There was only one person who could help her.

***

Jim Breslaw watched the press conference, listened to Jerome Jaden's disparaging comments about him, knew that his removal from the station had been strategic. With a lifetime of experience, he had known that change was inevitable. Reality shows, with a group of people, supposedly picked at random but heavily screened and their banality scripted, irritated him. And he knew that cooking shows, once a staple, cheap to produce, had had their day and that programmes that had a pretty host at the forefront, an excess of cleavage, a tight skirt riding high, were doomed.

He had to agree that Tricia Warburton was the last best hope, the programme well thought out, and with initial success, the result of more money spent on promotion and production costs than recouped from advertising revenue, the viewing figures would be guaranteed. But when the programme needed to be turned into a cash cow and with less money spent, the quality would suffer. Tricia Warburton, no longer staying in five-star hotels, relegated to four, flying economy instead of business class.

Vindication was his. He gloated, gained satisfaction, worried about his garden and life, saw no point in either. Grabbing a coat from a hook in the hallway, wrapping a scarf around his neck, and picking up the keys to his car, he left the house.

After driving around for what to him seemed hours but was no more than one, he found himself outside the television station.

It was calm, the time before the majority of those who worked in the building arrived. Parking next to a Mercedes, Jaden's car, Breslaw entered the building, flashed his magnetic card at the sensor on the front door, not expecting it to open, but it did. A fear came over him, not sure if what he was doing was right, knowing there was no going back.

On the fifth floor, Jaden appeared startled when Breslaw walked in. 'Jim, how?' he said.

'We need a word,' Breslaw said as he pulled up a seat opposite Jaden. 'You and me.'

Unsure what to do, aware that there was no one else in the building he could call on, security having failed to do their job – he'd deal with them later – Jaden adopted a relaxed pose.

'How's life been treating you? Good to be away from here? It's no fun having to deal with the current situation, what with Simmons's death and the new programme. Tricia will make a go of it, and I could do with you here to help out. How about coming back on a contract basis, paid by the hour or the day?'

Breslaw could see that Jaden was nervous. He was pleased, not yet appeased.

'Why now? Why not when you had the opportunity? I'd always played fair by you. I could have taken a lesser role, given the snotty-nosed kid a hand.'

'Not you, Jim. You're not the sort of person to let go, no more than I am. I've still got people I need to answer to. You were regarded as a liability, a legacy of the past.'

'The same as you, Jerome, or don't you believe it? After all, we were friends once.'

'Friends, but this is about the survival of the fittest. And you, Jim, aren't. Time will tell if I am.'

'With your money, you'll survive.'

'Money is not the motivator, never was. It was what I did, set up television stations, invest, speculate. You programmed, did a great job, but time moves on, the future is for the young, not for us.'

'Then why didn't you deal with my departure better? Why did I get the rough-hand treatment?'

'Hardly that. We paid all monies outstanding, and I personally wrote a reference for you.'

Breslaw felt calmer talking to Jaden, reminded of the early days when they had worked hand-in-hand, pleased to make a small profit, but then Jaden had been the owner, and he, Breslaw, an employee.

'The new programme, it's not going to fly, you know that,' Breslaw said.

'The last roll of the dice? The *Titanic* has sailed, an iceberg looming?'

'Poetic, but true.'

'It may be, but I won't go down without a fight.'

Platitudes, metaphors, neither did much for Breslaw. He had liked Jaden, the tenacity of the man, his generosity, and regardless of what had happened, he still did.

Jaden pulled himself up from his chair and went over to a desk in the corner. He withdrew a file of papers. He handed them over to Breslaw.

'Read these,' he said.

'What are they?'

'Projections of the new programme's revenue, operating costs, how much we're going to pay Tricia.'

135

'Why show me?'

'Eyes and ears.'

'You want me to spy, but how?'

'I want your advice. The station's going down, and yes, it's inevitable; believe me, you got out in time. But for me, it's not so easy, too much money tied up in stocks and shares, and they're heading south. I'll be cleaned out if we don't lift the share price, allow me to offload enough, use a middle man, someone to cover for me.'

'You want me to act illegally for you? Insider trading, is that it?'

'Nothing's illegal, not until you're caught. I'll agree I was wrong to disparage you at the press conference, but then I had that awful Ashley Otway asking questions. What could I do?'

'You could have spoken to me beforehand. I might have gone along with you.'

'Jim, it doesn't work like that, and you know it. There's no A to Z on this. Your presence here shows me possibilities that I hadn't seen before.'

'Simmons, you knew about his stunt.'

'Did I? It's not written down anywhere, not that I was overthinking about it when you told me. I believe I told you to make sure he didn't fall.'

'Which you will deny.'

'I will, as you must.'

'Tricia knows the truth.'

'She'll not talk, not as long as she's employed here.'

'And if the programme fails, the station is under threat?'

'Then we'd better make sure that none of those eventualities occurs. Are you on board?' Jaden said.

'I didn't come here to work for you.'

'Then why come? Bored at home?'

'You know I am. Who took that shot?'

'I don't know, nor do I care. He had to go, one way or the other. Macho man, the great adventurer he might have been, but the viewers, most of them no more than a dozen brain cells between them, want tits and arse, and for that, Tricia is ideal.'

'More than adequate,' Breslaw said. 'Tom Taylor?'

'He'll stay as the head of programming. You'll report to me. I suggest we don't meet here, not for now.'

'Do you intend to slag me off to Ashley Otway again?'

'If I must.'

'I might regret it,' Breslaw said as he shook Jaden's hand.

'Just like old times.'

It was, Breslaw thought, apart from two differences: he had come to the building with physical violence on his mind, and someone had killed Simmons.

***

Bacon and eggs weren't on the menu as Kate Hampton drew up at her sister-in-law's farmhouse. Deb Hampton was in the yard, a shovel in her hand, cleaning up the mess left by the cows that had come into the barn for milking.

'What are you doing here?' Deb said, wanting to throw a pile of manure over the woman.

Winding down the window, Kate looked over at the shovel and the woman. 'Do it if you want. I deserve it,' she said.

'What's happened? Skinner give you the heave-ho, tired of seeing your fat arse bobbing up and down, found himself someone younger and tastier?'

'I dumped him. I've wronged Mike. We need to talk.'

'You're still a bitch, told the police you were,' Deb said.

'I am, and so are you. Let's not pretend to like each other. You're a snivelling toad of a woman, a man dressed up in women's clothing.'

Deb Hampton put down the shovel and laughed raucously. 'Women's clothing? A pair of overalls, steel toe-capped boots?'

'Maybe not today. A truce?'

'For Mike, not for you.'

'Yes, for Mike.'

Buster, Deb's faithful companion, sensing the animosity, sniffed around Kate's ankles as she got out of the car, looked up at the woman and snarled.

'More sense than me,' Deb said.

'Still hanging in?'

'Buster loves me unconditionally, doesn't care if I look like the witch from hell.'

'I never thought that of you.'

'You did. Did you ever introduce me to your parents or your friends?'

'You're right. I didn't. A stuck-up bitch, that's me.'

'Seeing that you're here, come inside and take a seat. Don't take Buster's. He's particular about who he sits with. You'll have tea?'

Buster maintained a neutral stance as calm settled in the room. Outside, the weather was overcast, but Kate had to admit that even though the house was pokey and not as clean as it should be, it had a homely, lived-in look.

Not unlike the house she had shared with Mike when they first moved in together. Back then, evenings in front of a fire, lovemaking on a sheepskin rug.

'Why are you here?' Deb asked. She placed two mugs of tea on an old table, one leg shorter than the other. It moved slightly. 'I'll fix it one day,' she said.

'On your own?'

'I've got a man, comes over occasionally, not that you'd like him.'

'Wouldn't I?'

'Not the brightest, never been anywhere, not even sure he's been out of the county. But he's honest, doesn't screw around…'

'Not like me.'

'What is it with you? Mike's a decent man, and even before, you were screwing whoever.'

'The thrill of the chase.'

'What chase? You're not a bad-looking woman; I'll give you that. All you need to do is hang a sign around your neck, and they'll be queuing up.'

Buster, sensing an accord between the two women, raised himself and went and sat down next to Kate.

'Even the dog thinks you're alright.'

'Will you?'

'Not that easy. A dumb animal or a man and you flaunting the assets, not much difference between them, come to think of it.'

'I'm not a shameless hussy. Sure, I cheated on Mike, but it wasn't that often.'

'Once is fine, two is pushing it, three's adultery. Is that how it works? Numerical screwing?'

'You make it sound dirty.'

'Kate, I've screwed around, a biker's chick. I know all about right and wrong, have seen the worst of people, but they had a code, not that others would understand. Their code was anarchy, do what you want, stuff the consequences, and the law was an arse. But you don't come from that background. Your values, the same as Mike's, the same as mine, were formed differently.'

'You went astray.'

'I did, and don't I know it. Every time I look at myself in the bathroom mirror, marked up like a harlequin's nightmare, unlikely to have children.'

'Sorry about that. I didn't know.'

'Don't be, not your fault.'

Brave words, Kate could see, but behind the harsh exterior of her sister-in-law, there was a sadness, regret about what could have been. The same as she felt about herself, but she hadn't run with the wrong crowd or been abused or passed from one biker to the next. All she had been was loved, not with emotion, but physical love.

She realised that Deb had a reason for her outlook on life; she, Kate Hampton, Mike's wife, did not.

'It's not easy living with Mike,' Kate said.

'What do you expect? Unable to get out, to do what he loved, Angus Simmons dead.'

'They were close.'

'I used to think they were into each other, used to tease Mike about it.'

'Were they?'

'Not Mike. Angus was a bit that way inclined, not that I ever had proof. Even if I had, what does it matter?'

'It doesn't. I shouldn't have told him that I was having an affair with Angus the day he left.'

'You shouldn't have, not sure if it would have made much difference if you'd given Justin Skinner's name.'

'They wouldn't have argued on the mountain, not about Justin.'

'You're to blame, made a right hash of it. If I had any sense, I'd kick you out of here.'

'But you won't. You'll hear me out?'

'Buster thinks you're worth it. I'll rely on his judgement.'

'Mike still believes I was unfaithful with Angus, but that wasn't true.'

'It's not important. It's what happened on Cerro Torre, that is. For me, Angus was responsible, but then that's Mike's version of events.'

'Angus always claimed that it was an accident, an explanation accepted by the majority. Are you willing to broach the possibility that Mike's statement was tainted by anger?' Kate said.

'No, neither should you, not if you want to get back with him. But then I don't trust you. For me, I know what I did, what happened; I've learnt to live with it, no intention of repeating.'

'The shaven head, the sloppy dress?' Kate said.

'Out in all weathers, tending to the livestock, mucking out. Not a place for a fancy hairstyle. Practical, that's what it is, not that I was ever fashion conscious, too masculine, too much of a tomboy.'

'A fellow mountaineer?'

'I could have been, climbed with Mike a couple of times, but the elite, they're fanatical, a dedication above and beyond the reach of mere mortals. I had a wild streak, men and drugs. Mike was ascetic, would have made a good monk.'

'How do I make it up with Mike? I assume you approve.'

'You assume wrong. You've been a bitch up till now. Why should you stop? Why should I trust you after all you've done before?'

'You can't, but you have to trust me.'

'Not me, not so easy. You might have been able to twist Angus around your little finger, get Justin Skinner and whoever hot under the collar, but all I see is a painted whore, screw for England if you could.'

Not surprised by Deb's effrontery, Kate, who had locked horns with the woman before, did not respond to the insult. Instead, she said, 'Think of Mike, what's best for him. How to bring him out of himself.'

'I'm considering. It's just that you'll get your fancy tickled soon enough, and then he'll be back where he started,' Deb said.

'It's worth the risk.'

'With risk comes reward.'

'Clichéd, but what's the reward?'

'Mike's peace of mind,' Deb said. 'You, Kate, are an unknown quantity, but I'll go along with you for now. Truce?'

'For now.'

'Great. I'll give you a pair of overalls, some boots. Your penance starts here. If Buster still likes you afterwards, no longer smelling like a Chinese boudoir, more of carbolic soap, then we can work on Mike's rehabilitation; yours, as well.'

'Did you take that shot?' Kate asked.

'Blunt and to the point,' Deb said as she handed over the overalls. 'No, I didn't. Forgive and forget, that's my creed, although I know who did.'

'How?'

'Another day, another conversation. I can't prove it, never will, and I'm not willing to involve myself in an infantile search for vengeance, not for Angus, not even for Mike, and certainly not for you.'

'You think I did it, don't you? Tell me, why?'

'Not murder, but your sins are worse.'

'The police?'

'I didn't tell them. If they're smart, they'll discover it. There's someone else, hidden in view, someone with little empathy, a callous nature, a person who treats others with contempt.'

'Justin Skinner?'

'Stop asking stupid questions. You remember that shovel from before?'

'Yes.'

'It's yours. Do a decent job, and I'll make you lunch, let you sample my home-made wine. It's got a kick to it, more than the hind legs of a donkey.'

'Deb, thanks,' Kate said.

'Don't thank me, not yet. You're still a bitch.'

Chapter 15

A check of those with the necessary skill to take the shot that dislodged Angus Simmons from the Shard had found four persons. Justin Skinner, an accomplished cross-country skier, had represented the United Kingdom at the winter Olympics, coming fifth in the Biathlon, shooting at a target on the route. Deborah Hampton shot rabbits on her farm and belonged to a local shooting club in Dorset. However, after what had been a shaky start, she was rapidly becoming the most reliable of the witnesses, in that she had phoned up Homicide after Kate Hampton's unexpected visit, told them about her. She told that about Kate mucking out the stable, falling flat on her face in a pile of manure, even laughing after it had happened, and then scrubbing down with carbolic in a tub of cold water.

'Justice for the bitch,' Deb had said, causing a chuckle from those in Homicide. She failed to mention that she had a suspicion as to who had killed Angus, though.

Another person with the necessary skill was Charles Simmons, the deceased's father, and last but not least, Mike Hampton. Angus's mother, Gwyneth, thought to have been a competent shot, had confirmed she was a pacifist and no longer owned a weapon.

The speed with which Maddox Timberley had moved on to another man concerned Homicide. However, a phone call to her while on a photo shoot in Barbados had received a blunt denial. 'Not me. I'm hot property, Angus's woman. My management company reckons they can milk my notoriety, splash it around on social media, wherever they can.'

'You approve?' Wendy asked on the conference line.

'My mother's not too keen on me being portrayed as easy, but I'm not against it. Celebrity and fame are illusive. You know how it works. It's not always the most talented or the most beautiful who makes it, not the most intelligent. To be honest,' Maddox said, 'I'm not that attractive, not when the makeup's off, blotchy skin, acne scars, and my nose isn't the one I was born with. Not mutton dressed up as lamb, not yet, but I choose this life; and I chose Angus, a decent man, not like some of the sleaze-buckets I have to deal with, think they can get a leg over any time they want if they're dangling a contract and a trip to the Caribbean.'

'You're there now,' Isaac reminded her.

'The photographer reckons he's God's gift; he's sidling up to me, trying to get a better angle, to make me remove more clothes, wiggle my assets in his face, but he's got no chance.'

'Clothes haven't been an issue for you in the past.'

'In the past, when I was starting. I needed an edge back then, not that I was cheap…'

'Sometimes you did things your mother wouldn't approve of?'

'I wouldn't be the first. You choose your life; I thought I knew the realities, but I was naïve.'

'No nudity now?'

'Depends.'

'On what?'

'Who's paying and how much. If it's classy, helps my career, why not?'

'Maddox, let's be honest amongst ourselves,' Wendy said. 'You're young, attractive, and your man's dead. You're not going to embrace virtue, are you?'

'No, and why should I? It's not that I was ever promiscuous, but Angus wasn't my first lover, not even my first love. When the time's right, but not with the man they're pairing me with. He's not a bad-looking man, but he's not my type. Sure, if it's good for my career, I'll be seen with him, arm in arm, dancing together, even the occasional kiss, but that's where it ends. No hanky-panky, topless photos, or bleary early-morning shots snapped by a long lens.'

'We've met with Mike Hampton's sister.'

'She was rude to me, looked me up and down, thought I was a piece of trash.'

'Did she? The truth?'

'That's how I saw it. She didn't speak, not to me, but Angus. She told him that Mike didn't want to see him and that he could go to hell.'

'It's important,' Wendy said. 'We've met with Deborah Hampton. She's not a person to grace a magazine cover or to get a trip to Barbados, but aside from her disarming manner and her appearance, she seems to be a decent person, not as you portrayed her.'

'I might have been harsh,' Maddox said. 'She was not pleasant. I know that.'

'She wouldn't have approved of you,' Isaac said. 'She would have thought you to be shallow, hanging off the shirt-tails of a famous man. Were you?'

'No. We lived together. It was serious.'

'Was it? Did he make love to you, sleep in the same bed? Or was it a stunt cooked up by his management company? Money paid to you to play along. After all, you've admitted that the man you're now going around with is a publicity stunt, and you're not opposed to milking it for what it's worth.'

'Angus wasn't the greatest lover, no animal passion, a bit of a dullard in the bedroom, but our relationship was serious, everybody knows that.'

'So do we,' Isaac said. 'I'm pushing you, need to. We've not got an angle on why he died, and your career seems insufficient reason.'

'That's a dreadful thought that I had wanted Angus to die.'

'People have died for less.'

'In your sordid world, they might. In mine, it's the casting couch; not much difference, I suppose.'

'Not a lot,' Isaac conceded. 'Good night. Give us a call when you're back in London.'

'Three days' time. Call my home at any time. I'll be alone.'

Isaac ended the call, looked over at Wendy. 'Did you believe her?'

'Not totally, but then I don't know of anyone we can trust, not completely.'

'Deborah Hampton?'

'I trust her more than Maddox,' Wendy said. 'It's the edge she talked about. What a person needs to do to get ahead, and she's done well, and Angus has given her a boost. But if his death has helped her, who knows.'

***

Two investigations were underway, one by Homicide, the other by Ashley Otway. After Jerome Jaden's attempt to ignore her at the press conference, her editor had given her instructions to do what she did best, to dig deep into the underbelly of the television station. And besides, the newspaper's owner had a vested interest in another television station, and in business, as in love, all's fair.

Invigorated, refreshed, and glad to be free of making small talk with another petulant celebrity with the intellect of a ten-year-old, she had offloaded the next interview to a nineteen-year-old junior. A fan of the man, she had been delighted to get the interview.

Homicide was aware that Otway was sniffing around, making waves, digging deep, getting under Jaden's skin, and especially irritating Babbage. He had tried the heavy tactics, threatened the newspaper, received a rebuke from their legal department.

So far, Otway had found someone at the station, a quietly spoken, thoughtful woman who had worked with Jim Breslaw, but had stayed the course, kept her head down, said yes and no to Tom Taylor as required, even after catching him and Alison Glassop on the floor in his office late at night.

'Gave me a fright, I can tell you,' Grace Shean said.

The women sat on a park bench two hundred yards from the station, near enough for Grace to have walked, far enough for them not to be disturbed or recognised.

'How did you find me?'

'A friend,' Ashley said, not willing to mention that Jim Breslaw had given her the name. 'Tell me what you know.'

'I'm not that important. You know that. Do my job, go home.'

'Inconspicuous, part of the furniture?'

'Nobody knows I'm there, left alone most of the time, that is these days. Young Tom, he calls me mum, not that I like it much, never had kids, you see.'

'Out of politeness or sarcasm?'

'He's a sweet boy, done nothing wrong by me, except for calling me mum, but it could be worse.'

'If you were a sweet young thing, he could have been chasing you around the station,' Ashley said.

She had judged it correctly. Grace Shean belonged to that army of decent people who give to charity, look for the cheapest items at the supermarket, pay their taxes, go to work, go home. A good person whose life had passed by.

'Alison?'

'I'm not sure she does much, other than look pretty, smiling all the time. Although with young Tom…'

'Not so much smiling?'

'Not something you want to see every day. My dear old mum, ninety-six years of age, if she'd been there, we'd be burying her now. She's from another time, prim and proper. I'm not.'

'A wicked soul, are you?'

'I like a bit of fun, not that I get out much, and my husband, bless his soul, dead and gone now. He was solid, a decent provider; mind you, we didn't want much.'

'The same as you? Invisible?'

'He was. Worked in a factory, making parts for industrial-grade air-conditioners, knew more about the process than anyone else, could have told them a thing or two about reducing costs, improving the product, but they never listened.'

'Is that the same with you?'

'I observe.'

'You see what goes on, who's sleeping with who, who's fiddling the books, creaming off the money.'

'I don't like to talk. Loyalty, not much of it left.'

'Not much fun being ignored, the target of ridicule.'

'Mr Jaden, he disapproves of disrespect in the office. Alison can be a cow, looks me up and down, sneers and pulls a funny face when I'm not looking.'

'Funny face to who?'

'To Tom, but he doesn't like it. He's had a good upbringing, respectful. He told her off once, I could hear them through the door, not that I'm an eavesdropper.'

'Her reaction?'

'She told him not to be childish, that it's harmless fun. He didn't say anymore after that, understandable if she's ringing his bell.'

'A quaint term,' Ashley said.

'It's better than what they say these days.'

'Too much crudity, I'd agree.'

'I know. On our street, where I live with my mum, the children shout it to each other all the time.'

'Jim Breslaw?'

'Not here,' Grace Shean said. 'We might be seen.'

'It's unlikely, but if you want, we can talk in my car, a restaurant if you're hungry.'

'Your car will be fine. I have to get back soon.'

In the car, the engine running, the heater on full blast, Grace relaxed. 'It's a lovely car,' she said.

'It is, cost me plenty.'

'I never learnt to drive. Dan, that was my husband, he drove me everywhere, not that we ever had anything like this; our car was old, and he was always fixing it.'

'Jim Breslaw?' Ashley said, returning to the previous question.

'He was a good man, treated me well.'

'Competent?'

'I thought he was, but we were losing money, not that it was his fault.'

'He was regarded as impeding progress, blamed for Simmons's death.'

'Angus Simmons didn't care about anyone but himself. I can't say I liked him.'

'Did you meet Maddox Timberley?'

'He brought her to the station once or twice. She was delightful, complimented me on my clothes. Not very sincere, her doing that.'

'You look fine,' Ashley said. 'She was polite.'

'Even so, I liked her. Him, I didn't care for, full of himself, not in a cocky way, but smug. That kind of look that says I'm better than you, which he was, climbing those mountains.'

'You admired him?'

'For what he achieved, but then he goes and climbs that building, falls off, flattened on the top of a truck. Mr Jaden was on the warpath when he heard, screaming out loud to anyone nearby: "Who authorised that man to climb that building? I want their name, and I want it now".'

'Anger or show?'

'Mr Jaden doesn't get angry, only pretends. He only worries about money, and Angus falling off that building was going to hurt him where it hurt most.'

'His back pocket?'

'That's it, but I know the truth. He knew that Angus was going to climb, a message from Jim Breslaw.'

'You can prove it?'

'I've got a copy of the email. I've also got a copy of Jim Breslaw's termination letter and the severance package he received. Very generous, it was.'

'Who took the shot? Any ideas?'

'Not at first. I thought it was an accident, but then more people are tuning into the channel, and soon after, Tricia is announced as the star of a new show, guaranteed to excite, and so on.'

'The so on?'

'The usual. You were there, but then you started asking questions. Mr Jaden, he didn't like that.'

'What's the truth? What are you hiding?'

'Jim knew about the new programme, even before Angus Simmons fell. It was his idea, not that he received credit. He thought Angus was starting to look old, not the great force he had once been, and that accident when Mike Hampton fell was still giving bad vibes. Angus Simmons was no longer the all-conquering, pure as the driven snow, bona fide hero. He was on the way out, and Tricia was in.'

'Do you like her?'

'She fancied herself, although she was careful not to let it show. Maddox, I liked, a genuineness about her, but Tricia, she's what she wants you to see, and as for Alison, thick as two short planks. More attractive than the other two, but Tom Taylor will soon dump her.'

'Tricia Warburton?'

'I'm sure he slept with her. You'll not tell Alison, lose my job?'

'I won't. Proof?'

'The invisible woman, sees all, says nothing.'

'You're talking to me.'

'It's not comfortable, knowing one of those in the office is a murderer.'

'Who?'

'I don't know, but Tricia's flirting with Bob Babbage. That man's slimy.'

'Not an attractive man,' Ashley said.

'Does it matter? Mr Jaden's no oil painting, but he's got women stashed around the city.'

Grabbing her handbag, Grace Shean opened the car door and got out, looking back at Ashley, shouting that she was late and had to get back to work, almost colliding with a car.

Ashley knew she was onto something. She considered whether to let the police know or wait and see. The latter option appealed more.

***

Maddox Timberley breezed into town, a man on her arm, a contract to pose nude for a lads' magazine. All in all, she was pleased with herself, her star in the ascendency, although her mother was distressed at her lax morals, not believing that the pretty little girl she had given birth to would be splattered once again across the pull-out centrefold of a magazine, showing what should be reserved for someone she loved, not every Tom, Dick, Harry and pervert.

'Don't worry, mum,' Maddox had said as she sat in the kitchen of her parents' council home. They had refused to move, even when their daughter could afford to buy them a small place of their own. 'It's where I was born, where I'll die,' the mother's rebuke, more to do with where the money had come from than the uprooting from familiar surroundings.

Isaac read the guff on Maddox Timberley's return, her new beau, speculation as to whether she was on the rebound or if she had found true love.

He knew it wouldn't be long before Maddox was asked her opinion on global warming, the damage to the

environment, rioting in America, feminism, and whatever
else.

Wendy met with Maddox, a suite at one of the
best hotels in London.

'You're making a splash in the media,' Wendy said
as she sat in a chair that almost swallowed her, such was
its plushness. Behind her, a view over the River Thames,
the London Eye off to one side, the tourists with their
iPhones snapping happy shots, oblivious to a heavy mist
rolling up the river.

'It's a show,' Maddox said. 'You must know that.'

A yawn from the other room, a bleary-eyed
Romeo staggering out.

'Realistic,' Wendy said, a smirk on her face.

'It's not what it seems.'

'I suggest you get rid of lover boy, and you and I
can have a serious chat, woman to woman, or else Challis
Street, bright lights and not those from a photographer.
What's it to be?'

'Make yourself scarce,' Maddox said, kissing her
lover on the cheek, securing the towel that was slipping
from around his waist.

'Whatever,' the response.

Five minutes went by, time enough for Wendy to
look around, to see the designer luggage, the underwear
casually strewn, to smell the air.

'Smoking pot?' Wendy said. 'We have been a
naughty girl, haven't we?'

'I've nothing to be ashamed of.'

'We'll see about that. It's offensive, not able to
control yourself for more than a couple of weeks before
you find another man.'

It wasn't the standard interviewing technique, Wendy knew. She felt it appropriate under the circumstances.

In the other room, the sound of a shower running, Romeo singing out loud.

'If he's not out of here in two minutes,' Wendy said, 'he'll be out on the landing with no clothes on, you as well. Miss Timberley, your credibility is in the garbage. You're now a hostile witness, and the next time we meet, you'll be in a prison cell, not living it up here.'

'You can't talk to me, not like that. My manager—'

'Your manager will do nothing, and as for him who's got one minute…'

'You said two.'

'I lied, no different from you. Proud of yourself?'

The police station was the best place for the interrogation. Still, Maddox Timberley, her taste in lovers questionable, hadn't committed any serious crime, although knowingly telling untruths to the police wasn't going in her favour.

Wendy knew why she was so hard; she had liked the woman, recognised good values, underlying decency beneath the pretty exterior. She was disappointed, and she was letting it show.

'What do you want me to do?' Romeo asked, his eyes bloodshot. He was barefoot, dressed in a pair of jeans, a white tee-shirt from the Caribbean, an image of a glass with a straw and a decorative umbrella.

'Anywhere, just don't be long,' Maddox said.

'Make it long,' Wendy said. 'Call in one hour. What's your name?'

'Why?'

'Sergeant Wendy Gladstone, Homicide, that's why.'

'I haven't done anything wrong.'

'Who said you had? I asked for your name.'

'Brett, Brett Valentine.'

'Not your professional name, not the name when you're prancing around, flexing your muscles, screwing Maddox.'

'John Saunders. You want an address?'

'Somewhere we can find you, in case you do a runner.'

'She's got it,' Romeo said, looking over at Maddox.

'I can give it to you, a phone number as well,' Maddox said.

'Criminal record?' Wendy asked.

'You've no right to ask.'

'Which means you do. What for?'

'Possession of drugs, dealing, time in jail, a couple of years, out early on appeal.'

'And this is the sort of trash you go around with?' Wendy said, looking over at Maddox. 'Angus Simmons, a man of substance, of achievement, and you'd rather screw this piece of garbage?'

'Angus? Substance, achievement? The man couldn't get it up, not unless he was half-drunk, dosed up with Viagra.'

'I thought you were decent, but you're not, just garbage crawled up from the same primordial slime as Brett Valentine Saunders over there.'

'It's Brett Valentine. I don't use the other name, not good for my image.'

'You've got no image. Now, get out and don't come back until I say so. Is that clear?'

'You—'

'I can, and the drugs in here? What if I got a sniffer dog in? What will it find?'

'Nothing. I'm not dealing now. I'm a model; make enough money.'

'Get out, now.'

Maddox Timberley sat quietly in a chair; she was crying.

Chapter 16

With calm restored in the hotel suite, Wendy phoned Larry, briefly explained the situation and told him to get over to the hotel.

Isaac had been informed of developments, not entirely comfortable with the situation, but willing to let his sergeant continue, his inspector supporting her.

Wendy and Larry, on his arrival, went into another room. Wendy admitted she had said and done things, not because she had wanted to, but because it was necessary.

'Drugs?' Larry asked.

'More than marijuana, although they may belong to the boyfriend,' Wendy said. 'No point in wasting our time on a search. We're here for murder and the truth. This relationship with Simmons is all-important.'

'Maddox, are you ready?' Wendy said.

'I should have a lawyer with me.'

It was the woman's prerogative; neither Wendy nor Larry could refuse.

'Anyone in particular?'

'I have a friend. I trust him.'

'Lover?'

'No. Sergeant, you've got it all wrong. I'm not like that.'

Wendy said nothing.

'We'll reconvene down at Challis Street, make it official,' Larry said.

'Not there. I don't want to be seen, my image.'

'You're hardly the virgin queen,' Wendy said. 'I thought there was no such thing as bad publicity.'

'Everyone thinks I'm on the rebound from Angus, that I'm heartbroken, finding solace in the arms of another man.'

'Aren't you?' Wendy said.

'I loved Angus, always will.'

'Here or the police station?' Larry said.

'Here is fine. I've broken no law.'

'We'll see,' Wendy said, pulling out a drawer next to the drink cabinet, recognising the packaging, not needing to sniff or to inspect, knowing that the contents were illicit. An arrest could be made, which she had no intention of pursuing.

Larry phoned room service, asked for tea and coffee, along with a selection of sandwiches. 'You're not picking up the tab, are you?' he said to Maddox.

'Not for here.'

'Who is?'

'Fame has its benefits.'

'It's strange,' Wendy said, 'that you, Maddox Timberley, who has all the attributes and the opportunities, should sell yourself as a slut, whereas Deborah Hampton, who you believe insulted you, we've found to be estimable.'

'If I am what you believe of me, then why are you here? Why do you think I can help?'

'It's not only you,' Larry said. 'You're not the only person leading a double life.'

'Double life? What does that mean? I don't understand.'

A knock at the door. A man, dressed in a suit, pushing a trolley. 'Afternoon tea for three,' he said.

'Put it there,' Maddox said, indicating a place next to her.

'Is that all, madam?'

'It is, thank you.'

The man lingered. Larry, not used to such places, put his hand in his pocket, withdrew a five-pound note and slipped it to the man.

In return, a slight bow and the man disappeared as quickly as he had come.

'What entitles you to such luxury?' Wendy asked.

'It's my fifteen minutes of fame, and if I play it right, a lot longer.'

'And it's that important?'

'We grew up poor, not dirt poor, food on the table, a stable home, but back then, plain Freda Sidebottom, a gangly child with braces on her teeth, knock knees and a speech impediment. This is what I wanted; I always have. I'll do anything to keep it.'

'Including screwing whoever, even murder?' Wendy asked.

Larry leant over, helped himself to a sandwich. 'No cucumber? I thought it was compulsory in the best hotels.' He was concerned that Wendy was allowing her angst to intrude on her professional duty. He looked over at his sergeant and lowered his head slightly, hoping that she got the message to lower the tone and use subtlety, not the bull in the china shop approach.

'Tell us, Maddox,' Larry continued, helping himself to another sandwich. Whatever it was in the last one, it was tasty, and he was hungry. 'In your own time, about you and Angus, and how come we find you here in the lap of luxury, a man in your bed?'

'My career was stalling before Angus's accident; there are always younger, skinnier, prettier girls coming through all the time. I'd been one of them once, but I was on the way out. It had been great, travelling the world, the fashion houses, the expensive clothes, parties, and I had a few more years left, but I wasn't getting paid as much, and I knew that one day the phone would stop ringing. Angus's death, I had to seize the opportunity.'

'Lines of cocaine, a perk?' Wendy asked as she grabbed the last sandwich.

'I wasn't addicted. My mum is teetotal; my father would have a couple of pints on a Friday night in the pub on the way home. I didn't even smoke until I was seventeen, and then only to look cool, to fit in with the gang.'

'Gang?' Larry said.

'Not the type of gang you're thinking of. Just a group from school, hitting puberty, getting through it, experimenting.'

'Sex?'

'I wasn't any worse than the other girls. It was cigarettes I didn't like. I tried marijuana once, thought it was okay, take it or leave it. Anyway, the gangly girl's filling out, the teeth are straight, no braces by then, and I'm working in a takeaway joint of a night time, at college during the day, studying economics. I had never given my looks a thought, although I could see that men were often giving me the eye.'

'What age were you?'

'I was close to nineteen.'

'Still a virgin?'

'If you call a fumble in the dark, sex, then no. But only once or twice, no one in particular. Just feeling our way, as I said before.'

'The fast-food joint?' Larry said.

'I'm at the counter. It was a quiet night, not much happening, and there's this man, in his forties, asking me if I've considered modelling.'

'Your response?'

'We used to get the occasional guy in, the grey overcoat brigade, twenty quid for a photo, thirty if you show your underwear. You can't avoid them where I come from, but this man, he looks different, and outside I can see he's got a fancy car.'

'You got in?'

'No way. I asked the manager to phone my dad. We didn't live far away, and he's there within five minutes, grabbed hold of the man, threatened to punch him. My dad, he's not violent, and the man is head and shoulders above him.'

'What happened?'

'As I said, it was quiet. The manager intervened. Separated the two of them, and then the man opens his wallet, shows my father his business card, told us he was a photographer. He says he's on the up and up, and I've got a look about me, tall and skinny. He gives my dad the card, another one to me, gave us both a lift home. A couple of weeks later, I'm in London. It's my first photo shoot, a magazine for a department store, a dozen changes of clothes, standing in front of green cloth, a bikini under palm trees, a sunny beach, or else a heavy coat with a hood, me on skis, although how you can ski with a coat on is beyond me. He said not to worry. He'd shoot a couple of hundred photos, and they would choose.'

'Your career's on the way?'

'Five hundred pounds for an afternoon's work. After that, another department store, then prancing up and down catwalks, trying not to fall or make a total cock-up, somehow succeeding and getting noticed. Soon I'm on a tropical beach, no green background, the real thing.'

'Men?'

'Photographers, those that weren't gay, fancied their chances. I slept with one or two, but never any pressure. We were valuable commodities, not to be mishandled.'

'Angus?'

'I'll come to that. After eighteen months, I'm not as fresh as I was, and they're looking for the next new girl, the quirky nose, the gangly walk, the skinny legs, or in my case, they wanted waifs, so skinny they were all bone, their ribs showing. I was slim, but I can't starve myself. There's a demand for centrefolds, bosoms and curves wanted. I wasn't too keen at first; it made me think of the lechers with no film in the camera, just getting off behind a screen while you posed for them.'

'You had experienced it?'

'Not me. Some of the other girls had though; upset some, didn't worry others.'

'You started posing for the magazines?' Larry said.

'At first, a couple of vodkas before the shoot made me relax, but nowadays, I don't bother. Just ensure there's some privacy, don't want the locals getting an eyeful, do I?'

'You don't?'

'Some of the places we take the photos are sensitive about female flesh, although the men make sure they get a good look before they start throwing the stones.'

'We're digressing,' Wendy said. Maddox's verbosity was either the result of a natural high or artificial, neither of which concerned Wendy and Larry.

'My career was waning, and I'm getting bad media, the photos becoming more risqué.'

'They always wanted a bit more?'

'Not that I always said no; it depended on the photographer and how much they paid. At first, topless, crossed legs. But they're insistent, and the more you relax, the easier it becomes, and then, soon enough, it's the full-on frontal, no holds barred.'

'It doesn't explain Angus.'

'It does, in a way. I was at a celebrity event, not sure which one it was, strutting my stuff, on the arm of someone or other.'

'You don't remember?'

'I do, but it's unimportant. The cameras are flashing, the Page 3 girl and her movie star boyfriend. It was a setup to get the clicks from the paparazzi. I get paid for my time, play along with it, sidle up to him, make him look good.'

'He wasn't that good without you?'

'A big name, you'd know it. He's a total loser, and his people know it, but in front of a camera, delivering his lines, he's magic. I'm known for my wild ways, not that there were too many, and for getting my gear off; he's there to promote himself, to make out that he's a regular guy with a knockout girlfriend, the sort of woman men lust after. It enhances his reputation as a lady killer, not that he was; barely work up a sweat, let alone kill one.'

'You didn't like him?'

'No one did, not those that knew him. As I said, put him in front of a camera, give him a few lines to deliver, and he was the stuff of legend. Sit him down next to you, try to engage him in conversation, and he was tongue-tied, disinterested, and a waste of space.'

'Whereas you are smart but known as a bit of a tart?'

'It was my manager's idea, improve my reputation, make me go upmarket.'

'Doing what?'

'Skinny waifs were on the way out. They'd had a couple of years, but then one or two died of heart failure or another ailment. Bulimia, starvation, exercising themselves to physical exhaustion, whatever.'

'And taking drugs,' Larry said.

'Him that left, he's more into it than me, not that I haven't tried, but it's not my nature. I know it looks bad, him up here with me.'

'It does,' Wendy said.

'You can't blame a girl, her man dead, feeling lonely.'

'I can, but carry on.'

'As I was saying, the market's changing, demand is back for the fuller figure, but I've been getting my gear off too often, posing more provocatively than I should. My manager arranges for me to attend a sports award, Angus's date. Similar to when I had been with the movie star.'

'You liked Angus?'

'He didn't play up to the camera, held the door for me, pulled the chair out when I sat down, the perfect gentleman. Not that it was meant to be more than that, him and me together on the night, a write up in the newspaper, shown on television. Angus was a natural showman, and he was always looking for funding for his next adventure.'

'A mutual trade-off, you and him. He got money; you got respectability.'

'He got me. He wasn't much into romance, but after some that I've encountered over the years, it was refreshing. And then, I'm his woman, which I was, not because it paid, but because I wanted it. Nobody touches Angus's woman, not with the admiration that he

165

engendered. I was in love with him, still am, but he's not here, not now.'

'And you're back on the slippery slope to obscurity and men in raincoats, a Polaroid camera in hand?' Larry said.

'Easy way down, hanging about in a hotel suite with Valentine, taking drugs,' Wendy said.

'Distraught, the love of her life snatched from her arms, a hero falling to his death, struggling to reclaim her dignity. Sounds plausible,' Maddox said.

'For a soap opera,' Larry said.

'For the servile celebrity-obsessed, it's reality.'

'Assuming we buy what you've just spouted, Maddox, it raises other questions,' Wendy said.

'Why am I sleeping with Brett?'

'That's one. What's the answer?'

'A few too many drinks, something else that you don't want to know about, and it just happened.'

Larry, frustrated by the puerile rantings of the vapid, broken-hearted paramour of a much-beloved adventurer and hero, raised himself from his chair and walked around the room. 'You must think we're stupid,' he said.

'I don't; really, I don't. I'm committed to making something of myself.'

'Inspector, sit down, please,' Wendy said. 'Getting upset with Maddox isn't going to help.'

'It's hogwash, and she knows it,' Larry said, resuming his seat.

'You're hot property now, more so than before. His death has benefited you,' Wendy said.

A knock on the door. 'Is it okay to come back?' Maddox's lover said.

Wendy went over to where he stood and opened the door wide. 'She awaits your pleasure.'

'Please, you're wrong,' Maddox said. 'It's not like that.'

'I'm afraid it is, Miss Timberley,' Larry said. 'We'll meet again soon enough, but don't leave England without telling us.'

'In the meantime,' Wendy said, 'screw for England if you want, swing from the chandeliers, and have your photo taken any which way with lover boy here. We're serving notice on you that your rise to stardom on the back of Angus Simmons's death is a motive.'

'You can't talk to her like that,' Valentine said.

'Shut up, go back to bed with her, snort whatever foul concoction you want, but never tell me to be quiet,' Wendy said.

Outside the room, down in the hotel foyer, Larry and Wendy sat.

'You were rough in there,' Larry said. 'Do you believe she's involved?'

'Probably not, but she's going to ruin her life. It's alright now, young and pretty, but another ten years, the fat piling on, the face no longer peachy fresh, and she'll be turning tricks in porno movies.'

'You think so?'

'It's a slippery slope to obscurity. I hope I'm wrong.'

'Do you think she cared for Simmons?'

'Yes, I do. Simmons had been good for her, and I don't believe Maddox had anything to do with Simmons's death, but others might be making the decisions, taking actions.'

'Do you, Wendy, honestly believe what you've just said?'

'I hope I'm wrong. If she was my daughter…'

'She's not. Don't get emotionally involved. She could be Dorothy or the wicked witch of the west.'

'I still think she's Dorothy, and without Glinda, the good witch of the south, she could be doomed.'

'It's not your problem. DCI Cook's said it enough, don't get involved, just do your job.'

Wendy knew that her inspector was right, but she had been around longer than him. She knew their chief inspector had become involved on two occasions, and he had survived each time. She only wished she could protect the young woman from her folly.

***

Karen Majors had worked the telephone, written numerous emails, visited with all of the companies that had previously placed advertisements at the television station. As head of sales, responsible for bringing in the money, she had failed.

'Tricia's not saleable,' Karen complained to Jerome Jaden.

'You said she was.' Jaden, known in the industry for his no-nonsense approach to the management of a television company, knew his laurel crown was slipping; he did not intend to let it slip further. The other stations were experiencing similar problems, undercutting on advertising rates, looking for a way out of the dilemma. The revenue pie was reducing in size, and the economists, those that could be trusted, knew that one station had to fold in the next three to six months.

Jaden did not follow the so-called experts. One piece of paper told him what he needed to know. Karen Majors was not to blame, and she had worked hard.

However, he had no intention of letting her off the hook. It was her job; she would deliver one way or the other.

'They see her as insincere, no substance, just a pretty face. Simmons had the pulling power, not her. You made the wrong decision.'

Sitting calm and composed, Jaden spoke. 'I don't like your tone.'

'Nor I, yours,' the reply. 'You give me a pig in a poke, expect me to work miracles. Well, I can't, nor can you.'

'Tricia Warburton's not a pig, and as for the poke, the market's large enough. You should be able to do something with it.'

'I have increased our market share. Tom Taylor is doing his best, but he's not up to it, and the production values are not as good as when Breslaw was driving them. The man was focussed on quality, regular screenings with a selective cross-section of the community.'

'Taylor's doing that.'

'Sending a boy to do a man's job doesn't work, and you know it. Why are you hanging onto him, not willing to talk to Breslaw, to make him an offer?'

'Because, regardless of what everyone thinks of him around here, I can't trust him,' Jaden said. He had Breslaw in his pocket, but so far, he hadn't used him, knowing that the former head of programming, regardless of what he said, would interfere.

'Trust, a two-edged sword. Does he trust you?'

'He's sitting in that house of his, fretting over his garden, slowly going mad with frustration and boredom. He lays the blame at my feet for how we got rid of him.'

'He was treated with respect,' Karen said. She was sitting down, her heart beating more than it should. She was tired; gardening sounded good to her. Her boss, a man she had respected, looked no better, and the twinkle in his eye, the enthusiasm that was always there, was gone, never to return.

'It was his life, as it is ours. Take a person away from their family, their home away from home, and see what it does to them.'

'What would it do to you? What would you do to stay on top?' Karen Majors said. 'Jerome, it's now or never, and you know it.'

Chapter 17

Ashley Otway's junior, now the newspaper's new entertainments reporter, was delighted that her first assignment had been to interview Chas Longley, an American rapper, one of the latest in a long string of warblers that Ashley didn't appreciate. However, Chloe, fresh out of university, did.

'He was great, so friendly. Did you know he broke up with his girlfriend?' she had oozed on her return from interviewing the man.

Ashley did because she had read the media briefing about how he had made his first record at the age of eighteen, growing up in a crime-ridden ghetto in Detroit. And from then on, a meteoric rise, a chart-topper, Midas wealthy.

Ashley, not wanting to hear any more, cut the woman off. 'Must go,' she said. 'Write it up.'

Outside the building, Ashley Otway climbed into a car's passenger seat; a balaclava hid the driver's face.

'How much is it worth?' the driver asked.

'How good is it?' Ashley, frightened yet excited at the same time, asked. Aware that she should have told her office where she was going, aware that others would have stopped her, she had drafted an email, set it to transmit in two hours, explaining what she had agreed to, where she thought she was going. Her smartphone was on; the details included how to track it.

'It's gold.'

'Why are you telling me this?'

'I'm not here for my health.' The voice was gruff, a nondescript accent.

Ashley judged the man to be above average height, carrying more weight than he should, more from a lack of exercise than an excess of food. He was dressed in light-coloured jeans, an open-necked blue shirt, and was wearing a sports jacket.

'Why the secrecy? How did you get my number?'

'I prefer to stay in the shadows.'

'Driving around London in disguise is hardly inconspicuous.'

The man drove too fast, weaving in and out of traffic, although he seemed more than competent. She thought he might be a racing driver, maybe a courier, or drove a taxi, as he seemed to know his way with ease.

'I saw you challenge Jerome Jaden, not that you got anywhere.'

'I didn't expect to, but I wasn't going to let him off that easy.'

'What if I told you he was broke?'

'That piece of information is worth a couple of pounds. It's common knowledge, and it's not only his station. You'll have to do better than that.'

'Do you trust me?'

'Your driving?'

'Do you get a thrill out of getting in cars with mystery men; think you're playing at espionage, letter drops, invisible ink, sultry sirens baiting honey traps.'

'Whoever you are, you've got a twisted sense of humour, if this is what this is,' Ashley said.

'It's not humour; it's terror. I need to know if you're worthy.'

'Worthy of what? Of you? Slow down.'

The car slowed; the man removed his balaclava. 'Sorry about that. You could have informed the police, had them follow us. I had to be sure.'

'I haven't, and why don't you go to them?'

'The name's McAlister, Otto McAlister. A German mother explains the first name. I've not gone to the police, not that I couldn't, as I can prove this, but because times are tough, and you'll pay me a king's ransom for information. I'd be lucky to get the taxi fare home from them.'

'And if I give it to the police?'

'Then do so, mention my name if you must. I'll have your money, and you'll have an exclusive. Deal?'

'It depends on what you're trading and how much you want,' Ashley said. Calmer now and in the company of an earthy, ruggedly handsome man.

'I was in Patagonia when Hampton fell. I was there; I saw it happen.'

McAlister drew the car over to the side of the road and parked. He leant over to the passenger side glove box, causing the woman to flinch.

'Don't worry. I've got something, a sample, to show you.'

The man withdrew an envelope. 'Take a look at what's inside,' he said.

After she had looked at the five photos, four of them fuzzy, one clear, Ashley Otway handed them back to McAlister. 'What am I looking at?'

'Squint your eyes, look at this one,' he said as he handed over the clearest of the five. 'You can see two men, one in blue, the other in dark grey.'

'The outlines of two men, neither recognisable.'

'Those two men are Angus Simmons and Mike Hampton. Anyone who knows mountaineering and those two would recognise them instantly.'

'Not in a court of law; invalid, I'd say.'

'But you've never seen photos when Hampton fell; no one has, not until now.'

'I've not. Have you hung onto these since then?'

'Accidents happen. People lose it up on a mountain, start acting crazy.'

'And you think that Simmons or Hampton did?'

'Or both. It doesn't matter, only that if you know what to look for, it's proof that Simmons was at fault. Hampton blames the man, and he's right to. Angus, whether it was intentional or whether he was scared or angry, that I don't know. All I know is that these photos are proof.'

'And you want how much?'

'Two thousand pounds.'

'A story about something that happened in the past doesn't amount to much.'

'That's the sampler. The real scoop, the proof of who shot Angus, is still with me.'

'Provable?'

'Yes. First, take those photos to your editor, get them blown up, run software over them, take out the fuzziness and print the story.'

'The police?'

'Don't mention my name until the final proof is in your possession. Until then, they can't sweat it out of me. You see, I'm getting your newspaper to pay, the police to get the evidence, you to get the glory, and for me, a chance to leave this country. But don't worry about me.'

'I won't.'

'Have we got a deal?'

'Cash or cheque?'

'Either. Debit card if you prefer. I've got a reader with me, a market stall at the weekend.'

Ashley flashed her card, entered her PIN, took hold of the photos and got out of the car. 'The originals?'

'I'll email them to you.'

'How much for proof of the murderer?'

'We'll talk. Check with your editor, find out how much a scoop is worth.'

'Withholding evidence is a crime,' Ashley said.

'So is paying for it and not handing it over to the police.'

'We've got smart lawyers who can deal with our misdemeanours. What do you have?'

'The proof they want. Mine's more powerful,' McAlister said.

'They could make you talk.'

'Strongarm stuff? Give me a good beating?'

'They could put you in the cells.'

'They could. The information I have is not written down, but I can still prove it.'

'Where can I contact you?'

'It'll be on the email. Don't call until you've published the first article. After that, I'll drip-feed you, sweeten the deal, and make your editor willing to part with the readies. Bank transfer in future; no need for a meeting, not unless you're keen.'

'I'm not,' Ashley Otway said.

***

Aware that withholding evidence was a crime, Ashley phoned Isaac to let him know that she was in contact with someone offering information in exchange for money. She failed to mention the photos, not intending to do so until the editor had seen them, approved them for publication, and the legal department was happy with releasing them. Only then would she hand them over to Homicide.

Isaac, unsure why she had contacted him, had no option but to remind her that she had to hand over evidence. He knew that stating the obvious was pointless, but he felt duty-bound to do so.

For his part, he did not believe her, not entirely, but powerless to do more. He had thanked her for phoning him and told her to be careful, as a person or persons unknown were still out in the community. A murderer was at large, a murderer whose motive could have been revenge or hatred, love even, fame possibly, Maddox Timberley in the back of his mind.

And Ashley Otway, sleuth that she was, was looking for glory, to solve the case before the police, getting too close, taking risks that she shouldn't. Isaac met with her, a small bistro off Oxford Street, the sort of place where the midday crowd congregates, where lovers get together at night. Her hand touching his over the table sent shivers up his spine. He did not want romance, not now, not with a wife and child, but the woman was attractive, and she was making the right signals.

'I've embarrassed you,' she said.

'Not at all,' Isaac lied.

'Don't worry. I'm not poaching other women's husbands. But if you want?'

'Ashley, be careful,' Isaac said as he pulled his hand back sharply. 'You're a risk-taker, nosing in where you shouldn't. Not that I want to lecture.'

'But you are, aren't you?'

176

Isaac did not want to be there. A waiter with a menu, a couple of drinks on the table, ambient music in the background. If it weren't for what she knew, he would have made his excuses and left.

'Why were you removed as a political reporter?' Isaac said. 'Access to the highest echelons of power in this country, privy to the intricate workings, the secrets of state, decisions that would shape our country for years.'

'Behind the scenes, Machiavellian scheming.'

'You sound as if you're a first-year philosophy student at a progressive university, not someone who has experienced the rough and tumble of reality.'

'You don't think they should be held accountable?'

'I'm trying to advise you. Finding out that a senior minister has got a bit on the side, and then losing your job over it is hardly a recipe for success.'

'He wasn't the only one; there are more: a secret love nest, another taking their parliamentary secretary on an all-expenses jolly to Switzerland.'

'That's left-wing Bolshevism.'

'It's unjust.'

'Believe me, I know as much as you do about government officials and what they get up to.'

'The government minister, the soap opera diva, a secret child?'

'Where did you find that from?'

'Whispers in the corridors,' the woman said as she held up her glass, clinked it with Isaac's.

'What else?'

'Rumours.'

Isaac felt fear for her. Aggressively ambitious, a talent for spotting wrongdoing, a willingness to make it known, the ingredients for a short and fulfilled life. 'Take care. You could be heading down a path of no return,' he said.

'I'll trade,' Ashley said.

'For what?'

'Tell me about the secret child, and I'll tell you what I've got.'

'Official Secrets Act, I can't. I'm telling you, be extremely careful. People who take shots at other people are unpredictable, and they have no intention of giving themselves up, more than willing to take another life. You could be playing with fire.'

'People died?'

'Innocent people. Please, don't become one of those who end up dragged from the River Thames on a Saturday morning, your face half-eaten by crabs.'

'I won't. You care?'

The waiter hovered; Ashley ordered fish; Isaac ordered meat.

Isaac felt uncomfortable, unable to leave, feeling swayed by the mood, and knowing that at home, his wife only wanted to talk about their son, what he had done that day, and why did he have to work so long. And him there, a beautiful woman, available and desirable and single.

'Sorry, can't do this,' Isaac said. Professionally, he should have stayed; personally, he couldn't. 'Be careful; call me anytime. Don't get into potentially dangerous situations.'

She already had that day with Otto McAlister. Checking her emails, she found the number.

Any port in a storm, she said to herself.

'Ten minutes, make mine meat.'

'I already have. Red wine okay by you?'

'Dessert?'

'We'll discuss that when you get here.'

If she couldn't have a suave and tall black police chief inspector, ruggedly handsome wasn't a bad substitute.

***

Perturbed that Jim Breslaw was back at the station, Tom Taylor made his concerns known to Jerome Jaden.

'Don't you worry,' Jaden said from behind his desk, a cigar in his mouth.

'But Jim's starting to order me around, treats me as if I'm the office boy, only fit for menial tasks, getting him this, getting him that, running errands.'

'Alison, how is she?'

'We argued.'

'About what?'

'She accused me of chasing another woman. What if I was?'

'Take a seat,' Jaden said. 'We'll talk this through. I might have something special for you.'

Taylor realised the seat was a command, not an option. He complied.

'It's like this,' Jaden continued. 'You're not up to the task of the head of programming, are you?'

'A fresh approach, the optimism of youth, an understanding of what the viewing public want.'

'And you believe that?'

'It's what you said, and Alison...'

'What did my relative say?' A subtle hint from Jaden to remind the woman's boyfriend of the importance of his relative.

179

'That you were a wily old fox. The ratings are down, and from what I know, the banks are hammering at the door.'

'Dear sweet, innocent little Tom Taylor, whining like a child in the school playground. Did you believe what I said when I promoted you?'

Taylor was at a loss for words.

'Cat got your tongue?'

'I'm not sure what to say.'

'Say nothing and listen. I know all about this other woman you've got on the side. Not that I care much either way but upset Alison, and you're out. Do I make myself clear?'

'But—'

'No buts. Alison is family, you're not, and I'm particularly fond of her mother. The Jadens look after their own.'

'She's a Glassop.'

'Don't be naïve. You're playing with fire, upsetting her.'

'Is Jim taking over?'

'No, he's not. Breslaw's making sure that Tricia Warburton does this right. She's the best we've got, not that I'd choose her, but we go with her.'

'You preferred Angus?'

'I preferred what we had ten years ago, but we deal with what we've got. The advertising revenue is down, and that's the primary consideration.'

'It's down everywhere,' Taylor said.

'And where did you read that? The *Beano*?'

'What's that?'

'A comic, what the young used to call entertainment.'

'I don't understand.'

'Of course you don't. Breslaw does, not that he likes it any more than me.'

'What do you want me to do?'

'Make Alison happy,' Jaden said. 'You're still green, full of yourself, believe that you know more than you do, no harm at your age. But remember, you know nothing about life. The viewers are not there, not the way they were, but they're fickle, easily swayed, putty in the hands of smart people.'

'You're one of the smart?'

'How far would you go for this company? For me?' Jaden asked.

'Anything. Are there any guarantees for me?'

'There's a woman, razor-sharp, likely to cause us trouble.'

'I won't do that.'

'Do what? Kill her?'

'No, never.'

'The killer instinct is not in you. You have a limit to what you'll do.'

'Angus Simmons was murdered. Whoever did it will spend time in jail.'

'Will they? What if they're not caught?'

'Are you saying that you know?'

'Am I?'

Tom Taylor sat back on his chair, the realisation dawning that career advancement came at a cost, which he wasn't sure he could pay.

'What do you want? Is she that much of a threat?'

'You know who I'm referring to?'

'Ashley Otway. She wanted to ask questions about Angus's death, accuse you of taking advantage.'

'She hasn't proof, not yet, but she's no dummy. Took on a politician once, got shafted, ended up interviewing washed-out singers and talentless actors. But now, she's back doing what she does best, investigating.'

'The station? You?'

'Us. And you're right. She's getting some dirt; I know that, although what it is and how much, I don't know.'

'Who's keeping you informed?'

'I've been around a long time; I've got contacts out there, some who owe me a favour, others who want money. The woman is playing it close to the chest, not letting anyone know, not until publication.'

'You know the editor where she works?'

'I do. A friend, or as much as anyone can be in this business. He'll not tell me, no more than I would if I was in his position.'

'So, what do you want with me?'

'Ashley Otway, older than you, not a saint by all accounts. Karen will get the advertising revenue after we've tickled the viewing public's fancy, a few titbits from you, courtesy of what you can get from Otway.'

Not feeling the heat as before, Taylor relaxed, felt more willing to talk. 'What sort of titbits?'

'What she's planning to publish. Prewarned, we'll head her off at the pass, discredit her. Pay her off if we have to. All I know is, we need Otway's feet cut from beneath her.'

'What do you know so far?'

'She came on strong with a chief inspector. When he wasn't biting, she phoned Otto McAlister, a colleague of Simmons and Mike Hampton. He and Otway spent the night together.'

'Your source is reliable?'

'The best. We know that McAlister's feeding her information, although what and how much, we're not sure. Could be insignificant, could be damaging, but whatever it is, Otway will make sure it's printed.'

'You could bribe McAlister, make him work for us, let him feed falsehoods to her.'

'You're learning,' Jaden said. 'However, paying McAlister off is now complicated by Ashley Otway having him in her bed. You've seen her?'

'Not so easy to throw away, is that what you reckon? McAlister's getting a bonus we can't give.'

'You're going to seduce her, get her away from McAlister. If you can find anything from her, or drip-feed her what we tell you, we'll decide how to proceed.'

'Alison,' Jaden shouted out from where he was sitting. The door opened; Alison Glassop appeared.

'He'll do it,' Jaden said.

'I knew he would,' Alison said, throwing her arms around Taylor, giving him a big kiss.

'You don't mind?' Taylor said.

'What option do we have? And besides, it's nothing, not to you. A woman who's twelve years older than you. She's almost ancient.'

Tom Taylor was unsure what to think. Sure, he had been unfaithful to Alison, but for her to agree to his seducing another woman seemed immoral. Alison had dropped in his estimation.

'Alison will work with you. McAlister's not attractive, not pretty-faced like you, Tom,' Jaden said. 'We've researched Otway, know something of her history. To you, it'll be easy, and no doubt, fun.'

'I hope it isn't,' Alison said. 'It's the only way, Tom, don't you see?'

He did; he just didn't like it, although he would do what was wanted.

'If McAlister's kicked out of her bed, he might turn hostile, sell his story elsewhere,' Taylor said.

'We're keeping a watch on him, and McAlister's broke, desperate for money. When the time's right, we'll meet with him, put a proposal to him. He'll go for it; we know that.'

'Know what?'

'Neither Simmons nor Hampton liked him much, used him as one of the team, reserving the glory of the summit for them. McAlister's not interested in Otway, not in the long term, prefers to be on his own out in the wild somewhere. He'll be no competition for you.'

Chapter 18

Publication of five photos on the third Sunday after the death of Angus Simmons and the accompanying article by Ashley Otway improved sales by eight per cent on the day.

Ashley's junior was elevated to the role of entertainments reporter permanently, the previous incumbent wishing her well. She cautioned her about sleeping with every rap artist and bedraggled would-be singer but knew that her advice fell on deaf ears.

'And watch out for boy bands. All for one, one for all, as the three musketeers would say.'

'Who are they?'

'Alexandre Dumas, a French classic, published in 1844.' In exasperation, 'Forget it, before your time,' Ashley said as she hugged the girl and left her to it. Either the young woman would learn that picking up strays could end badly, and as for a future in journalism, there would be no Pulitzer Prize for her.

'What's next,' the editor asked.

Ashley, sitting in a leather chair to one side of the office, enjoying the afterglow of the controversy on the television and YouTube, wondering whether Simmons's action in Patagonia had been accidental or intended.

Mike Hampton, confined to his home, Kate at his side, attempting a reconciliation, not succeeding. She knew what was right, but she also needed excitement, not negativity. Justin Skinner was fun but facile, and she knew that her husband was the best bet, but apart from a momentary lifting of spirits, he was still the same: dull, someone who did not want to come near her. She knew she couldn't stay, not for long.

'It was because of you; he did it on purpose,' Mike said.

'I was angry, and besides, you suspected something even before I said his name.'

'Maybe I was occupied, focussed on a climb.'

'You were always focussed. Back then, it was mountains, setting another record; now, all I get is negativity. Does it matter if Angus did it on purpose or not? He's dead; you're not.'

'It would have been better if I was.'

Vindication was all that Hampton wanted, no longer to be a leper to the mountaineering community he once proudly embraced.

As much as she could, Kate had done her duty. She phoned her sister-in-law, explained the situation, received a string of four-letter words in return, packed her case, and left. She had no intention of returning.

In Dorset, Deb Hampton roused Jock. 'Look after the place. I'm going up to stay with my brother for a few days.'

'Uh. Alright. Whatever you say?'

Deb had to admit he was decent and undemanding. Her age was starting to go against her, and as a father, Jock would be good, although genetically, he was a poor choice. Barely literate, he could shoe a horse, shear a sheep, tell you which crop to plant and when, and what the weather was going to be for the next few days, but ask him about the world and politics, he was a complete dunderhead.

On her return, Mike was coming with her, whether he liked it or not; rushing up to London every time his wife did a runner or found herself another lover wasn't sustainable.

A registry office, that's what she thought. 'When I come back, we'll get married. Alright?'

'Whatever you say,' the sleepy response.

'You can live here if you want.'

'Okay.'

For some reason, she felt calm. Life had been rough, but a remote farm, a good man, even if neither was any more than mediocre, suited her fine. She had come from a privileged background, an emotionally distant father, a controlling mother. Her man would do her fine.

At Challis Street Police Station, the photos were studied. Ashley Otway had been reminded again that withholding evidence was a crime; the newspaper's legal department replying that they pertained to a period before Simmons's death and they were a matter of public record, and only proved the reason for the apparent animosity of the two men.

Isaac knew they were right, and even though enhancement of the photos showed clearly two men, a sign of anguish from one, an open mouth from another as if shouting, there was still enough blurring not to be sure as to whether it was Hampton or Simmons shouting.

Otto McAlister enjoyed the first of the money he would fleece from the newspaper, their star reporter, an unexpected and much-appreciated bonus.

'You've got to give me more,' Ashley said during their cosy weekend getaway.

'Next week,' McAlister said as he drank his champagne, looked across at the bed, knowing that no was not an option from her.

A one-night stand was not an issue; a more extended period was, and Ashley Otway knew she was trapped; her ambition thwarted by a man whose idea of foreplay was rough, his calloused hands on her skin not conducive to love. She wanted to be rid of him, but she took him by the hand and led him to where he wanted her to be.

Another couple, romance not on their mind, listened to Otway and McAlister from an adjoining room. The squeaking of the bed didn't interest them. 'A waste of time, if that's all they're going to do,' the man said.

Satisfied, albeit only for a while, McAlister lay beside Ashley. He had resumed drinking his champagne.

'Otto, what will you give me next?' Ashley said, attempting to get the man to look over at her.

'Proof that it wasn't an accident. Simmons hadn't been with his wife, that I know, not before he left for South America.'

'How?'

'How did I get the proof, or how do I know Angus hadn't been Kate's lover, regardless of what she said?'

'Both.'

The man was tiresome, the lovemaking stolid and one-sided. Ashley Otway was not enjoying her time away from London.

'I have a recording of them arguing at the base camp.'

'Why?'

'It was Angus, always looking for ways to make money. A documentary of the climb, a chance to sell it to a media company. I have a copy of the original, the unedited version.'

'What does it say?'

'It reveals the level of animosity between the two men; one of them unjustly accused, the other adamant that his one-time friend had cheated with his wife.'

'Do people argue when climbing?'

'Usually, they're too focussed or too tired. They shouldn't have been climbing, not that day, but they were determined men, alike in many ways, like brothers.'

'That's been mentioned before. What else?'

'That's it for now.'

'Monday?'

'Five thousand pounds, cash or bank transfer. Can that be arranged?'

'It can. This weekend?'

'The icing on the cake,' McAlister said.

Resigned to her fate for the weekend, Ashley Otway realised the man wanted money more than her and that her compliance wasn't going to make a difference. She got up from the bed, put on a pair of jeans, a top, and walking boots. 'I'm going for a walk, be back in a couple of hours,' she said.

'When you get back,' the reply, nodding over to her side of the bed.

Outside, away from the reluctant love nest, she breathed out loud, said to herself, 'That's the last sweetness you're getting from me. From now on, the information is in exchange for money.'

As she walked along a scenic track nearby, she knew that she had to remain close to the man, not because she wanted to, but because it was vital. The information he had was valuable, and other people would pay for it, even more than her editor.

She turned around and returned to the hotel room and the loving if brutish hands of Otto McAlister.

***

Mike Hampton had been upset at Kate leaving, not that he would have told her. He was even more upset when his sister entered the house, going so far as to ask her to clear off, not that she was taking any notice of him. Thirty-five minutes after Deb had arrived, the knock on the door by a chief inspector and an inspector was enough to make the man blow his top.

'Why don't you—'

'It's homicide, Mr Hampton,' Isaac said. 'Here or at the police station, your choice.'

'It's better if you talk to them,' the sister said.

'When they leave, you can go with them.'

'And leave you on your own? Kate's taken off, back to whoever.'

'It was your damn fool idea that she came back. I was better off without her.'

Isaac wasn't interested in family conflict, only in asking questions, getting answers. Mike Hampton wasn't the first belligerent interviewee he'd encountered.

'Mr Hampton, there appears to be some vindication for you.'

'It wasn't an accident, not down there in South America.'

'Tell us about the events leading up to it.'

'Again?'

'Yes, again. There may be something you missed before.'

'Before? Throwing him off the mountain before he threw me wouldn't have been a bad idea. How would you feel if your wife was cheating on you?'

'Your reaction was understandable, but it wasn't Simmons, was it?'

'It was Skinner, a snake in the grass. I always preferred someone else when we were climbing, but Skinner's good, very thorough, checks the equipment, deals with the logistics.'

'You didn't like him?'

'He was always a bit snide.'

'What do you mean?'

'Always trying to boast about his importance. It was either Angus or me who was the team leader. It should be us discussing the climb, not one of the team, not that we didn't treat them well.'

'Did Skinner believe he was a better climber than you?'

'He was.'

'Yet, he didn't make the summit, not that first time on Everest.'

'Not everyone can. He was physically the strongest, but he had trouble at height, shortness of breath, fatigue. Some people handle it better than others; you never know until you're challenged. Besides, on Everest, it's already known who is going to attempt the summit. It was our expedition; it was our summit. Skinner understood. I didn't like his attitude sometimes, a surliness, but it wasn't that important.'

'Otto McAlister is feeding the newspaper information. Did you know?'

'I didn't, but I'm not surprised. He wasn't good with money, and once the climb was over, he'd want to party on, a few drinks, a woman.'

'That wouldn't be uncommon.'

'Only he went overboard, spending more than he should, looking to borrow more from whoever.'

'We assume the newspaper is paying him. What did you think of the photos?'

191

'It's the two of us, but not that clear. Even so, as you say, vindication. I've received some phone calls, fellow mountaineers willing to press my case.'

'You've accepted?'

'Not yet, not sure I want to. Whatever the outcome, I'm still not going to climb again.'

'Your reputation will be restored.'

'Not important. Now, if you don't mind.'

'When did the truth dawn on you about Simmons and your wife?'

'A lot of facts are becoming clearer. If I'd known back then, Simmons would be alive, and I'd still be climbing.'

'That would appear to be the case. You've spent a long time hating a man who hadn't wronged you.'

'Then why did he try to kill me?'

It was an interesting observation. Was there something else? Isaac thought.

Larry had been silent so far, taking the opportunity to look at the awards framed on the wall, the cups on the mantelpiece, the sister in the kitchen.

'We didn't expect to find you here,' Larry said.

'Nor did I. Why do you keep bothering my brother?' Deb's reply.

'You knew about Justin Skinner?'

'Not at first, but I realised afterwards that something was amiss when they had returned from South America, Angus always asking after Mike, wanting to meet with him.'

'You've seen the photos?'

'I have.'

'What do you reckon?'

'I don't believe that Angus could have done it.'

'The photos indicate otherwise,' Larry said.

'Talk to McAlister. You'll find him under a rock somewhere,' Deb said.

'You overheard?'

'Hard to miss from here.'

Isaac continued to talk with Mike Hampton; Larry stayed with the sister. One was agreeable and approachable, the other reticent, even though acknowledging that Simmons hadn't been his wife's lover at the time of the climb in Patagonia.

'You know McAlister?' Larry asked Deb.

'McAlister's regarded as a reliable team member.'

'Did you climb?'

'I told you in Dorset. When I was younger, I wasn't as dedicated, and besides, my rebellious behaviour got in the way. Even so, we stayed close, not unusual given our upbringing.'

'Rough?'

'Difficult. Don't dwell on it. It made me do what I did; made Mike climb mountains. We're all shaped by our parents, and ours weren't perfect, but then, whose are?'

Larry could still remember his father's reaction when he told him that he would join the police force.

'You're smarter than that. Go to university, study law,' his father had said.

A stable home life, loving parents, but to him, policing had always been what he wanted to do. As to becoming a lawyer, he knew that he wasn't academically inclined, unable to devote the hours to study.

'Tell me about McAlister,' Larry said. 'Is he a loose cannon or strategic in what he does?'

'If you mean, does he have proof?'

'I do.'

'He may. As I've said, and Mike knows him better than me, McAlister is a fatalist, takes one day at a time. If he has money, he spends it; if he doesn't, he scrounges.'

'Attractive?'

'To some women, he would be.'

'To you?'

'He's got an earthiness about him. Don't expect sweet talk. He's more likely to try it on within five minutes; make his intentions clear.'

'To you?'

'Once he did, in this house. Mike had a group around, Angus included. It was before they all went climbing that damn mountain. Kate's here, arm around Mike, giving Skinner the eye, but that's her nature. Otto McAlister's brought a girl along with him. No idea where he picked her up, the gutter, I suppose.'

'Not your style?'

'Otto used to find plenty of women, some classy, some not as much. She could have been a paid escort, but I don't think so, as halfway through the night, him pawing her, she slaps him hard and walks out, takes his car.'

'Did that worry him?'

'Otto's not a worrier, not about assets and women. His philosophy, don't sweat the small stuff.'

'A car? Small?'

'I've told you this before; Otto doesn't care about such things. If he's got money, great; if not, there's someone with a car or a place to stay, and someone will feed him.'

'He stayed the night?'

'Mike was out of it. Drunk and a blazing row with Kate at the end of the evening. Everyone else had peeled off, thanked Mike for the night, the usual handshakes, kisses on the cheek, but Angus, not a great drinker, was embarrassed for Mike and Kate.'

'Did Simmons bring a woman?'

'He came with someone, not sure if it was Maddox Timberley.'

'After they left, you hooked up with McAlister.'

'It's a big enough house, and both Otto and I had had a few drinks. It just happened, no big deal, no protestations of love. The next morning, I dropped him off at the train station, let him find his way home.'

'You could have done that the night before,' Larry said.

'I could have, but you know.'

Larry did.

***

Tom Taylor met with Ashley Otway, ostensibly to discuss the negative publicity she was bringing to the television station.

'Sending a boy to do a man's job,' Ashley said. Not that she didn't find the man attractive, she did, but she had dealt with politicians, devious and underhanded, not all that they seemed to be. She was suspicious.

'Your assistant set this up,' Ashley continued. 'Is this official, or are you fishing?'

'I thought we should talk,' Tom said.

Alison had chosen the location, a pub in Chelsea, loud enough to drown their conversation, seductive enough if that was where it was heading.

Ashley Otway looked Tom up and down, liked what she saw, but she wasn't in the mood for love, and certainly not after the mauling she had received at the hands of McAlister. She detested the man; he represented everything she disliked: rough and inconsiderate, as crude in his manner as in his behaviour. Jerome Jaden's head of programming was more her style, even if he was younger than her, and Jaden's puppet.

'Who's speaking? You or your company?'

'I am. But yes, they're concerned, felt that we should make contact.'

'They could have sent Bob Babbage or Karen Majors, even Jaden himself. Why do they send a boy?'

'Not a boy, but the head of programming.'

'Was it Alison Glassop who phoned me? And by the way, mine's red wine. You may as well get a bottle and two glasses.'

Taylor picked up the menu and let the woman choose. As he had expected, she chose the most expensive. He went and paid, asked them to send over food as well.

'Alison, yes it was,' Taylor said on his return and at Ashley's insistence.

'Your girlfriend?'

'We spend time together, but we're not exclusive.'

'You are to her. Does she agree with you meeting me here?'

'She does.'

'You know who's giving me the information?'

'I have a name.'

'Good in bed, are you? Alison, appreciates your technique?' Ashley said. She knew why he was in the pub with her. Either he'd become embarrassed and leave, or he'd admit to it.

Flustered, not sure what to say, Taylor knew he had been called out. 'We're here to discuss the photos, what you hope to achieve.'

'Jaden put you up to this, didn't he? Don't be bashful. I'm not about to run off, and I'll not deny that I'm interested.'

'In me?'

'Not here, not today, and not while I'm finding out about Angus Simmons.'

'And destroying Mr Jaden and the station.'

'It's not personal, but I've got a job to do, and until it's finished, my source is not going anywhere.'

'Not even if you don't fancy him? Good weekend, was it?'

'You've got people watching me?'

'No, but we know some of it.'

'My source?'

'Let's come back to what you have.' As he picked up his glass, Taylor grabbed hold of a couple of soggy chips that had come over with the bottle of wine. 'A better meal than this?' he said.

'Smarter than you look, young Tom. You've fielded me off better than I thought you would. Jaden trained you well.'

Taylor didn't say that it wasn't Jerome Jaden, but Alison who had practised with him. That time, the seduction had gone through to completion; he was sure it wouldn't this time. Ashley Otway was no pushover, even if her seduction of McAlister had been swift.

Grabbing their glasses and a bottle of wine, the two walked through the bar and to the adjoining restaurant, Ashley choosing a corner setting.

'Now, young Tom, tell me what Jaden wants, and don't give me the sanitised version of the truth and fair play. Television's passé, the same as the print media. Sure, there'll always be a place for both, but they're changing.

Jaden's no dummy, he knows that, and he's no more concerned about Simmons's reputation than you are.'

'You've done your homework.'

'Another bottle?'

'We should order,' Tom said.

'Call over the waiter, tell her to send over the fish of the day, a side of salad, and something to wipe that lecherous look off your face.'

'I like you, Ashley,' Tom said. 'You're a lot of fun, not what I expected.'

'What did you expect?'

'A pretty face, a hard-nosed bitch.'

'Right on both counts. Cross me and Jaden will go down.'

'How?'

'The pen is mightier than the sword, or haven't you heard?'

'I have, but the truth will prevail.'

'The truth is that Mike Hampton did have murderous intent towards Angus Simmons and that halfway up a mountain, he probably realised that only one was going to come off it. Forced into a situation, people make decisions they have to live with, and whether they regret them or not is another issue. I will prove that Simmons is guilty; I will also solve his murder.'

'McAlister?'

'Don't assume it's only him. I found out about a government minister and his love nest, exposed it as well, lost my job as a result.'

'You could have lost your life.'

'If he had found out in advance what I was going to write, I might have.'

'And you don't think that could happen this time?'

'Tom, dear sweet Tom,' Ashley said as she touched him on the arm, 'don't say things you don't understand. Nothing's going to happen to me. Jerome Jaden's not a bad man. He'll fight to keep his television station, his money, but he won't commit violence against me for it. And even if he considered it, which he won't, it needs others more capable of carrying it out. Jaden's not taking this personally, and nor should you.'

'Someone shot at Simmons. We don't know the reason.'

'Don't we?'

'Are you saying…?'

'I'm not saying anything. The truth is out there, and I'll publish it first, let the police have the evidence afterwards, and Jerome, enough time to issue a statement.'

'If I'm not going to sway you?'

'It'll take more than a night of passion.'

'If not that, would you be open to a counteroffer?'

'Of what? Money?'

'It's possible.'

'It's not money I want. It's the prestige, being respected as a serious journalist, never again having to interview head-up-their-arse talentless actors and singers. That's what I want. Would you take some advice from someone older than you?'

'If you like.'

'Jerome Jaden is going broke. He won't say it openly, but he's in debt, and Tricia Warburton's not going to cut the mustard. Sure, she looks good, but she doesn't have the depth of Simmons nor the credibility, and as for heights, she would shake at the top of a ladder.'

'Tonight?' Tom said.

'Eat your fish, and go home to Alison, tell her you lucked out. No doubt, she'll be pleased, put you out of your misery.'

Chapter 19

Angus Simmons's parents parted company after spending two weeks together. She, back to Scotland, to resume her solitary life, and for him, his mistress and his life of mild eccentricity.

Maddox Timberley, her relationship with Brett Valentine a matter of social interest, continued to find solace in his arms.

By his own admission, Valentine's future as a model would only last as long as the demand for chisel-jawed, flat-bellied and slightly effeminate men lasted. Being an adjunct to Maddox didn't make him a murderer.

Karen Majors beavered away, realised that she was losing the battle and that the advertisers were looking for a discount, something she couldn't give, not beyond a certain point.

Bob Babbage continued to look out for other opportunities, aware that the financials don't lie.

The young Cook, the first-born of Isaac and Jenny, was now taking tentative steps around the house, becoming more adventurous, banging into things, crying until either parent came to soothe.

Isaac was not enjoying himself; the hours were long, and when he got home, invariably late at night, he wanted peace, the sort that Jenny had given him, but now there were issues to discuss. Which school would be best? So intelligent, so beautiful, from Jenny. He had to agree, but it was sleep he needed, and he knew he was irritable, likely to snap at his wife, something he didn't want to do.

Apart from Homicide, there was nothing he would have preferred than spend time at home with his wife and his young son, to see the world through their eyes, the simple pleasures, the contentment, the joy. But it was not to be for him, not yet, probably never as long as people committed crimes and killed.

A Thursday night, close to midnight, Isaac was in bed, Jenny by his side, their son in the other room. He had worked every day for the last twenty-two. Tomorrow, he intended to lie in, arrive at Challis Street Police Station at midday.

The phone rang; Isaac ignored it. Others could deal with whatever drama it was, he thought.

It rang again. 'You can't ignore it,' Jenny said.

Isaac put the phone to his ear. 'Yes, what is it?' he said.

'Sorry to disturb you, and usually I wouldn't bother you, but…' Larry Hill said.

'Is it important?'

'Maddox Timberley's attempted suicide. She's in the hospital.'

'Will she live?'

'It appears that it was a half-hearted attempt, sleeping pills washed down with vodka.'

'Even so. Which hospital?'

'Praed Street, St Mary's. Just up from Paddington Station.'

'I know where it is. I'll be there in thirty minutes, maybe thirty-five. Uniform?'

'I've got one outside her room.'

'Tell him to be vigilant.'

'Sorry about the hour.'

'You were right to call, and besides, Jenny's already running the shower for me.'

Isaac arrived forty-one minutes later; at Jenny's insistence, he wore a clean shirt, knowing that he wouldn't be back until late that day once he left the house.

'Make sure your inspector takes you for breakfast,' she said as she kissed him goodbye.

'I'll make it up.'

'You won't. Besides, I signed up for this. I knew what it was going to be like.'

Isaac found Larry propping up a vending machine, a paper cup in one hand, a bar of chocolate in the other.

'Milk, no sugar,' Isaac said.

'Here, take this one.' Larry handed over the cup. 'I saw you parking your car.'

'Maddox?' Isaac said as he drank his coffee, the taste of the paper cup.

'They've pumped her stomach. We can see her in a few minutes. Don't expect much from her.'

'Any idea?'

'Not yet. Valentine found her after he came back from a night out with friends.'

'Drunk?'

'Drunk and drugged. I've left a uniform there. Once he's conscious, we'll go and talk to him.'

Inside the hospital room, Maddox Timberley revived, a nurse giving her a drink, an intravenous drip in her arm.

'Not so smart,' Isaac said when the woman looked at him. He thought that asking her how she was wasn't the best approach. He knew how she felt – sick as a dog and aware of her stupidity.

'I suppose it wasn't, but you wouldn't understand,' Maddox said.

'Try me,' Isaac said. Larry had left, gone to visit Brett Valentine, as the uniform had phoned to say that the man was stumbling around the kitchen, looking for something to eat, burning his hand on the hob as he attempted to fry bacon.

'It just got too much, this pretending, a new love, the world at my feet.'

'Whereas you're a decent person from a stable background, seduced by the bright lights, is that it?'

'It's empty, and as for Brett, he's not my boyfriend.'

'You're sleeping with him.'

'That doesn't make him my boyfriend.'

'Why the pills? The truth.'

'Sure, I'm making a lot of money, flying around the world, living in great places, but it's shallow. With Angus, it was fine. He kept me grounded, and he never let it go to my head. I'm lost without him.'

'No help from Valentine?'

'Testosterone-charged, drug-addicted man-child, what do you think? His career's on the wane, not that he's sober long enough to realise it.'

'You could find another man.'

'I don't want another; I want Angus.'

'Your future after here?'

'My mother's coming down to London. I'll spend a couple of weeks with her.'

'Valentine?'

'Not a chance.'

'You shouldn't have slept with him,' Isaac said, realising that he was close to lecturing the young woman.

'On the rebound, don't you see?'

Isaac thought it a weak excuse.

***

'Your side of the story?' Larry said to the man propped up in bed, a towel around his head, shivering from the after-effects of a wasted night out.

'I came home, found her on the floor,' Valentine said. 'Nothing more to say, nothing to do with me.'

'Aren't you interested in how she is?'

'I phoned for an ambulance. What more do you want me to do?'

'How? You weren't in a fit condition to phone anyone, let alone emergency services.'

'I knew the number, used it before.'

'The perils of a drug addict, overdosing?'

'Not that I've done it myself, not yet, but I've friends who have.'

'But you will?'

'Inspector, you might not think very much of me, but I'm not stupid. Okay, you're right. I'm not stupid when I'm sober or clean, but I'm addicted, and addicted people make bad decisions, go over the limit. You don't need me to tell you, do you?'

'You could get treatment.'

'You've got the look of a man who drinks. Are you an alcoholic?'

'Not now.'

'Inspector Hill, once an addict, always an addict. Denial doesn't count for anything. One day, when you're down, and life's kicking you in the guts, you'll find the bottle, the same as I will with drugs.'

'Did Maddox have any reason to commit suicide?'

'You mean with me?'

'Yes.'

'Maddox is a good person, probably too good for the life she leads, the life she thinks is important. There are sharks and rogues out there, unscrupulous people who'll bleed a person dry, and when there's no more to give, kick them in the guts.'

'You have experience of these people?'

'Maddox does as well. Believe me, Inspector, she's the homely type, happy to be at home with a good man, a budgerigar in a cage and a couple of kids.'

'She's not said that.'

'She doesn't know it herself, not yet, but she will soon enough. The pretty face doesn't last forever.'

'What do you feel for her?' Larry asked.

'We were thrown together, made to look as though we were in love, but we're not. I agreed. Who wouldn't? And Maddox is obliging, although at night she sometimes cries.'

'For Simmons?'

'Who else? If she's got any sense, she'll walk away from this life, find herself a steady man, pop out a couple of kids, throttle herself with a mortgage and be happy. Simmons would have given her that, but he got himself killed, damn stupid thing to do.'

'Not something you'd do?'

'My future's mapped out. No long life for me. It'll be drugs, drink and women. After that, when my time's up, I'll grow old disreputably.'

'You've not made plans for the future?'

'No point. My parents were losers, so am I. For a while, I made myself some money, had a good time, got to sleep with some classy women. It was as if I'd won the lottery. No regrets from me.'

Larry, believing there was no more to be gained, left the man and headed back to the police station, giving

Isaac a call to join him for breakfast. He knew just the place in Notting Hill: full English, bacon, eggs, toast, the works.

***

As he looked at the woman beside him in the bed, Otto McAlister believed that life couldn't get any better. Not only was Ashley Otway giving him money, but she was also giving herself. He knew she did not like the second part of the deal, but he didn't care. He felt as little for her as she did for him.

The same hotel as before, one floor up from the previous visit, a view out over the countryside, idyllic to some, but McAlister was not interested, and it bored him. He had money; he wanted action.

'Ashley,' he said as he nudged her, 'we need to talk.'

'I thought that was why we're here,' the woman replied, keeping to her side of the bed, drawing the sheet in close to her. 'Who fired the shot? Are you saying you've not got it, and I'm here under false pretences?'

'No, not that.'

Sitting up in bed, the woman pulled a jumper over the top of her body. She didn't want him getting excited again, not sure she could hide her disgust of him, of herself for what she was doing.

'Then what?' she said, moving further away from him, putting her feet on the ground, pulling on a pair of jeans. 'We need to keep the story alive. You need to give me more.'

'The slower this goes, the more money I get paid. Is your editor ready for this?'

'The cost or the information?'

207

'The cost,' McAlister moved over near to her, put his arm around her. 'We wouldn't want to sour our relationship, would we? Not when we're so near.'

'Near to what?'

'I want more money.'

'Is this for the final proof?'

'Not yet. In the meantime, you have to make a decision.'

'Whether I continue to sleep with you or not?'

'There are others who would be willing to pay me what I want?'

Ashley weighed up the options; she didn't like the choices presented.

'How much and how soon before you give me the final proof, the name of the murderer?'

'Today, if you'll pay what I want.'

'Which is?'

'Two hundred thousand pounds.'

'No one will pay that much.'

'Jerome Jaden will.'

'Are you inferring…?'

'I'm inferring nothing.'

Ashley knew the man enjoyed his control over her.

'I'll need to talk to my editor, see what he has to say.'

For now, the man would have to remain with his tongue hanging out; she wasn't going to whore herself anymore.

'Are you going to play ball?' McAlister said, patting her side of the bed.

'I'll get you the damn money. You need to be prepared to give it over, whatever it is.'

'I will be. A down payment?'

'Not from me. Otto, you're slime.'

'From you, Ashley, I take that as a compliment,' McAlister said.

***

Jock, an uncomplicated man, waited at the farmhouse in Dorset.

Deb, tired of her brother's belittling and complaining behaviour, had finally walked out of the door, phoning his wife to get off whoever she was shacking up with and to get back and look after him.

'How could you,' Kate had protested, 'leaving him on his own.'

'He won't be, once you get down here. I've got better things to do.'

'Such as?'

Jock received a kiss on Deb's return, never asked one question about her time away, nor how she was. She went to a cupboard, took out a bottle and poured two whiskies, one for her, one for him.

'It's good to be back,' she said.

'One of the cows calved,' Jock said.

To Deb, they were the most romantic words she had ever heard.

'We'll talk to the vicar tomorrow; tell him we're getting married,' Deb said.

'The calf's not feeding properly, and the cow's not sure what to do, and then the others need milking, and by the way, you've got to do something about the chickens, that cockerel's not pulling his weight.'

No holding of hands or overt signs of affection, Jock continued as he always did. To him, the world didn't exist outside of the farm and the nearby village. He had never been to London, nor did he want to go, regarding Dorchester, the nearest town, with a population of twenty thousand, too big and too busy for him.

Deb was sublimely happy, and as for Jock, once he had finished eating the meal, he left the cottage, walked over to the wayward cockerel, wringing his hands to let it know its fate if it didn't perform.

'I've got to go and check my place,' Jock shouted. 'Back later.'

And that from Jock was the limit of his romantic inclinations. Deb knew that others wouldn't understand, especially her sister-in-law.

Ashley, feeling dirty and soiled and abused and used, all in the cause of a story, felt cheapened, more so than her former junior, Chloe, who had been elated at seducing one of her idols.

Neither did she want to meet with Tom Taylor, even if he was attractive and young, knowing that he and McAlister were peas in a pod. One was rough and ready, the other was soft and fresh-faced, but neither cared deeply for their women, only for what they could give.

'Jerome,' Ashley said, 'we should meet.'

She had thought long and hard before phoning Jaden, not sure if she'd get a favourable response. But there was a dilemma in that McAlister was demanding, and he would want her again, something she didn't want to do, so she'd have to find someone who'd pay the money, get him off her back. Her editor had given a flat refusal to McAlister's outrageous demand. 'Not even if pigs fly,' he had said.

Reaching out to Jaden would dash her career in journalism, sever her job at the newspaper, but she was determined.

'Should we, Miss Otway?' Jaden said. 'After all, you're bad news around the station. Somewhat of a tart, whoring for a good story.'

'You've had someone following me? Bugging my phone? Or hacking my computer?'

'Nothing so dramatic. We had someone at the hotel, the first time you shacked up with McAlister, but after that, nothing more.'

'You sent Taylor to charm me.'

'You think I would do better?'

'Not with me. You, Mr Jaden, are a shrivelled old prune.'

'We'll meet tonight, at 8 p.m. Is that fine?' Jaden found Ashley Otway's retort humorous. He had to admit to liking her tenacity, a sneaking admiration for a strong-willed person, but he had no intention of letting her know.

'Fine by me,' Ashley said. 'Where?'

'Savoy Hotel, my treat.'

'Downstairs?'

'Savoy Grill, nothing untoward, not with you. You're a smart woman, Ashley. If you weren't such an annoyance, I'm sure I could find a job for you.'

'I've got one, finding out who killed Simmons,' Ashley said.

'McAlister not to your taste?'

***

Justin Skinner stayed in Wales, spent more time with Rachel. His trips down to London curtailed due to Kate Hampton's unwillingness to meet.

As Deb Hampton had said when Wendy phoned her, 'The woman's trying her best, and Mike's not such a pain now, not after some of the mountaineering community came around, starting to believe his story. Although some are giving her the brush off, the Jezebel who caused it in the first place.'

'Remorse on her part, making amends?'

'Kate? Unlikely. That day she was down at the farm, I almost liked her, I never thought I would.'

'When you were the main course for the bikers…'

'When I was putting it about, is that what you're saying?'

'Succinctly,' Wendy said. 'You weren't too particular back then, or were you?'

'I wasn't, but that was my time to rebel. I couldn't see anything wrong with it at the time, still can't, and as for Jock, he doesn't care one way or the other.'

'Have you told him?'

'None of his business. We all make mistakes, do things we shouldn't. I made mine when I was younger; Kate's still making hers. Even when Mike was whole, she was with Skinner. Not often, and who knows what Mike got up to when he was overseas.'

'Good for one, good for the other?'

'Something like that, not that I'd accept it with Jock, but then, he's not the type, not the type for much other than making me happy.'

'He'll not be much of a provider if what you say about him is true.'

'Money's not an issue, never has been. I've got enough for the two of us. It's the same with Mike, able to afford the best medical treatment there is. It's not as if he's totally incapacitated.'

'Isn't he? Wendy said. 'It's the first we've heard of it.'

'There's still some movement in his legs, not that he exercises, and it would take a lot to get him out of the chair. I'm not saying he'll climb again, but he might be able to get around with a frame, maybe a couple of walking sticks. But that takes determination and a positive attitude, something he's sadly lacking. Maybe with Kate, but then, she's unreliable.'

'Even before Mike had his accident?'

'It wasn't as bad, only when he was away, which was a lot of the time. He's not cut out for marriage, not really. An obsessive man, capable of great things, not a great conversationalist, tends to get focussed on something, and then that's all he can talk about. I can understand Kate being bored, seeing that she's an extrovert, full of life. A lot of men in her life, more than me, I daresay.'

Wendy looked around Homicide, waved for Bridget to come over.

Her phone on mute, Wendy spoke. 'Check out Mike Hampton, his medical records, any treatment he had – physiotherapy, traction, medicine – and his prognosis. Find an expert to advise us if you can.'

'Sorry about that,' Wendy said when she resumed the call. 'Another phone ringing. I needed to answer it.'

'That's fine,' Deb said.

Chapter 20

It wasn't Ashley Otway's first visit to the Savoy Hotel. Built by D'Oyly Carte in 1889 with profits from his Gilbert and Sullivan opera productions, it was the first luxury hotel in Britain, replete with electric lights, electric lifts, and bathrooms in most of the lavishly-furnished rooms, and constant hot and cold running water.

To her, that first time, a birthday treat from a boyfriend, it was a magical place, frequented by movie stars, musicians and royalty. The second time, in the company of Jerome Jaden, the lustre had tarnished. She was more world-weary, her idealism tainted by her trade and the people she had met, and now, those who checked in to the hotel.

Chas Longley had stayed there, as the newspaper's new entertainments reporter had attested to. It was on the third floor that he had seduced Chloe, given her a scoop that he was coming back in six months, a brand-new show, more dancers, guest artists, the works.

As Ashley sat down, a waiter pulled the chair back for her, telling her that Winston Churchill had sat in the chair. It seemed that he had sat in many chairs as she distinctly remembered that first time that another waiter had mentioned the same thing.

Jaden had chosen the D'Oyly Carte room with its 1920 features; her first visit had been to the other end of the Savoy Grill, more modern, more accommodating to those walking in off the street.

'Tom Taylor treated me to a pub meal and a bottle of wine,' Ashley said. 'You're spoiling me.'

'He had youth on his side; all I've got is money,' Jaden said.

The mood was upbeat, the restaurant's ambience sublime, the sort of place where a person could succumb to drinking more than they should. Ashley was aware, determined not to lose control. This man was not Taylor, nor was he a McAlister; he was altogether more dangerous.

'Lobster Thermidor, or do you prefer something else?' Jaden said.

It was the first time she had been close to the man, and she realised that the shrivelled old prune comment had been extreme. In his sixties and shorter than most men, shorter than her, he was wrinkled but not shrivelled and certainly not a prune. Jerome Jaden had the look of money. His nails manicured, his greying hair, balding on the top. He was dressed in a suit and, on his wrist, a Breitling watch. She had to admit that the man was someone she could respect, but someone she would take down if he was behind Simmons's climb, behind his fall.

'Lobster would be fine.'

'A Chardonnay, or would you prefer champagne?'

'I didn't know we were here to celebrate.'

'A truce before the battle.'

'A Chardonnay. I don't think we'll be celebrating, not today,' Ashley said.

Jaden waved over to the waiter. 'My usual for the two of us, and your best Chardonnay.'

'Aren't you going to check the price?'

'Why? We are not here to worry about money, only what you intend to do.'

'To expose Simmons's murderer.'

'Yes, I understand, but McAlister is hardly the most credible source.'

'He has been so far.'

'Ashley, I don't want to sound patronising, but at what cost to you?'

'I'm not sure what you mean.'

'We've not met before, not like this, but let me be frank. You're still young, ambitious, all credit to you for that, but McAlister's not your type.'

'Are you suggesting?'

'You know enough of me to know I'm a tough bastard, but that's business. I have little sympathy for my competitors or for those who don't pull their weight. But you, Ashley, don't do this, not with McAlister.'

'Do what?'

'Don't cheapen yourself. He's not worth it, and if he does give you something, will it be reliable?'

'It could discredit you,' Ashley said. She felt uncomfortable, unsure if she should stay, although the ambience and the man were soothing but not seductive, as he was old enough to be her father.

'Jerome, I've run in the fast lane before. I know what I'm doing.'

A bottle of wine appeared. Jaden sniffed the cork, tasted a sample, proclaimed it fit for consumption.

'Cheers,' he said, clinking his glass with Ashley's.

'The first of many,' she responded.

'I'm not the first older man you've dined with, am I?'

'They didn't succeed, either.'

'Please, that is not my intention, and besides, the Savoy Grill is hardly discreet.'

'You could have a room upstairs. I doubt if many in here would raise an eyebrow if you whisked me up there.'

'An interesting thought, but no, you're wrong on the first count. There is no room, but on the second, you're right. Look over to your left. Can you see a man, older than me, open-necked shirt, a blue jacket?'

'I can.'

'A banker from Berlin; comes to London every month.'

'That sounds feasible.'

'The woman he's with, a lot younger, beautiful, a lot of class?'

'His daughter?' Ashley said before laughing.

'High-class escort. A wife back home, socialising with her friends, doing charity work, and he's here sampling the local wares.'

'He could be seen.'

'What does it matter? Middle-class morality doesn't concern him, and his wife knows.'

'How do you know this?'

'The same way I know that McAlister's not reliable, and you shouldn't be sleeping with him.'

'If you know so much, then you must know who shot at Angus Simmons, what the reason is.'

'I know enough to be cautious. Ashley, let me be blunt. You're playing with fire, sleeping with a rough man, making a bit of a fool of yourself.'

'Isn't that up to me?'

'Your lobster, madam; yours, sir.' The waiter, silent as a breeze, appeared alongside them and put the plates on the table.

'Not one of yours?' Ashley said.

'He should be, glides in and out. He could have been standing there for thirty seconds, and we wouldn't have known.'

Ashley, seduced by the meal and the wine, not by the man, could feel she was losing control of the situation. 'Before I get too drunk, what is the point of us here?' she asked.

'I'll level with you, Ashley,' Jaden said, clinking his glass with hers again. 'Whatever happens, the television station is going under.'

'You'll be forced to take it off the air?'

'Unlikely, but it'll need restructuring, and for that, I need money. Bad publicity, the sort you could bring me, would make banks nervous.'

'How much do you need?'

'Twenty-five million pounds, give or take a few million. Not chicken feed.'

'You've got that sort of money?'

'On paper, but yes, if I cashed in everything, mortgaged the house, sold the boat, then I could get the money.'

'You sound almost bourgeois. And as for your house, an eighteenth-century stately home in the Palladian style, and the boat, hardly a dinghy.'

'Very well, seeing you've been checking on me. Fifty metres, state of the art, parked in the South of France, worth upwards of twenty million, but it's not mine, belongs to a credit company. Regardless, my wealth is separate from my business interests.'

'A long way separate: overseas bank accounts, companies in every offshore jurisdiction, all of it untouchable by inland revenue in the UK.'

'You're well informed,' Jaden said as he put a piece of lobster into his mouth.

'Not about you, but I know how it works. You're not going broke, although the station might. What about Babbage, Karen Majors, Tom Taylor?'

'And the others. I'll not cheat them, and besides, it's academic. With you helping, I'll survive, and you'll end up well rewarded.'

'Is that a bribe?'

'How's the meal?' Jaden asked.

'You're changing the subject.'

'Am I? You've not heard me out yet.'

The waiter appeared, topped up the glasses. 'Another bottle, sir?'

'Of course.'

'Are you sure you haven't got a room upstairs?' Ashley said. 'Getting me drunk.'

'Please purge that from your mind. I want to put a proposal to you. Will you hear me out?'

'Go on.'

'Someone took a shot at Simmons; we both know that.'

'So do the police,' Ashley said, placing a hand over her glass when the waiter tried to top it up again.

'Let's not forget them, but they're floundering, annoying his girlfriend, although she's into someone new, up until she tried to top herself. The Hamptons must be sick of the police now, and he's a misery, and the sister is a reprobate biker's moll, tattooed from head to toe. And as for Simmons's parents, he's a lecher, and she's reclusive. No wonder Angus felt the need to prove himself to them.'

'I believe you're maligning his parents.'

'Maybe I am, but that's not important. Simmons died, that's all I know, and McAlister might know the truth. He'll string it out, milk as much money for as long as he can, and as long as you're there for sweeteners, why wouldn't he?'

'Is that a roundabout way of giving me a compliment?'

'If you like. You're in a different league to him. It cheapens you. She doesn't have a conscience over there with the banker, just a cocaine habit and a taste for the good life. You, Ashley Otway, are not obsessed about money, would like more, everyone does, but it's not an all-consuming passion.'

'What are you getting at?'

'You want a story; I want to restructure the station, or if it can't be, then to get out with as much money as I can. For that, I need us to work together. You scratch my back; I'll scratch yours.'

'Platonic?'

'Don't go down that road,' Jaden said. 'You whored once, not enjoyed the experience, leave it at that. What if McAlister put his iPhone somewhere in the room, pointing at the two of you going hell for leather? Those videos last forever, and you'll be the butt of jokes, not to mention ridicule. Whatever you do, don't sleep with him again.'

'I've no intention.'

'Does he know?'

'I told him he was a piece of slime.'

'Which he thought hilarious, believing that you'd be back.'

'He did. What's the deal?'

'We mutually agree to release McAlister's information at times that suit us.'

'Which is never.'

'Is it? Think about it. I can't be connected to his death, although Breslaw might have known about Simmons and his stunt.'

'You'd damn him?'

'Breslaw's bourgeois, to use your cute term. He can go back to his garden and his vegetables or whatever else he does in his spare time. He'll not be that concerned, not if I make a deal with him to take the blame for allowing the climb.'

'Did you agree to the climb?'

'My conscience is clear.'

'That's not an answer.'

'Hear me out,' Jaden said. 'Those photos you published of Simmons and Hampton, not very good, but good enough for the public. Whatever's next could be more damning.'

'It will not reflect badly on the station.'

'Very well, but what I need is a copy of all that McAlister has.'

'He wants two hundred thousand pounds.'

'It's not worth that,' Jaden said. 'He'll not get it.'

'He'll trade.'

'A discount if you put out?'

'That's what he has in mind.'

'Would you?'

'Not with him, no.'

'Your editor? Have you put a proposal to him?'

'I have. He'll pay for a recording of Simmons and Hampton's conversation, but he won't pay the full amount.'

'I'll pay.'

'Why? What possible use could it be to you?'

'We, and I mean the two of us, will go through what we've got, decide on when to release it, making sure

221

you get the credit from the newspaper, and I get to release it soon after on the television. That way, both of us get what we want.'

'If it's damning to the station or one of your people?'

'As I said, we agree on what we say, on how we report it.'

'Concealing the truth? Ashley said. 'I'm not sure I'm comfortable with this.'

'Not concealing, choosing the time of release. Do you agree?'

'I'll consider it,' Ashley said. 'You were willing to have Tom Taylor seduce me. Why?'

'I needed you on my side.'

'You hadn't thought this through.'

'Not in total. No plan is set in concrete, and certainly not this one. All I know is that we both need McAlister to hand over the goods.'

'And Tom Taylor?'

'McAlister's not the first one you've slept with for a story.'

'Maybe we're both a couple of old whores,' Ashley said.

Jaden laughed, then caught the eye of the waiter. 'Your best champagne,' he said.

***

McAlister brooded on why Ashley wasn't returning his phone calls. Justin Skinner consoled himself with Rachel in North Wales. Kate Hampton attempted to stay in the same house as her husband.

Homicide met at Challis Street Police Station, unaware of the scheme being hatched by Jaden and

Ashley Otway, only knowing that the motive for a man's death was as unclear as on the day Simmons had died.

A jealous lover didn't seem likely, given Simmons's ambivalence on matters of the heart, and Tricia Warburton's complicity in the death seemed a long shot. After all, she was a capable woman, smart enough to find another job if Simmons had taken over the programme's hosting.

'McAlister's feeding Ashley Otway the proof,' Isaac said. He was tired; it had been a long day, and he had only slept three hours the night before, as the young Cook had a nasty cough, the mother fretting, the father providing moral support.

'He's out for what he can get,' Larry said.

'Fringe benefits,' Wendy said. 'You do know she's sleeping with the man?'

'We do,' Isaac said. 'She tried it on with me that time when I met her.'

'Run a mile, DCI?' Wendy asked, a broad smile across her face.

'Two,' Isaac's reply. He tried to maintain a straight face, but in the end, he had to smile as well.

'A man-eater?' Bridget asked.

'Not from what we know. Ashley Otway's ambitious, a good investigative reporter, demoted after she had exposed a senior politician for corruption.'

'The man's been given a more senior position since then,' Larry said. 'One law for the rich and influential, another for the rest of us.'

Wendy didn't comment. Her politics were well known, and she didn't expect anything better from those in power.

'He's not important at this juncture. Who took that shot is,' Isaac said. 'Any luck on the rifle?'

'It's in the report,' Bridget said.

'Humour me.'

'A person of medium height, a universal rifle mount you can buy at any reputable gun store. Forensics and the crime scene team can't be more specific than that.'

'Trajectory, wind deflection? How about impact velocity?'

'Lucky the first time. Even if the person had taken a couple of trial shots to check the rifle's scope, there was still the wind, and in between the two buildings, it's funnelled into a narrow canyon.'

'And the person had time to pack up their belongings, not taking the mount, believing it was unimportant.'

'A professional would have left it, possibly the rifle, certain that it couldn't be traced back to him.'

'We know that Charles Simmons is a good shot, and Skinner is. Who else?'

'Gwyneth Simmons. Angus used to go hunting, but he was more traditionalist, setting traps and tickling trout.'

'Discount the mother, and besides, it's a long way down from Scotland to shoot your son, and we've found no evidence that she made the trip.'

'Mike Hampton, but he wouldn't have been able to make the climb,' Larry said.

'Unless he's fooling us all. People do recover from back injuries. Bridget, you were looking into his medical records. Anything of interest?'

'After the accident, Hampton spent time in a hospital in Argentina. Unable to move his lower body and in pain, he was doped out on morphine for most of it.'

'Did Kate Hampton go down?'

'She was there five days later, although the morphine was kicking in and he was becoming addicted to it. In the end, she chartered an air ambulance and had him repatriated to England.'

'Expensive?' Larry asked.

'Anywhere between eighty thousand pounds to one hundred and ten thousand.'

'Who paid?'

'Hampton came from money. All I know is that his wife paid for the trip.'

'Can you transport a person in that condition?' Isaac asked.

'I have a copy of the form that Kate filled in, as well as a medical report from a doctor in Argentina. It was in Spanish, easy to translate online these days. According to the doctor, Hampton's spinal cord had been severed, and that, apart from some pain, dealt with by the morphine, he wouldn't walk again, and no further damage could occur.'

'No need for an air ambulance, then,' Larry said. 'They could have saved the money.'

'Commercial airlines aren't set up for a man in a stretcher, and besides, medical advice in this country disputed the Argentinians. They had access to the x-rays, and one doctor had flown down from the UK to see Hampton. I've got his name, not sure how much he'll tell you, but he felt that if the diagnosis weren't correct, he'd go along, get the man out of the country and into his care.'

'How do you know this?' Isaac asked.

'Most of it is common knowledge.'

'Where's Simmons while this is all going on?'

'He was in Argentina with Kate Hampton, and then he flew back commercial.'

225

'Why not on the charter?'

'It was dependent on his need to be there. Kate Hampton flew on the charter, as did the doctor out from the UK, and it's fair to assume Mike Hampton, if he hadn't been semi-comatose on morphine and sedatives, wouldn't want to see Simmons. The man, regardless of whether he was right or wrong about Kate's affair, or whether he had tried to kill Simmons, or if it was the other way around, was still seriously ill. They wouldn't have wanted any more trauma on the flight.'

'McAlister?'

'He stayed in South America for ten days, made sure all the equipment from the climb was packaged and shipped back to England, over two hundred kilos. Even if he's a louse, as people seem to believe, he's still competent and conscientious.'

'Was the spinal cord broken?'

'The medical reports in the UK are not so easy to obtain, although it has been reported that Hampton did have slight movement in his lower body.'

'Conclusive?'

'I'm not competent to comment,' Bridget said. 'From what I've researched, I believe that the damage to Hampton is not as severe as first thought. That doesn't mean he's regained the use of his limbs or ever will. I found another mountaineer on the internet, a broken back, spinal cord intact. Even so, it took ten months of intense treatment and considerable pain before he walked out of the hospital. Two years later, he climbed Mount Everest.'

'And Hampton sits in a wheelchair, complaining about his lot in life,' Wendy said.

'The doctor, where is he? We need to contact him,' Isaac said.

'I've pre-empted you,' Bridget said. 'You have an appointment tomorrow morning, at 10 a.m. Royal National Orthopaedic Hospital, Stanmore, Middlesex. It'll take you less than an hour to get there, assuming the traffic's not too heavy. You're meeting with Dr Matt Henstridge.'

'Is he the doctor who went to Argentina?'

'He is the most eminent in his field.'

'You were right to make the appointment.'

'I can't guarantee how much he'll tell you, patient confidentiality.'

'We'll deal with that after we've met with him. As for me, I'm off home and try to get some sleep.'

'The joys of fatherhood,' Wendy said.

'Sometimes, I could do with a little less joy,' Isaac said. 'Larry, pick me up, 7.30 a.m. sharp.'

Chapter 21

The Royal National Orthopaedic Hospital, one of eleven centres in the United Kingdom specialising in spinal cord injury and rehabilitation, did not impress either Isaac or Larry. A modern building, but from the outside, it looked like a building site, surrounded on two sides by construction barriers, a crane hovering over the roof.

'Expansion,' the young lady at the reception said. 'It's not so easy, and the demand is increasing, too many fools in powerful cars showing off how good they are.'

'They should keep it to a race track,' Larry said.

Isaac felt the woman was talking out of turn; sure, she was right, but the hospital was there to heal, not express an opinion.

'Dr Henstridge,' Isaac said. 'He's expecting us.'

'Is this about Mike Hampton?'

Too many questions, too nosy, the woman needed a session with the hospital's human resources department. Patient confidentiality extended beyond the doctor.

'It is.'

'Dr Henstridge asked me to check. You're DCI Cook and DI Hill, am I right?'

'You are. The doctor?'

'Five minutes. We're busy, and the doctor's been here since four this morning. If he's not the most agreeable, you'll have to make concessions. I'm sure you understand.'

'We do,' Isaac said. The two officers went and took a seat.

Larry picked up a magazine that was on a table. 'It's older than me,' he said as he put it down.

Isaac looked around him, knowing that he and hospitals didn't get along. In his youth, a broken arm, an overnight stay at the hospital. And then, at the age of fifteen, he had watched a childhood friend die in the hospital from a knife wound.

A weary man came through the double folding doors at the far end of the reception area.

'Sorry about the delay. I'm Henstridge,' he said as he shook hands. In his mid-fifties, balding, with bloodshot eyes ringed by horn-rimmed spectacles, the man looked the part.

'Pleased to meet you,' Isaac said. 'This is Detective Inspector Hill.'

'Please to meet you, Inspector,' Henstridge said. 'Sorry that I'm not brighter, but I've just finished in the operating theatre.'

'The patient transferred here from another hospital?'

'We primarily deal with orthopaedics, so the answer to your question is yes. Anyway, you're not here for that, and I could do with something to drink, a stale sandwich in the canteen if there's one left.'

Larry tried one of the sandwiches, not stale as Henstridge had said.

'We can talk here,' Henstridge said. 'The canteen's as good as anywhere, not sure I'll be able to help you.'

Isaac would have preferred somewhere more private, but he wasn't about to complain or confuse matters. 'Doctor, Mike Hampton?'

'That's what I was saying, not sure I can help you much. I went down to Argentina, checked the man out, signed him off to fly.'

'You came back with him?'

'I did. It was a bun fight down there, too much paperwork, and the authorities thought that his returning to England would reflect badly on their medical expertise.'

'Did it?'

'The hospital near to where he had injured himself was basic, not set up for spinal injuries, but apart from that, it was clean, efficient and no worse than some you'd find in this country.

'But here was better for him?' Larry asked.

'Definitely. There are other facilities throughout the UK specialising in spinal injuries, and even if I say so myself, here's the best. Hampton's wife couldn't have chosen better.'

'Expensive?'

'Look around you; what do you reckon? And besides, the cost isn't the most important factor.'

'It is if you don't have the money.'

'True, but people come here under the National Health Service, and if you have insurance, or you're a genuine hard-luck case, we'll not turn people away.'

'The construction work outside?' Isaac asked.

'Expansion. We've got forty beds, need another twenty. We're expanding out the rear of the building, trying to keep the disruption to a minimum, not always succeeding.'

'How long to complete?'

'Twice as long as it should take, strict hours when they can work. No weekends, nothing after 4 p.m., nothing before 7 a.m., and if they're using heavy equipment, driving in piles or jack-hammering, they need to put in a request two days in advance, and even then, we're likely to knock it back. Frankly, we shouldn't have started the work, but now, we're committed.'

The general chit-chat aside, Isaac knew they needed to focus on the one patient. 'Mike Hampton?' he said again.

'Has he been charged with a crime?' Henstridge asked.

'He's a person of interest,' Isaac said.

'No doubt you don't have a court order, nor do you have a letter of consent from the man.'

'Neither. It's Mike Hampton's former friend whose murder we're investigating.'

'I'm bound by the General Medical Council, by the law of this country, and something called the Hippocratic Oath. Much as I'd like to help, I can't. Frustrating for you, no doubt, but I can't see a way around the dilemma.'

'We understand,' Isaac said. 'Why don't we go over what is general knowledge, and if you feel comfortable, then you can answer accordingly.'

'We can try, but remember, I am limited in what I can say.'

'Very well. You went down to Argentina, correct?'
'Correct.'

'You signed off on the man, dealt with the Argentinian authorities and then came back to England with him, checked him into here?'

'In essence, you're correct. The only item is the Argentinian authorities. The air ambulance's personnel dealt with the majority of the paperwork. I was primarily concerned with confirming to Kate Hampton and the air ambulance that it was safe for him to fly. Although I did have some contact with Argentinian medical personnel, on account of this facility's reputation and my name.'

'You signed off because you believed his spinal cord was damaged irreparably, that he'd never walk again.'

'In part, and that was my belief at the time. The facilities in Argentina did not allow a more intensive evaluation of his condition.'

'Mike Hampton, what part did he take in all this?'

'Not a lot. He was on morphine, and he had other injuries. The only problem was that they gave him too much. He developed a mild addiction to it.'

'What did you do about it?'

'Weaned him off it once we were back here.'

'What else can you tell us?' Larry asked.

'So far, I believe I've told you what is common knowledge. I gave a speech at a seminar, used my trip to Argentina, the difficulties, our treatment when we got back to England.'

'Mike Hampton agreed?'

'He did. I saw him myself, got him to sign off on the speech.'

'From our contact with him, he's showed no interest in anything or anyone. A down on life; surprised he doesn't blame you for saving his life.'

'As injured as he was in that hospital in Argentina, he wasn't going to die.'

'Since then?'

'I see him every couple of months. The man is physically well apart from his disability. Mentally active, having to deal with a changed situation. We've given him counselling, advised him to continue, but that's not my area. I believe that's it.'

'One more question,' Isaac said.

'You can try.'

'It's been reported that Hampton had some movement in his toes. Does that indicate that the spinal cord might not be permanently damaged and that it could self-heal?'

'I'm afraid you're now asking questions I can't answer. I sympathise, but I can't discuss the case further.'

'It's been reported.'

'Not by me, it hasn't. Get a court order, not so easy, given that he's not the victim, nor has he been charged with a crime. Otherwise, get Mr Hampton to sign a letter of consent. I'll give you a form before you leave.'

Larry regarded the visit as wasted; Isaac wasn't so sure.

'Henstridge clammed up when we asked about Hampton moving his toes. He was right, gave us more than I expected, but he's not going to be drawn on a contentious area.'

'It's not his responsibility,' Larry said. 'What are the chances of a court order?'

'On what grounds?'

'Then we need Hampton to sign the letter of consent.'

'You or me, or should we leave it with Wendy?' Isaac asked.

'She can talk to Deb Hampton, to the man's wife, see if they can talk him around.'

***

Otto McAlister, his phone calls to Ashley unanswered, was unsure what to do next. He had seen her leaving the Savoy with Jaden, smiling at each other, sharing a taxi.

Desperate and believing that she was leaving him for Jaden, he went to the pub, drank five pints and then drove to her home. If she were there with another man, he'd deal with him, then her.

'Who is it?' a voice called out from inside the house.

'Otto,' he said.

It was after one in the morning, and no one was in the street, apart from a drunk staggering home, a couple of cats and a stray dog.

'Go away. It's late; I need to sleep,' Ashley said.

'With who? I saw you with him,' McAlister said. He was feeling unsteady, swaying from side to side. He wasn't a drinker, and five pints had been too much for him, but it was Dutch courage, the courage to approach the woman, to find out what was going on, to plan for the future.

He had already decided that once he had the money, the two hundred thousand, he was off to Thailand or Cambodia, somewhere he could live cheaply, and with that sort of money, he could live well.

'I'll phone you tomorrow.'

'Now, we need to talk now.'

Along the road, bedroom lights were going on, residents wanting to know what the disturbance was. A voice shouted out, 'Shut up, go home.'

'Bugger off,' McAlister said in response.

'I'll phone the police,' Ashley said. She stood on the other side of the door. He bent down, pushed open the letterbox flap; he could see her, dressed in a bra and panties. He was wild, desperate and drunk.

'You have to let me in, or I'll shout the place down.'

It was either the neighbours or opening the door. Ashley Otway chose the latter.

'I've got a Taser,' she said as he lunged forward.

'I wanted to see who you had upstairs.'

'Nobody, I'm on my own.'

234

'I don't trust you, and what were you doing with Jaden?'

'Trying to get your money. What do you think I'd be doing with him? He's old enough to be my father, and I'm not whoring myself with him, not with you, not anymore. You'll get your money, and then I don't want to see you again.'

'But tonight, I'm here.'

'You can have a black coffee, something to eat and then leave.'

A move forward by the man, and she levelled a spray and pushed down on the plunger.

McAlister bent over double and collapsed to the ground.

'You asked for it. It was either mace or the Taser. Now, will you be calm?'

'I will.'

More relaxed than she thought she would be, she phoned Isaac. 'My house, as soon as possible. Otto McAlister's here, and I don't trust him.'

'Lock yourself in a room; give me ten minutes.'

'If he moves, I'll use a Taser.'

'They're illegal.'

'I brought one back when I was covering a story in the Middle East. Arrest me if you want, but I'll use it on McAlister if he makes a move.'

'You bastard,' McAlister said.

'Lie down flat, put your hands behind you.'

'What for? It's not as if we haven't slept together before.'

'This is my house, and you've invaded my personal space.'

'I'll not comply.'

'Suit yourself. I'll use the Taser, and don't think I won't.'

'Just a coffee, not the Taser.'

'Don't move, not until the police get here.'

'Water for my eyes?'

'When the police are here. For now, don't move, and I mean it.'

Realising that the front door was still open, Ashley made a move to close it. McAlister, drunk and angry, tried to grab her ankle. She took aim with the Taser and pressed the trigger, the man writhing in agony. Regardless of his situation, she grabbed hold of a cable tie and fastened him to a radiator in the hallway.

'Sit yourself up. I'll get you coffee and water for your eyes.'

'You bastard,' McAlister garbled. The effect of the mace, the power of the Taser, had rendered him barely capable of coherent speech. And on the floor, a rapidly forming puddle where he had wet himself.

A knock on the door. 'Ashley, are you alright?' Isaac shouted out.

'I am now,' she said as she opened the door. 'I don't think he is, though.'

'Tasered?'

'Mace, as well.'

'You'd better hope he doesn't want to press charges.'

Isaac took out his phone, requested an ambulance. 'Hopefully, they'll treat him here. What's this all about?' he said.

'Drunk, thought I was cheating on him, as if.'

'Remove the cable tie, and we'll make him comfortable,' Isaac said. 'McAlister, we're going to pick you up, put you into a comfy chair. Miss Otway's going to fetch us a drink. Is that alright, Ashley?'

'How is he?'

'He'll be alright. I was tasered at the police academy. They were looking for a volunteer; it hurts like hell, but recovery doesn't take long.'

'Why, Ashley, why?' McAlister said. His voice was calmer, although still weak and tremulous.

'A change of clothing might help,' Isaac said.

'I've got some that'll fit.'

'A man upstairs?' McAlister said. To Isaac, the man was a lovesick puppy, although Ashley Otway, in underwear, was enough to turn any man's head.

'My brother, if you must know. He stays over sometimes, keeps some clothes here.'

An ambulance came and went, a medic washing McAlister's eyes, checking his heart rate, his physical condition. Standard procedure would have been to transport the man to the hospital for observation, but on Isaac's surety and a signature to confirm that he took responsibility, the medic left.

Wearing trousers three inches too short and baggy around the waist, McAlister leant back, a mug in his hand, apple pie on a plate in front of him.

'Why were you here causing trouble? After all, you two are friendly,' Isaac said.

'She's my meal ticket.'

'Mercenary, but it doesn't explain why she had to take you down.'

'I was jealous and drunk. A man is entitled to make a fool of himself over a woman.'

'A fool, for sure, but it's more than that. You're feeding Ashley information; she's publishing it and letting us know afterwards. The priorities are all wrong here, and withholding evidence, especially in a homicide, is a criminal offence. I'm sure I don't need to tell you this.'

'I'm not withholding anything, only letting her know what I know. You can put it together, make what you want out of it. I'm not giving any guarantees, am I?'

'I wouldn't know. Level with me, do you have proof as to who took a shot at Simmons?'

'Ashley wants the story; I'm giving it to her.'

'He thought I was sleeping with Jerome Jaden,' Ashley said.

'Why would he think that?' Isaac asked.

'I spent a pleasant evening with him at the Savoy. Not upstairs, but in the Grill. I drank too much, maybe said more than I should.'

'Why were you there?'

'Otto wants money. I can't get it from my editor, but I can probably get it from Jaden.'

'Why would he pay, and how much are we talking about here?'

'Two hundred thousand pounds, enough for me to live like a lord in the Far East,' McAlister said.

'Ashley, explain Jaden's logic, yours as well.'

'He gets to control the release of the information, gets the maximum bang for his money. I get the credit for the story and a chance to work with him.'

'You know what you are?' McAlister said.

'Don't you think I know, and if I had to make up the one hundred thousand my editor wasn't going to pay, I'd be flat on my back until this time next year. And you, Otto McAlister, weren't a price I was willing to pay.'

'The more you get angry, the more I like you. Come to Thailand with me, live like royalty, make love on a sun-drenched beach.'

Ashley Otway looked away, pretended to retch, which Isaac could see, but not McAlister.

Isaac liked the woman, a fiery spirit, able to stand up for herself against a man twice her size, although sleeping with McAlister for a story didn't sit easily with him. She reminded him of a government-paid assassin he had had a fling with years before.

'Are you going to charge me with possession of illegal weapons?' Ashley asked. 'And what about Otto?'

'Are you pressing charges, McAlister?'

'I was pushing my luck.'

'I'll make a note, caution you both,' Isaac said. 'Any more nonsense, and I'll charge the two of you. However, my leniency comes at a cost.'

'You want the truth?' McAlister said.

'That's it. If you and Ashley want to keep stringing Jaden along, get the money out of him, I don't care.'

'If I tell you, Ashley will print it, and Jaden won't pay.'

'I'll play my part,' Ashley said. 'After all, we're not breaking any laws, or are we?'

'If you want to fleece Jaden, that's up to you two, but I can't guarantee you much time to pull this off,' Isaac said.'

'As long as I get my twenty-five per cent. Okay with you, Otto?' Ashley said.

'Very well,' Otto said.'

'Are you sure you can trust me?'

'You might be high and mighty with your fancy accent, your upmarket house, but you're not much different from me. You enjoy the chase, the challenge, as much as I do. You won't cheat me, and besides, I could always deny it afterwards, say it was taken out of context.'

'Would you?' Isaac asked.

'No need, she won't cheat, not if she's got Jaden in her control. That man's a rogue. Did he try it on?' Otto asked.

'He was a perfect gentleman, told me not to sleep with you; almost fatherly,' Ashley said.

'What do you have, McAlister?' Isaac felt like a gooseberry, the interplay between the two former antagonists taking a turn in another direction.

'I've got a recording where Hampton and Simmons threaten to kill each other on that mountain,' McAlister said.

'Not good enough for two hundred thousand pounds,' Ashley said.

'Okay, try this. Mike Hampton isn't crippled.'

'Can he walk?'

'He'll not tell anyone, and after he had criticised Simmons, he was an outcast, but now his former mountaineering friends are starting to flock around him. One of these days, he'll make a statement that the encouragement of others wrought changes in him, that he can feel the strength returning in his lower body.'

'Is that true?'

'I know it is.'

'How?'

'I saw movement in his legs when we were down in Argentina, and then, here in England, I visited him once, not that he was pleased to see me. I made him hot soup. Kate wasn't there, probably shacked up with Skinner.

'Anyway, I spilt the soup onto his lap. He moved, placed weight on his feet. He's milking the sympathy vote, and remember, he was always a miserable sod, no idea why his wife put up with him. Later, I sneaked back and

240

looked in a window, and there he was, balancing himself against a table in the dining room. He was standing.'

'We've had our suspicions, spoken to his doctor, but he's not told us the full story,' Isaac said.

'I don't know about that; I just know he's capable of movement. If anyone could have taken that shot, it would be him.'

'Hatred is a great motivator,' Isaac said.

'So's love. How about you, Ashley?' Otto said.

'You'll need a bath and a rest. You can stay here for tonight; plan our next move.'

Isaac discreetly made for the front door. It had been a bizarre visit, and how Ashley Otway and Otto McAlister got together that night was the most bizarre of all.

Chapter 22

Tricia Warburton considered her position. She had gone from the co-host of a successful programme to redundant and rehired to great fanfare. And now, apart from putting up with Jim Breslaw's interfering and Tom Taylor's incompetence, she felt as though she had been set up, an attempt by the television station to force life into a defunct programming format.

'A bit more, Tricia,' Breslaw shouted. 'Lean out further. We've got the cameras on you.'

She knew as she dangled perilously over the chasm, a cord secured to her ankles, that the stories she was going to bring in, the travel to all four corners of the globe, was not going to occur. And that it was her, Tricia Warburton, who was putting her life at stake, attempting stunts that Angus would have done.

'Pull me back,' she screamed.

'Why, it'll be great.'

'If you're so keen, you can get out here.'

Unhitching herself, removing the radio mic and taking off the helmet with the GoPro mounted on it, she walked off the set and got in her car. She was furious.

Jaden waited at the television station, forewarned by Breslaw of an impending visit from a presenter who, in his estimation, was unstable, fighting angry and not suitable for the new programme.

Across from Jaden, two people who interested him more: Ashley Otway and Otto McAlister, his eyes still red from yesterday's mace, his body bruised from where he had collapsed to the ground after being tasered.

'I want you to make yourselves scarce when Tricia arrives,' Jaden said. 'In the other room, Alison will make sure you've got a drink.'

'Are we in agreement?' McAlister asked.

'I agreed to the deal with Ashley, not sure how I'm going to maximise on this. It's a matter of timing.'

'My money isn't. I want it now, or else I'll offer it to the highest bidder.'

'Otto, you should heed Ashley's wisdom on such matters. You are, quite frankly, out of your depth.'

Jaden, who did not care for McAlister's bombastic manner, also didn't care whether the man heeded Ashley or not. What he needed for now was time, and Tricia Warburton was heading up in the lift.

'Next room, now,' Jaden said. 'Give me whatever time I need, and we'll come to a mutually beneficial agreement.'

'If that's a smart way of saying you'll drop the price, I'll not buy it.'

'Leave it to me, Otto,' Ashley said. 'You'll get your money.'

Alison came in, took one look at the woman who would have slept with her boyfriend if she had been willing, and gave McAlister a casual glance.

'If you'll follow me,' she said. 'We've not got long before Tricia's here.'

'You've seen her?' Jaden asked.

'Breathing fire. I saw her on the CCTV downstairs, arguing with reception, insisting she didn't need an appointment to see you.'

'She still got through.'

'I wasn't about to stop her. There's a press briefing in later today, as you know.'

'It may be that we'll have updated news for them.'

'Jerome, Jim's impossible,' Tricia said. The other three had left the room before she entered. 'And besides, I thought I was there to present, not to get myself killed.'

'Bungee jumping?'

'I'm not a dancing parrot, nor am I Wonder Woman. I like my feet planted firmly on the ground, looking pretty if that's what you want.'

'It's what you agreed to.'

'Risking my life, I didn't. And why is Jim taking control? I thought we were working on a new programme that would bring in the viewers.'

'And we are, but times are tough, the revenue's not there. We might have to curtail the travel, three months, maybe more.'

'But…'

'There are no buts, only yes. Get back out there. Do what you need to do.'

'I won't do it,' Tricia said. 'And if you force me, I'll make it known that you intend to force up the price of your shares in this company, then to offload as much as you can, to let the station survive on its merits or die.'

'An interesting speculation,' Jaden said. He leant back and thought about what to do with a woman who was starting to become a nuisance.

'Do you deny it?'

'Whether I do or don't is unimportant. What is important is that you signed a contract with very favourable terms, that you would front the programme.'

'I didn't agree with jumping off a bridge.'

'I'm afraid you did. Tricia, you are the decoration on the cake, as well as what's inside. If you have to stand there looking pretty, that's what you'll do, and if it's getting dirty and jumping off a bridge, you'll do that too.'

'I'm scared of heights.'

'So am I, so what? We'll beef it up, make sure we get a couple of days' worth of promotion out of it.'

'I could fall.'

'You won't. I've got someone who'll come along, make sure it's safe. He can even take a jump before you. Didn't your manager explain the contract before you signed?'

'She said there had to be a catch.'

'She was right. Did a lawyer check it?'

'I knew what I was signing.'

'Which means that you didn't. If you had, the lawyer would have found a clause that says you're liable for failing to comply with any reasonable request and that this station has the right to reclaim costs for money lost.'

'Would you do that?'

'Sue you? Without hesitation, the same as I would expect any individual to sue me if I reneged on a deal.'

Cornered, Tricia knew that she had to make a decision. 'If you'll promise my safety. I don't want to end up like Angus.'

Jaden did not comment, only shook her hand, kissed her on the cheek, and showed her out of the door.

***

'Are we in agreement?' Jaden said. Three hours had passed since Tricia Warburton left, and McAlister and Ashley Otway were still in Jaden's office.

'It depends on Otto,' Ashley said.

'I agree,' McAlister said. 'Fifty thousand pounds today to my account and that I'll work with Tricia Warburton, advise her on the stunts, check them for safety, not that I couldn't have done them myself.'

'You'll hand over a copy of the recording once the money is in your account, and you'll give us indisputable proof that Hampton can walk; two days after Tricia makes the jump.'

'You'll pay the balance before I do?' McAlister said.

'McAlister, my word on it.'

'I'll test that cord for her, twice if she likes. All she's got to do is jump, and if she dithers, I'll give her a gentle nudge.'

'My exclusive?' Ashley said.

'Just lay off the station and me for now, let me boost Tricia, get the share price up, some more advertising revenue, and I'll see you right. Twenty-five per cent of what McAlister gets. Do you trust him?'

'About as much as I trust you, Jerome.'

'You've got the carrot; dangle it. Like a duck to water, so predictable.'

'Are you referring to me?' McAlister said.

'Will you use the carrot?' Jaden asked.

'Sparingly,' Ashley said, 'but Otto will uphold his part of the bargain.'

'McAlister, do this right, and maybe I'll have extra work for you,' Jaden said.

'I won't be dashing off anywhere quick,' McAlister said.

Ashley knew she might dangle the carrot, but the donkey would never get to eat.

***

Wendy visited Mike Hampton, a letter of consent in her hand. She found the man in his usual place, sitting by a bookshelf, a book on his lap. In the corner of the room, a television, its volume muted.

'The only damned thing to talk to,' Hampton said.

'You're on your own?' Wendy said.

'There's a woman who comes in twice a week, tidies up around the place, leaves me food and drink.'

'You cook?'

'If I have to.'

'With your wife gone and Deb down in Dorset, it must get lonely.'

'Not so much these days. A few of those who had treated me like a leper have found their way here.'

'You were pleased to see them?'

'I was civil, the same as I am with you, but I'd rather be on my own.'

'Mr Hampton, there's something we need to know.'

Hampton picked up the book from his lap, put it to his face. 'If you don't mind, I've got a book to read.'

'My sons, if they had been as rude as you, I would have given them a clip round the ear,' Wendy said.

'What is it that you want?'

'A letter of consent.'

'What for?'

'We need a release of your medical records from the Royal Orthopaedic Hospital, from Dr Henstridge.'

'What are you trying to find? Proof that I sit in this chair all day because I want to?'

'There have been reports that you had some movement in your foot.'

'Did Henstridge tell you this?'

'He wouldn't reveal any more than is generally known. Only your time in a hospital in Argentina, your relocation to this country, your stay at the Royal

Orthopaedic. He was adamant that he could say no more, not without a court order or a letter of consent from you.'

'Then it's a court order. I won't give my consent. I'm here, and I'm going nowhere, and I certainly didn't take a shot at Simmons, not that I wouldn't have once.'

'Are you a good shot?'

'I am, not that I ever competed. Sometimes, on the days when I feel better, I go out the back of the house, tin cans on a fence, shoot them off.'

'What did you think of the shot that took down Simmons?'

'Complicated shot. Not for an amateur.'

'Are you an amateur?'

'I am, but I could have taken the shot.'

'What type of rifle do you own?'

'Ceska Zbrojovka 452 bolt action rifle with a scope. 0.22, more than suitable. The only problem is it wasn't me.'

'The letter of consent?'

'Not that it matters if I sign it, but it's the principle. I can't see the point of you knowing my condition.'

'And what principle is that?'

'Accused of something I couldn't have done.'

'I suggest you reconsider the letter of consent, Mr Hampton.'

'Don't slam the door on the way out,' Hampton said as he picked up his book.

***

Jim Breslaw did not like it. His return to the station had been in an advisory capacity, but now he was front and centre, in full control of the new programme. Not that it wasn't a good outcome for him, but Tricia Warburton was no Angus Simmons, and the stunt advisor, Otto McAlister, wasn't either.

'There's nothing to worry about. I've checked the equipment myself, and I'll make a jump before you do,' McAlister said, a man richer by fifty thousand pounds. However, the fringe benefits hadn't resulted – Ashley Otway was keeping her distance.

The three of them, Tricia, McAlister and Jim Breslaw, were standing on a bridge to the north of London. A steel construction that had endured the test of time for more than a century, and two hundred and twenty feet below, a slow-flowing river.

Ashley Otway stood at a vantage point thirty yards away, aware that she wouldn't trust herself to McAlister, cheapened by her involvement with the man.

'Are you sure, Otto?' Breslaw asked. 'We don't want a repeat of what happened before.'

'Don't worry. I know what I'm doing.'

'How long to go?' Tricia asked. The short dress, the curvaceous figure, concealed by green overalls.

'Down and dirty,' Jaden had said the day before. 'Show them another side, a daring personality.'

Even so, she wasn't sure; she hadn't slept the night before, wondering if the fame she craved was worth the fear.

In Homicide, Bridget watched the event, live-streamed by the television station; Wendy was looking over her shoulder.

'Not me,' Wendy said. Bridget could only agree.

McAlister took his position, gave a thumbs up and launched himself, arms splayed. On his return, he declared it safe for Tricia to jump.

After a snatched gulp of alcohol, Tricia took her place after her weight had been double-checked, the length of the bungee cord adjusted.

'There's nothing to worry about, Tricia,' McAlister said. 'Your heart will beat stronger, you may feel an adrenaline buzz, but it's over within seconds.'

There was a weak smile from Tricia, a wave to the camera, and then she followed through with what McAlister had done, crossed herself for luck and pushed off.

A feeling of exhilaration as she fell, not enough time to achieve the sense of accomplishment, a camera tracking from a distance, the sound of screaming, and then at the maximum trajectory, the recoil of the cord, drawing her back up some distance before dropping her again. A shout of '*I did it*'. And then, at the lowest point of the second time down, when the cord should have recoiled again, a sound of sheer horror as it snapped.

Tricia Warburton was in free fall. She hit the river headfirst, soon bobbing back up to the surface. Pandemonium up above, disbelief, people were standing around, others overwhelmed by what they had just seen.

McAlister was rushing down a track to the river; the rescue crew at the bottom, not used to what had just occurred, not snapping into action, valuable time lost.

In Homicide, Bridget and Wendy watched the unfolding drama, the commentators on the early-morning show at the television station unsure what to say or do, and then, over to a commercial break.

Wendy was on the phone with her DCI, updating him on the unfolding events. Larry in the office, but not watching, was on the phone to Tom Taylor or whoever he could get, rushing to pick up his phone and car keys, Wendy not far behind him.

'She couldn't have survived,' Bridget said.

'It's murder,' Larry's comment.

Publicity was what Jaden had wanted; publicity was what he got. The other stations started to pick up on the unfolding events, and it was on YouTube within five minutes, on Facebook in an even shorter time.

McAlister was down at the riverbank, wading into the water to grab the woman and pull her in. On one side of her face, blood was pouring out, the result of hitting shallow water, a rock below the surface. Tricia Warburton was dead.

Larry and Wendy arrived forty-five minutes later, a still stunned crowd of onlookers watching, McAlister with his head in his hands, wandering around, zombified.

'How could it happen?' he said. 'I tested it myself.'

The bungee jump owner, a pugnacious little man, was there, having arrived five minutes before Larry and Wendy. 'The first time,' he said. 'The cords are checked regularly.'

'You knew Tricia Warburton was to jump?' Wendy asked.

'Her people asked for permission to film, wanted to see all my certificates, our level of insurance.'

'Is that unusual?'

'Filming for commercial purposes is, but usually, no one asks to see the certificates, nor the insurance, not that we don't have them, we do. But you don't expect an accident, and certainly not death. The rules and regulations in this country are stringent, unlike in some countries overseas, and accidents are rare. It's not that dangerous. People have jumped into their nineties.'

'Has anything been touched?' Larry asked.

'Nothing. Everyone's stunned, never seen this before.'

Isaac arrived within the hour and made his way down to the river. The crime scene investigators were with the body, as were McAlister and two people from the bungee jump company.

'You checked it?' Isaac asked.

'I made a jump myself with the same cord,' McAlister said.

'You compensated for her weight difference?'

'I checked that those up top shortened the cord. It was right what they did, she stopped at the right level, and then the cord tensed, brought her back up. It was on the second drop that the rope snapped. It could have been a faulty cord.'

'You don't believe that likely?'

'I'm not sure what to think. It's a different discipline to mountaineering. We're not looking at the same thing. They want the cord to stretch, but in climbing, it's whether the rope will support the weight, although we allow a certain amount of stretch. A bungee cord is no more than a glorified elastic band.'

Larry was on the bridge, watching the crime scene investigators.

Gordon Windsor, overseeing his crime scene team's work, looked over the bridge briefly.'

'No head for heights?' Larry said.

'Suspicious, that's what it is,' Windsor said.

'It's too coincidental for us. Two deaths from the same programme, both of the hosts attempting stunts.'

'Climbing a building with no safety gear is foolhardy; bungee jumping isn't, not that I've tried it, but my children have, so's my wife. And from what I've seen so far, this appears to be a professional operation.'

'The cord snapped, plain and simple.'

'If that was intentional, then someone must have interfered with it.'

'Before or after McAlister jumped?'

'It might not be so easy to prove that one way or the other. After all, there was only a few minutes' difference between him and her. He could have been the target.'

'If he was, then why? McAlister doesn't seem viable.'

'Whereas Tricia Warburton was, is that what you're saying?'

'I'm not sure yet. And why kill the woman?'

'I can't help you there.'

Larry took one look down. He knew one thing: he would not attempt a bungee jump, not now, not ever.

***

Homicide was convinced, even if Windsor had been noncommittal, as to who the intended victim had been.

Jerome Jaden sat transfixed in his office chair, barely able to comprehend the situation. Jim Breslaw sat opposite; Bob Babbage took a neutral position.

'The programme's not going to work,' Tom Taylor said. He had remained standing, not sure what to say or do.

'Legally, we're covered,' Babbage said.

'Is that all you can think of at a time like this?' Karen Majors said on entering the room. 'Tricia's dead. The police will be swarming over this place. I'll be lucky to keep any of our advertisers, not after this is splashed over the media.'

'She was murdered,' Jaden said.

'How do you know?' Taylor asked.

'It's a conspiracy.'

'Do you believe what you just said?' Babbage asked.

'We need to act fast.'

'It sounds callous,' Karen Majors said. 'Tricia was one of us; so was Angus.'

'Emotions are not for now. Action is, and for that, I need you all on board. Jim, how about you?'

'This has become too grubby,' Breslaw replied. 'Count me out, wherever this is leading.'

'It leads to survival,' Jaden said. 'Within a couple of hours, the police will be here. Whoever or whatever is responsible for Simmons's and Tricia's deaths is not important for now; the rumours are just hearsay, innuendo or downright lies. Either we take advantage, or we might as well shut up shop now. Do you want that, Tom?'

'No, of course not.'

'Great. You've got twelve hours to put together a fifteen-minute documentary: the history of the programme they hosted, interesting excerpts, Simmons's mountaineering exploits, Tricia's if she's got anything of note. He's to be the outdoor adventurer, following in the footsteps of Andrew Irvine and George Mallory, mountaineers from the 1920s. Lay it on thick, a man who had no fear, a man's man, charismatic, loved by all. You know the sort of thing.'

'I'll need help,' Taylor said. 'I'm not sure I've got the skills to do this.'

'Take Alison. Grab hold of the production team. Jim, you're in?'

A nod of the head from Breslaw.

'Great,' Jaden continued. 'In the meantime, schedule one of Simmons's documentaries. The news team can show the necessary sympathy. And as for you, Bob, you can check out our legal liability, make sure Tricia's daughter is looked after, payments to whoever as soon as possible.'

'Can we afford this?' Karen Majors asked.

'Get whoever it is that we have – Helen Moxon, I think that's her name – to run through the figures, also what it'll cost to set up a new programme, murders that have never been solved, that sort of thing. Time is of the essence, and you, Karen, have got to sell it. The world's watching, and we're taking note.'

'And what of Tricia Warburton?' Breslaw asked.

'If McAlister killed her, for what reason we can only guess, he'll be charged. Maybe he got a knockback from Tricia. After all, he was sleeping with Ashley Otway, and she gave him the push. Who knows what goes through the mind of such a man?'

'If he didn't?'

'Jim, don't worry about this for now. Focus on preserving this station; the station of law and order, compassion and love. Karen, can you work with this?'

'Was this planned?' Karen asked.

'Tricia's murder? Why would you say that?'

'It seems that her death has given this station another lease of life, that's all.'

'It's providence. There's always a solution. Only sometimes it's not so easy to see,' Jaden said.

Chapter 23

The consensus in Homicide after Tricia Warburton's death was that whoever had taken the shot at Simmons could have tampered with the bungee cord. Gordon Windsor confirmed the probability that it had been partly cut with a sharp knife, enough to have weakened it, the reason that it took two jolts before it snapped.

Although, as Isaac said at the first meeting in Homicide after the tragedy, that speculation came with provisos, in that no one except McAlister had been alongside the woman as she jumped.

'Then it's McAlister,' Wendy said.

'What possible motive could he have for killing Tricia Warburton?' Larry said.

'Or the intended target wasn't the woman,' Wendy added.

'Are you suggesting the cord had been cut earlier, and she wasn't the target?'

'McAlister was the first to jump that day. We know that the woman wasn't keen and that he jumped to show her that there was nothing to worry about.'

'This is common knowledge,' Isaac said, 'but where's this heading?'

'McAlister has the dirt on Hampton. We know that well enough. He's a liability and possibly to others who know the truth.'

'Others?'

'I'm not sure of who, so maybe nobody.'

'There's a flaw in your argument,' Larry said. 'Even if we agree with you that McAlister's the target, there's still the question of the damage to the cord.'

'Is there?' Wendy said. 'Hampton knows ropes and what to look for, and even though a bungee cord is not the same, he'd be able to research on the internet how much to cut the cord.'

'It would have been seen,' Isaac said.

'Would it? A cold morning, high on a bridge, a tight schedule. And how often do they check them? Once a week, once a month, every time someone jumps?'

'Hampton's not on the bridge. How could he do it?' Larry said.

'Wasn't he? And even if he wasn't, couldn't he have got to the cord beforehand? The company has somewhere they store the equipment. Not so difficult for a determined person, and Hampton's single-minded. What if it was McAlister that was to plummet to his death, and somehow it held? Tricia Warburton could have died instead of him.'

'Larry, you and Wendy, bring Hampton to the station. Bridget, use a Section 29 request form, get DCS Goddard to sign it, prepare a court order, make sure all the salient points are there, and I'll phone up Doctor Henstridge, tell him I'm on my way and that I'll expect full cooperation.'

***

Henstridge sat firmly on his office chair, adamant that he wouldn't discuss the matter further or open up Hampton's file without a court order.

'Events are moving fast,' Isaac said. 'I suggest you prepare the information that we want.'

257

'That's not the issue. As you say, you intend to arrest Mike Hampton on suspicion of murder, so that must mean you are very confident of his guilt.'

'Not murder, not yet, but he had the motive, if not the ability. He is the crux on which our investigation hinges.'

'And if his medical report says otherwise?'

'If it does, then we'll look elsewhere. In the meantime, you can either deny or confirm that Mike Hampton has reacquired the use of his legs.'

'Section 29 of the Data Protection Act gives me some leniency in this, and I'm aware that your chief superintendent has signed the form, but due to the seriousness of the matter, I'll still need a court order. You, as a police officer, can understand that,' Henstridge said.

'I can, and I do. However, Hampton may well have been responsible directly or inadvertently for the deaths of two persons. I wouldn't want another to be on your conscience.'

'I will follow the letter of the law, no other.'

'When was the last time you saw Hampton?'

'It will be in the information I give you.'

'It's only a question.'

'To you, it is, not to me.'

At Mike Hampton's house, calm reigned. Larry and Wendy had arrived, told the man his rights and informed him of his removal to the police station.

'In a wheelchair?' Hampton's comment. 'Me, involved in a murder? How? I can't leave the house, not unless I go down a ramp, and you expect to charge me with cutting a bungee cord.'

'It's not been reported, the cutting of the cord,' Larry said.

'It's on Twitter.'

The curse of social media. Those interviewed had been told of the need for confidentiality, but others, with their smartphones, hadn't.

'You'll need to come with us to the police station,' Wendy said.

'Why? I don't need a cell; I've got one here.'

Even though a woman came in during the week to check on Hampton, the house showed neglect. An electric heater, turned up too high, closed windows, and a smell that permeated the place.

Wendy excused herself and went outside. It was cold, but not so cold that the heater needed to be on high.

'We're taking your brother to the police station; to help us with our enquiries,' Wendy said on her phone.

'How? Why?' Deb Hampton's reply. 'He couldn't have shot Angus.'

'He could have been responsible for the death of Tricia Warburton.'

'He never knew the woman.'

'We believe the intended target was Otto McAlister, and the woman was an unfortunate consequence. We are obtaining your brother's medical records. You spent a lot of time with him. You must have seen him move.'

'And if he can, he's a murderer, is that what you're saying?'

'We still have to place him at the second murder site.'

'How, I used to help him into the shower?'

'Surely the house has been set up for a disabled person,' Wendy said.

'Mike wouldn't hear of it. He relented with a ramp into the garden, but when he first came back, he wasn't as bad as you see him now.'

'Yet, he's on his own. Neither you nor Kate.'

'You know what he's like. He's my brother, not a millstone around my neck, and as for Kate, more interested in herself than her husband.'

'Still, a millstone around hers.'

'She married the man for better or worse, and now that's what he is, the worse. You'll not convince me that he's faking his injury. Where is his *loving* wife?'

'She's not answering her phone.'

'Justin Skinner?'

'She's not with him. He's abseiling in Wales. It was Rachel, his on-again, off-again girlfriend who had answered the phone.'

'Then she's with someone else,' Deb said.

'How's your man?' Wendy asked, an attempt to draw the woman away from damning her sister-in-law, to get her to refocus.

'Three weeks' time, a quiet wedding in the local church. You'll come?'

'I'd be pleased to,' Wendy said.

'Jock's moved in with me, so we can skip the honeymoon, too much work to do around the place.'

'Kate spent time with Mike. Did she ever believe he wasn't as bad as he said he was?'

'She didn't say anything to me, but then we never spoke much, argued mainly, apart from that time she turned up at the farm.'

Four hours later, Isaac had the court order.

***

Kate Hampton's visit was unexpected, but there she was at the police station, asking after her husband.

It was Larry that spoke to her. 'How did you find out?'

'I received a phone call from your sergeant, assumed it was serious,' the woman's reply, which didn't ring true, not to Wendy when told.

'It's either Deb Hampton or Justin Skinner that phoned her,' Wendy said. 'And I never told Skinner's girlfriend what it was about, only Deb.'

'It must have been her,' Larry said. 'Suspicious?'

'With those two, I can't see it.'

Mike Hampton was in the interview room. An ambulance had brought him to the police station. The man's condition, whether good or bad, was uncertain; however, exacerbation by the police bundling him into the back of a police car couldn't be allowed.

Kate Hampton sat in another room, no more than thirty feet from her husband.

With the court order, Dr Henstridge's reluctance had changed to obliging.

'Mentally, the man's regressed into a dark place,' Henstridge had said. 'The brain is a powerful organ, able to wreak havoc, conversely able to heal the sick.'

'Dark place, what does that mean?' Isaac asked.

'Mike Hampton's injuries were not as severe as first thought, and with time he could have regained limited mobility.'

'Fully?'

'The man was ideally placed for a return to basic normality. Physically fit at the time of the accident, a positive attitude, determined to succeed at any cost. There was damage to some of his vertebrae, and for Mike

Hampton to achieve remarkable results, there would be severe pain.'

'Treatment, the fusing of two vertebrae, bone grafts, plates, rods, any or all of the aforementioned?' Isaac asked, having checked on the internet the issues confronting Hampton.

'We have inserted rods and fused two of his vertebrae. The next stage is up to him.'

'Which is?'

'Application, a rigorous regime of exercise and rebuilding of wasted muscles.'

'Could Mike Hampton, unbeknown to you, have committed himself to what you've just said?'

'What I'm saying, and I saw him two months ago, is that if he wanted to, he could probably walk, if not for long periods, and more than likely with the aid of one or two walking sticks.'

'Could he in that time have recovered sufficiently, applied himself, and now be walking?'

'Inactivity for so long causes wasting of muscle, and he had put on weight. Unless he has overcome the mental barrier, then I would say no.'

'If he had, would others have noticed?'

'Those near him for extended periods might have.'

'His wife, his sister?'

'Have you spoken to them?'

'They deny any improvement.'

'They could be defending him,' Henstridge said.

What was clear, and Isaac had told Larry and Wendy back at the police station, was that Hampton could have been responsible for Tricia Warburton's death. However, he could not have taken the shot at Simmons.

At the station, Kate Hampton, agitated and emotional, continued to say that her husband needed medical care, a stress-free environment and to be at home where he belonged.

In the interview room, Mike Hampton sat and waited. To his side, a man he had climbed with, a well-credentialled and immaculately dressed lawyer.

Isaac arrived at the station, spoke to Kate Hampton as he passed, offered the usual: following through on our enquiries, and we have sufficient to have brought your husband into the station.

Not far behind him on his entry into the station, Deb Hampton, sister of one Hampton, the antagonist of another.

'DCI, what's this nonsense?' Deb Hampton bellowed.

'Your brother is helping us with our enquiries,' Isaac said.

'How? The man can't move, and even if he could, he's not a killer. Sure, he's difficult, but you can't blame him.'

Isaac could, but the woman would not be waylaid by a comment from him, smart or otherwise.

Kate Hampton sat nearby, watching the interaction, not saying anything.

'We believe he has regained mobility,' Isaac said, waving the folder Henstridge had given him.

'Henstridge?' Deb said. 'Doesn't know what he's talking about. He baffles everyone with medical mumbo-jumbo, gives this speech about the power of the mind.'

'He's an expert in his field.'

'Do you think a person like Mike wouldn't have tried? I was with him for a long time, so was Kate. Neither of us saw as much as a twitch.'

'It still doesn't obviate the fact that medically, and we have to place our trust in Dr Henstridge, your brother could possibly move to a varying degree, subject to muscle improvement, rigorous exercise and a positive frame of mind.'

'The third one he hasn't got.'

'Revenge is a great motivator, as strong as love.'

Wendy came out from Homicide, made an excuse and extricated her DCI from the ire of one woman, the sneering glances of another.

'I wasn't prepared for that,' Isaac said.

'Nor are you for Hampton's lawyer. The man's aggressive, sharp, and he's definitely on his client's side.'

In the interview room, five minutes after his extrication and long enough for him to phone Chief Superintendent Goddard and update him on the current status, and the fact that they might have to release Hampton, Isaac went through the formalities.

Larry was on the left side of his DCI; on the other side of the table, Mike Hampton and Duncan Harders, the man's lawyer.

'Let me make it very clear at the outset,' Harders said, leaning over the table for emphasis, 'that bringing my client in here in his condition is a violation, and I will be filing an official complaint on his behalf.'

'Mr Hampton is assisting us with our enquiries,' Isaac said. 'We did not transport him in the back of a car but an ambulance. I don't believe that we were in error.'

'When my client leaves here today, after this interview, I will arrange for him to have a medical to check his physical condition, to clarify the harm done to him by the incompetency of the police.'

'That is your prerogative, Mr Harders. However, his leaving here is subject to the clarification of certain facts.'

'If you mean proof, where is it?'

Good question, Isaac thought. He knew the evidence against Hampton was not as robust as it should have been.

'Otto McAlister was the target of the latest murder. Fortunately for him, the cord held, but not for the next person.'

Mike Hampton sat still, his hands folded, his head down, not looking across the table.

'A half-baked theory as to intent, coupled with no substantive evidence, gives you no option other than to release my client this instant.'

'Mr Hampton,' Larry said, 'the report we have from the Royal Orthopaedic Hospital states that with sufficient application, you could gain some ability to walk. Do you agree with that?'

Hampton's head lifted, and he placed his hands on the table. 'Hobbling around is not walking.'

'Most people would agree that hobbling is better than the alternatives.'

'I'm not most people. I'm a mountaineer, plain and simple. What do you expect me to do? To pull myself up?'

'Do you have the willpower to improve?' Isaac asked.

'Chief Inspector, you have brought my client into this police station for a crime he couldn't have committed, based on no evidence and no proof,' Harders said. 'This is a farce, and you are the perpetrator of this, dare I say it, a witch hunt.

'Yes, that's what it is, a witch hunt. It may serve your purpose to arrest a man of great achievement, but at the end of the day, you will rue that you ever considered my client guilty of a heinous crime.'

Isaac didn't need the end of the day; he regretted it now. But he was not going to give in so easily, determined to find a chink in Hampton's armour.

'Mr Hampton,' Larry said, 'let us discuss Otto McAlister.'

'There's nothing to discuss. He was a good climber, dependable, team player.'

'Yet, he was willing to sell photos of you and Simmons. And he was ready to sell a tape recording of you and Simmons arguing about his affair with your wife, which we now know not to be true.'

'Do we?' Hampton said.

'You've had adequate proof of that now. Do you believe that Simmons was having an affair with your wife?'

'Not now, I don't.'

'And finally, not yet released, is the proof from McAlister that you can not only move your feet but you can walk.'

'What proof does he have, this McAlister?' Harders asked. 'I'm aware of your reputation, DCI Cook. A man who goes out on a limb; latches onto the truth at the last minute more often than not. But believe me, it's not going to work here. Unless McAlister can prove that my client can move, your case is worthless.'

'McAlister visited your client, made soup for him. Do you remember that, Mr Hampton?'

'I do. Too hot, if I remember rightly.'

'Some of it spilt onto you, causing you to react, to place your feet on the ground.'

'I moved my legs, so what?'

'You didn't use your arms to do that, not according to McAlister, and that, coupled with the doctor's report, shows us that you've been lying all along. This has been a remarkable performance, but the curtain's about to come down, and you're on the wrong side of it.'

'My client refutes your accusations. It's good that I'm here to act for Mr Hampton, a man whose mental health is not strong.'

'Regardless of what you're saying, Mr Harders, I will require an independent examination of your client's medical condition, as well as a complete psychological examination. Two murder investigations hinge on Mr Hampton. The second murder required limited mobility, although Angus Simmons's death would have required a person in good physical condition. At this time, we're willing to concede that Mr Hampton did not commit the first crime, although he had the strongest motive, but believe that the second crime continues to point in his direction.'

'You're right,' Hampton said. 'I wanted Simmons to pay for what he did to me. I was pleased when he fell, but I didn't kill him.'

'McAlister was about to expose you as a charlatan; you couldn't allow that,' Isaac said.

'He saw me place my feet on the ground, I'll not deny that, and there is some movement, but it's limited and erratic.'

'Yet up until now, you've denied any movement. Why?'

'I'll tell you why. A few steps, what use is that?'

'Do your wife and your sister know this?' Isaac asked.

'Deb does, but Kate's not the caring type. She wouldn't have noticed.'

'Your leg muscles?'

'Weak.'

'But with time, you could walk again?'

'What good would I be? What could I do? Get a job in an office?'

'You've lied about your medical condition. Are you as depressive and miserable as you make out?'

'I am, no lying there,' Hampton said.

'Mr Harders, I have no option but to retain Mr Hampton in custody while we conduct further investigations, to lay a charge against him of obstructing justice.'

'I would request that he is returned to his house on his surety for now,' Harders said.

'I will agree to that under the circumstances,' Isaac said. 'However, he will need to be available for a complete medical by an independent doctor.'

'I agree,' Hampton said. 'Now, can I get out of this hellhole?'

'Your wife and sister are outside. We will need to talk to them before they leave. In the meantime, do you want to wait here, or do you want us to return you to your house?'

'Get me home. As for Kate and Deb, they can come and keep guard if they want to; no more than a prison back there, anyway.'

Chapter 24

Jerome Jaden sat in his office; he was holding court.
McAlister sat beside Ashley Otway, but at a distance, no
longer as close as they had been the last time.

Tom Taylor, an eye for Ashley, Alison clinging to
him tenaciously, stood close to the window. Karen Majors
sat on an uncomfortable chair brought in from outside.
Bob Babbage, confident he would be accepting a rival
company position, sat alongside Karen.

The only one not in the room was Jim Breslaw.
No longer on contract, he had been terminated after
Tricia's death, sulking at his home.

'The deal stands,' McAlister said.

'Otto, I don't see how,' Jaden said. 'Hampton's
under investigation by the police, and they don't believe
he killed Simmons. What use is your proof now?'

'He could have taken that shot.'

'Could, would, maybe, perhaps – all mean
nothing. And besides, you were the target, not Tricia, or
doesn't that concern you?'

'Not as much as your money does.'

'So far, I'm down fifty thousand pounds,' Jaden
said. 'How much more do you think I should give you
and why?'

'I can prove that Hampton took the shot.'

'The police have his medical report. If he did, and
I doubt it, what's the point of paying you more money.'

'We need to be careful,' Babbage said. 'Discussing
on air what happened with Tricia and Angus, given that

they are both murder investigations, could leave us open to criticism and prosecution.'

'We're aware of that, Bob,' Jaden said. 'However, this television station is going broke, and not only don't we have our new programme or our star host, but we've also got to contend with McAlister here, who thinks I'm a fool. As for you, Bob, you're ready to leave a sinking ship.'

'I'm still here,' Babbage said.

'Let me remind you that if you hand in your resignation, your chance of a performance bonus, stock options and whatever else you squeezed out of me when you signed your employment contract is gone.'

'Jerome, I'm a lawyer. I know what I signed, not what you want to interpret.'

'And if I declare bankruptcy?'

'You won't.'

'Wouldn't I?'

'Whatever happens, you'll figure a way out.'

'You're right. We're not finished yet. Ashley, what's your take on this?'

'Mine? I'm not sure I have one, other than Otto's here, and if he was the intended target, we must be able to do something with it.'

'How do you feel, knowing that you jumped with that cord?' Karen Majors asked, looking over at McAlister.

'At the time, I didn't give it much thought. If it was Mike Hampton who cut the cord, then why try to kill me at the bungee jump?'

'Tom, that fifteen-minute spot for tomorrow's sunrise show, the life and times of Simmons and Tricia?' Jaden asked.

'We'll be ready.'

'Good. Add in that Otto was a probable target and that Tricia's death was unintentional. Tom will run it past Bob, make sure the wording is crafted. No direct mention of who killed who, only suppositions. Karen, focus the advertising for that time slot.'

'Tricia had a daughter,' Alison said.

'If you can get her to say a few words, tearful would be better.'

Babbage didn't like it, but Jaden was right. The contract he had signed, eager as he had been at the time for the position, did have loopholes, loopholes that Jaden would use.

'Even if we can generate more viewers, increase our advertising revenue, where does it leave us?' Karen Majors asked.

'Another day's grace,' Jaden said.

'Otto's money?' Ashley asked.

'And your cut?'

'That's not what I asked.'

'If Otto can prove it was Hampton who took the shot, then we'll come to a deal. In the interim, I'll pay him for services rendered. If he appears on camera, discusses that day at the bungee jump, says a few words about Tricia, then he'll be paid for that. As for you, Ashley, I'm not sure that you have much to offer. You're no longer required.'

'You can't do that. I protest.'

'Protest as much as you like. Where's the contract?'

'You paid fifty thousand. That served as a contract.'

'Then, Miss Otway, you're not as smart as you believe yourself to be. Alison will show you the way out.'

'You'll be hearing from my lawyer,' Ashley, indignant and angry, said.

'If you want to waste your time and your money, that's fine by me. But for now, get out of my office.'

'Otto?' Ashley looked over at him.

'Sorry, Ashley. It was fun while it lasted,' McAlister's reply.

'Miss Otway, if you would be so kind as to follow me,' Alison said.

***

Apart from a charge of murder, Mike Hampton had the added burden of Deb and Kate in the house. To him, neither woman was welcome.

If Deb was in the kitchen, Kate was upstairs making beds; if one was in the garden, the other was in the house. The conversation between the women was muted, and when they did speak, it was in low voices, the type used in the presence of death, but Hampton knew he wasn't dead, not yet.

He had been careful to conceal his improving mobility. At times that had been difficult, and if McAlister hadn't dropped that soup on his lap, the man wouldn't have seen the pressure he had applied on the floor. Deb had sensed something before, but not Kate, thinking of other places and other men.

'Your dinner's ready,' Deb shouted from the kitchen. 'In here, or do you prefer it where you are?'

For him, it made no difference. He wasn't about to move from the chair he was sitting in.

'I'll be glad when you two leave me alone,' he said.

'No doubt you will, but murder is serious. We're here for moral support.'

'In here. That way, I won't have to listen to you. And besides, what about this man of yours, won't he be missing you?'

'Jock? Barely acknowledges me when I'm there.'

'Do you love him?'

'In my own way. He'll never climb a mountain or do anything great, nor will he murder anyone.'

'Do you believe I did?'

'What I believe is unimportant.'

'And if I had, could I rely on you?'

'You know you can.'

'What about Kate?' Hampton asked.

'She's a selfish woman,' Deb said. 'You can't rely on her.'

'Where has she been the last week? Where did you find her?'

'I left a message on her phone.'

Hampton flexed his leg muscles, a cramp in one leg. He wanted to stretch it out to massage, but not with Deb in the room.

'Ask Kate to come in here,' he said.

After two minutes, long enough for her to end her phone call, Kate entered the room.

'I can't prove that I didn't kill that woman,' Mike Hampton said.

'But you couldn't have killed her, not from here.'

'The police will check my medical condition, conduct tests to check nerve impulses, muscle density. They will know.'

'Know what? That you can't walk,' Kate said.

'Kate, so blind, too busy enjoying yourself. Who is it now? Not Skinner, or could it be McAlister?'

'Is this important?'

'Not really. Some fancy man you met somewhere or other. And besides, what do I care?'

'He's a doctor,' Kate said.

'I want you to leave the house,' Hampton said. 'Today, as soon as you've packed your case.'

'You need our help.'

'You were doing your duty, and I'll thank you for that, but I don't need your help or Deb's. Both of you can leave.'

'What will you do?' Deb asked.

'I will survive, the way I always do.'

Removing the blanket covering his legs, Mike Hampton took hold of his upper left leg and placed a foot on the ground in front of him. He repeated the action with the other leg. Then, with his hands on the chair's armrests, he pushed himself upwards.

The two women watched, unsure of what to say.

Standing up, Hampton moved one foot in front of the other, halting steps, slowly improving.

'Some days are better than others.'

'How long?' Kate asked.

'Slowly over the last few months. McAlister was right, what he told the police, what he attempted to sell to that reporter.'

'We need to be by your side,' Deb said. 'They will convict you of Tricia Warburton's murder, of Angus's.'

'They can prove one, not the other. Kate, don't stay here. You haven't committed a crime.'

'It's my duty,' Kate said.

'It's not. What I am saying is rational, not embittered. Go!'

'Deb, will you look after him?' Kate said, looking over at the woman.

Kate put her arms around her husband, kissed him on both cheeks, packed her case and left. He did not expect to see her again.

'Deb, I don't want you here when the police return,' Hampton said. 'Go back to your farm and your man, raise cattle or children, whatever you want, but don't come back here, not for now.'

Deb knew her brother was right, and the bond that had tied them as children remained. She would comply with his request, the same as when they were both young in that house of misery with their parents.

***

Mike Hampton opened the front door of his house. He was standing.

In the time since Kate and Deb had left, Hampton had exercised his legs, ambled around the garden twice, stopping three times to catch his breath. He felt that an almost complete recovery might be possible, but time was not on his side.

Before the walk around the garden, he had phoned the police, told them to come down, and he would make a full confession to the murders of an innocent woman and a guilty man.

'As you can see, I can walk,' Hampton said, standing in the house's kitchen with Isaac and Larry.

'Are you telling us that you climbed that building carrying a rifle?' Isaac asked.

'I will subject myself to any tests that you want.'

'Doctor Henstridge stated that you could walk in time, but he hadn't seen any evidence of it.'

'He was right. The feeling in my legs started to come back after the last time that I saw him. At first, I ignored it, but with the improvements, my mood started to change, although it did not go from depressed to optimistic, but instead to hate.'

'Did you hate McAlister?'

'I did. You would never have considered me for the murder of Angus Simmons, not without McAlister's accusation.'

'He never said that you could, only that you had strength in your legs.'

'You would have continued to probe, come up with the only logical conclusion: that I am a murderer.'

'The rifle?' Larry asked.

'I threw it in a river, not far from here. You can trawl for it if, not that you'll find it.'

'Then, Mr Hampton, we have conjecture but no proof. If an admittance of guilt is what you're ready to give now, then where does that place us? Sure, your charge can hold, you could be convicted, but your mental state is still questionable. Do you believe that you will be declared mentally incapable of standing trial? Of conviction?'

'Inspectors, I do not. I will provide you with evidence as far as I can. I'm sorry about the woman; I hadn't wanted to kill her.'

'So are we. But why did you leave it open to error? No doubt you had researched the subject extensively.'

'I'm not familiar with bungee jumping, always regarded it as more frivolous than serious. I could see that the cords, regularly tested, changed as needed, were subject to wear and that there were weak spots over the length.'

'You miscalculated, and how could you be sure that McAlister would go first?'

'It was simple. I was there.'

'We didn't see you?'

'I suggest you check your footage, a man in his fifties, a peaked cap, dark-skinned, standing to the rear of the group on the bridge.'

'We have the names of all those who were there,' Larry said.

'Have you interviewed all of them?'

'All except one.'

'Ivor Putreski?'

'Yes.'

'You didn't interview him because he wasn't there, not after I heard that McAlister was to jump first.'

'How could you be sure that cutting the cord was sufficient?'

'Research, meticulous research.'

'Which proved to be wrong?'

'It was correct, but I failed to take into account that he had lost a lot of weight over the last year after contracting typhoid in Nepal.'

'When did you realise you had made a mistake?'

'They checked his weight just before jumping. Even so, I was certain that what I had done was sufficient.'

Isaac opened his laptop, played the television footage from the day, ensuring that only he and Larry could see the screen. A man at the rear of the group on the bridge, the mysterious Ivor Putreski.

'Describe the clothes you were wearing,' Larry said.

'Blue jeans, a red shirt, a greyish-coloured jacket, zip up the front.'

'And you intended to jump?'

'I was down for the last jump of the day, a last-minute booking. I was certain it wouldn't come to that and that McAlister would be of more interest. The man, if he continued with his aspersions, would have damned me, and I wasn't willing to allow that to happen.'

'But you've damned yourself.'

'It was the woman, don't you see?'

'Were you there when she died?'

'No. With the cameras and everyone excited on the bridge, I managed to get through unseen and cut the cord. I knew that once McAlister died, there would be an attempt to make sure no one left the scene. I melted into the background before he jumped and then disappeared. No one missed me, and if they did, they probably thought I'd chickened out.'

Isaac went into the other room, phoned Henstridge and updated him as to the situation.

'I've seen it before,' Henstridge's reply. 'Although a plea of insanity won't go far.'

Isaac expanded on Hampton's condition to Henstridge, his ability to walk, his determination to confess. He had possibly said more than he should have, and it would be imperative for independent and police-accredited personnel to check Hampton, but Henstridge was on the phone. More importantly, as the senior officer in Homicide, Isaac could see that the confession, so freely given, was lacking in crucial details. And if Hampton was also confessing to climbing up twenty-one flights of stairs and shooting Simmons, then where was the rifle, which river had he thrown it in.

Isaac wasn't a psychoanalyst, but he knew inconsistencies when he heard and saw them.

'Will he improve from here?' Isaac asked.

'It depends if the physical recovery is complete.'

'He killed the wrong person, feels remorse. With his confession, we can't leave him at the house.'

'If he can walk, then he can travel in your vehicle.'

Isaac ended the phone call, went into the other room. Hampton was writing a confession.

Twenty minutes later, Hampton looked up. 'There you are,' he said as he pushed three sheets of paper across the table. 'Either you type it up here, and I'll sign it, or we do it at the police station.'

'You seem anxious,' Isaac said.

'Tired of living a lie.'

'Sign them for now,' Larry said. 'We'll get it typed up at the station, get you to sign that it's an exact copy of what you've just written, but the original remains the primary document.'

'Have you included both murders?' Isaac asked.

'Only Tricia Warburton's for the present. She's the only one I regret. I'm sure you understand.'

Isaac didn't, but for now, what they had would suffice.

On the trip back to the police station, the wheelchair folded up, and in the boot of the vehicle, Hampton said nothing, only closing his eyes and falling asleep.

'I'm not sure what to make of this,' Isaac said to Larry, who was sitting alongside Hampton in the back seat.

'An itch you can't scratch?'

'That's it.'

No one spoke again until the three arrived at the station. Hampton preferred to walk to the interview room than to take the chair that Larry wheeled behind.

Chapter 25

Chief Superintendent Goddard was delighted. Two murders solved, one with a signed confession. It was to him a red-letter day, a chance to praise his team in Homicide, to let his superiors know that once again, under his tutelage, his people had delivered.

Isaac Cook, a man who had known Goddard from the first week he had joined the force, could not share in his senior's evident joy. Something niggled him, or as Larry had said, an itch he couldn't scratch.

'You worry too much, Isaac,' Goddard said as the two men sat in the Chief Superintendent's office, up high on the top floor.

Isaac had taken the stairs up the three storeys, preferring not to use the lift, conscious that he didn't exercise as much as he used to, a thickening around the waist, a flabbiness in the jowls.

Now free of his chief superintendent, Isaac sat in the interview room with Larry; Hampton was on the other side of the table with his lawyer friend, Duncan Harders.

'I've advised my client that he was unwise to give a confession,' Harders said.

'It's signed,' Isaac said.

'Even so, I will argue that it was a confession made under duress: a disabled man in a precarious mental condition, badgered by the police.'

'Mr Harders, the facts are damning. Firstly, Mr Hampton was at the bungee jump, and secondly, and more importantly, he has consistently hidden from us and those closest to him that he is not confined to a wheelchair. You do acknowledge that last fact?'

'I acknowledge both. It would be pointless to deny the evidence.'

'Duncan, I appreciate what you're doing,' Hampton said, 'but it's not necessary. I was there; I cut the cord.'

Ignoring his client, Harders continued. 'A man confessing without the supporting evidence is not guilty. I've seen the footage, and nowhere can I see where Mr Hampton bent down and cut the cord. My client may well feel sadness that his hatred of McAlister was indirectly responsible for an innocent woman's death, but the facts don't point to murder.'

'Why was Mr Hampton at the bungee jump? Surely you're not going to say that he intended to make the jump later on?'

'I'm not. My client had intended to confront McAlister, to argue with him, and try and reason with him if it was possible. After all, they had been friends once.'

'Fellow mountaineers, two men who placed trust in each other, doesn't make for a friendship.'

'The chief inspector is right,' Hampton said. 'I didn't like him, never did. Although if he said the bungee jump was safe, it was.'

'Yet you managed to sneak through, cut the cord and then get away?' Larry said.

'I did,' Hampton replied. To add emphasis, he stood up, pushed the wheelchair away, grabbed a chair in one corner of the room, pulled it up to the desk and sat down.

'The knife?'

'I tossed it out of the car window as I drove. Don't ask me where because I can't remember.'

281

'Why? You've just doomed a man to his death. People usually experience heightened emotions after committing a murder, and they can remember everything in infinite detail.'

'It was on the radio that the woman had died. I wasn't thinking straight. I tossed the knife not far from the house. I could show you, but I doubt if it's still there.'

'Why? It's hardly likely to have got up on its own and moved.'

'My client is confused. I am requesting a thorough mental examination be conducted before we proceed further,' Harders said.

'The purpose of this investigation is to confirm that your client committed the murder, not whether his mind was disturbed,' Isaac reminded the lawyer.

'I'm protecting my client from himself, arguing that he is not in a fit state and that any confession he has given is invalid.'

Isaac thought Harders' approach unusual but saw no point in pursuing it further. Instead, there was another murder that he needed to focus on.

'Mr Hampton, you admitted to shooting Angus Simmons,' Isaac said.

'I did.'

'Yet, you have still not written a confession.'

'I will be tried and sentenced for one murder. Why should I give you the benefit of two? The first death was justifiable. I do not regard Angus Simmons's death as murder. My lawyer would back me up on this.'

'Would you?' Isaac said to Harders.

'I would advise my client to act in his best interests.'

'You're not concerned that two people have died?' Larry asked, perturbed at the man's attitude.

'I am here in a professional capacity; your question is irrelevant.'

'The defence of your client is more important,' Isaac said. 'That's understood. However, a confession for the first murder is required; otherwise, we will continue to investigate. Whether he is tried for both is not for us to debate here.'

'I'll confess, I was there. It was me that took the shot,' Hampton said.

'Is that it? Three sentences, no more?'

'What more do you want?'

'You wrote close to one thousand words detailing how you were on the bridge, how you severed the cord and threw the knife away. Yet, Angus Simmons dies, and you give us platitudes.'

'It was soon after I found that I could walk again. My mental state was confused after so long, with no movement. How would you feel?'

'I imagine I would be confused,' Isaac said, 'although revenge would have been the last thing on my mind, more a need to tell those nearest and dearest, to tell the world.'

'What you would do is not relevant,' Harders said. 'My client couldn't have committed the first murder, not up those stairs. How could he?'

'I agree,' Isaac said.

'It was me; I killed him,' Hampton said. 'I've told you the make of gun, and I had the anger. McAlister's proved that.'

'Has he? He's got a recording of the two of you arguing, and he was the first one to say you could walk, but that's it. And are you telling us that with your life returning, revenge was all you could think of?'

'It was.'

283

'Mr Harders, Mr Hampton is either lying or confused,' Isaac said. 'I just walked up three floors to the chief superintendent's office. I'm relatively fit, but I had to catch my breath at the top. Yet Mr Hampton can climb over twenty floors of a high-rise under construction, clambering over builders' rubble on the way, negotiating rebar and concrete.'

'He couldn't,' Harders said.

'I did,' Hampton remained adamant.

'I suggest that we wrap up the interview for now,' Isaac said. 'It's clear that Mr Hampton could not have shot Angus Simmons and that either he is delusional, or he's protecting someone. This will require further investigation by Homicide.'

'Mr Hampton's status?' Harders asked.

'Mr Hampton will remain in custody. He will receive the appropriate medical care.'

***

Larry and Wendy met with Jim Breslaw to see if he remembered anything untoward at the second murder and if he had further recollections of the first.

There was a look of decay in the man's garden, the lawn too long, flowers wilting, a pile of rubbish next to a bin.

'Gone off gardening?' Larry said.

'Life in general,' Breslaw, unshaven, unkempt and slovenly dressed, responded.

'You must be used to it by now,' Wendy said.

'If you mean receiving the sharp end of Jerome Jaden's boot, then I am.'

'Do you blame him?'

'Not really. He'll come out of it smelling of roses.'

'What does that mean?'

'I've known the man a long time, know what makes him tick, what drives him.'

'Are you suggesting that he's come out on top?'

'No need to prove it; I just know he has.'

'Is that because you believe it?'

'In the early days, Jerome would stake his house to get the money, constantly take a risk, always keeping an eye on the bigger picture. Whatever's happened, whether he was responsible or not, he will have been weighing up the angles, looking for maximum effect, the chance to fill his pockets, to let others take the loss.'

'You, for instance,' Larry asked.

'Not me. I'm only a small fish, but he used Simmons's death to deride me publicly, and now, with Tricia, he'll do the same if it's to his advantage.'

'Do you think he feels sorry for the two deaths?'

'Not Jerome. A charming man to those he likes or wants to influence, but he's devious, as slithery as a snake, twice as dangerous.'

'Mr Breslaw,' Larry said, 'you were there when Tricia Warburton died.'

'I was, but not on the bridge. I had stood back, ensuring that everything was in place, looking at a monitor, interested in camera angles, making sure the focus was on Tricia, as nervous as she was.'

'She wasn't happy to be there?'

'Happy to be in the limelight, but not the jump. It was Jerome who had persuaded her and McAlister who had guaranteed her safety.'

'In which McAlister had failed. Did you see the other man, this Ivor Putreski?'

'I would have seen him, not that I would have taken too much notice; after all, it was Tricia that the viewers were interested in. We thought it would look better if we got a few paying customers up there on the bridge with her, make out it was a regular jump.'

'Wasn't it?'

'It was, but if it were her on her own, then the public would have thought she was getting privileged treatment.'

'Not in the overalls she was wearing,' Wendy said.

'Even so, she still looked glamourous. The two other women who were to jump later didn't look as good as her, but that we had agreed. We couldn't have Tricia overshadowed by one of the paying customers.'

'Coming back to Putreski, and allowing for the fact that he wasn't the primary focus, you must have spoken to him, asked him to sign a video consent form.'

'I wouldn't have, but one of the production crew would. Nothing untoward in that, just ask the man's permission, get him to sign a form: name, address, phone number, email address. No need for a person to prove their identity. No one ever refuses.'

'If we look at the video you took, we can't see when Putreski cut the cord,' Larry said.

'Focus was on Tricia and McAlister, nobody else. Most of the time, those in the background wouldn't have been in focus, so it's not surprising if nothing was seen. How he did it, I've no idea, and McAlister checked everything twice, made a nuisance of himself.'

'You didn't approve?'

'I did, but we were running to a tight schedule, and the cutovers to us were scheduled down to the second, no room for error, no possibility of telling them to hang on for a few minutes while we get sorted out.'

'McAlister jumped to the second?'

'He did. After that, he's pulled up and a cutaway to a commercial break. Long enough for McAlister to adjust the cord length for her weight, and then there's Tricia in place, one of the bungee team instructing her, tying the cord to her legs, telling her to splay her arms and to scream on the way down.'

'The radio mic?'

'She had one; it was working, but we removed her earpiece, didn't want it falling out, or getting jammed in her ear.'

'Was that likely?'

'The jamming? Not really, but we didn't need it, and besides, once she's completed the jump and she's dangling there, she could speak, tell the viewers about her excitement, what was coming up in the new programme.'

'Even if her voice was shaky, her nerves were on edge?'

'All the better. We weren't worried about Tricia, and, as I've already said, McAlister was thorough.'

'Could Putreski, or someone else, in your opinion, cut that cord without anyone seeing?'

'I'm not sure. We had more than one camera. One focussed on Tricia, another on McAlister, and another off to one side of the bridge,' Breslaw said. 'We should have picked up anything out of the ordinary, and as you've seen the footage and not found anything, there's no more I can say or do.'

'The first death?' Wendy said.

'I wasn't there.'

'But you approved the climb?'

'I did, so did Jerome, not that he'll admit to it now.'

'Does that annoy you?'

'I never expected any more. Nor did I expect Angus to fall. After all, it's not as difficult as it looks, and if you check the building close up, there are plenty of places to hold on to. Easy for a man of Angus's abilities.'

'Even so, Jerome Jaden knew that the station's revenue is going down and that there was a cost-cutting exercise in place.'

'He would have had a contingency plan. I'm glad I got out when I did, not my choice at the time, but those remaining better hope they get a full payout.'

'He'll cheat them?'

'He won't see it that way.'

'You appear to have given up,' Wendy said.

'I've embraced retirement. I am no longer chasing after work or pandering to Jerome Jaden. It used to be fun, but now, too many deaths, others thrown on the scrapheap. I've no intention of becoming one of them. The house is paid for, my needs are few, and here, I don't need to worry unduly. I'll slowly wither on the vine, as it should be.'

Outside in the street, Larry lit up a cigarette and blew the smoke up into the air.

'Any wiser?' Larry said to Wendy.

'He's right about Tricia Warburton's death. Someone must have seen something.'

'Hampton's confession?'

'He could have killed the woman by accident.'

'But not Angus Simmons.'

'Are we certain McAlister was the intended target?'

'We have to be. Who would have wanted Tricia dead? And if they did, where does she fit into the saga?'

Chapter 26

Isaac and Wendy made the trip down to Deb Hampton's farm in Dorset. 'You've arrested Mike?' she said after opening the door at the farmhouse.

'You've not visited him?' Wendy asked.

'No reason to, and besides, I've got a wedding to organise, and Mike will never see the inside of a prison.'

'He's in a cell,' Isaac said.

'You know he'll spend his days in an institution for the criminally insane.'

'It seems as if you're pleased,' Wendy said.

'Our mother was unstable, not that she ever killed anyone. Madness runs in the family. What do you want me to say or do?'

'Compassion wouldn't be a bad place to start,' Isaac said. 'We need to talk.'

'Five minutes while I find Jock, tell him what needs doing.'

Inside the farmhouse, after Deb Hampton had removed her overalls, washed her hands, rubbed a flannel over her face, the three sat down close to an open fire, the dog in between them and the flames.

'He'll not stay long, prefers the cold outside most of the time,' she said.

'Jock?'

'He's good for me, and he'll not let me down, not like others.'

'Your father? Your brother?' Isaac said.

'Our parents ensured we had food in our bellies, a decent education, but children want more than that. They want love, to be told they're wanted.'

'You weren't?'

'Rarely, and then it was begrudgingly. At Christmas, a hug. Apart from that, never. It stuffed me up for a while, the reason for the bikers' gang, and Mike, well, you know about him.'

'What do we know?'

'His depressive nature, his single-mindedness.'

'His ability to walk.'

'I didn't know, honestly. I know what the doctor had said, but Mike said there was no reason to try. I can't blame Kate for running out on him, but that Skinner, what a choice.'

'If she had chosen Simmons?'

'I would have understood.'

'And yet, you hated Angus,' Isaac said. 'Is it because of your childhood, forged in adversity, that you and Mike remained connected as adults, a unique closeness?'

'I don't understand.'

Wendy didn't either. She looked at her chief inspector, a perplexed look. 'Nor do I,' she said.

'The inseparable bond, brother and sister, finding solace in each other, and Kate in the middle, but she was an inconvenience. And there's Deb, patronised by Angus, treated as a sister, wanting more.'

'I did love him, you're correct there, but as a brother,' Deb said.

'It was more than that. Your brother, you couldn't have, but his greatest friend you could. Did you make a play for him, get a knockback? Is that why you were unpleasant to Maddox Timberley, the woman who had what you couldn't?'

'I was unpleasant because she was using him for her benefit.'

'She loved him,' Wendy said. 'With him, she felt safe.'

'I've seen her on the media, a new man, making out in public.'

'I can't say I approve of her behaviour, but she's back with her mother now.'

'Did Angus reject you?' Isaac asked. 'Did you love him, not as a brother, but as something more?'

'Always, from the first time I met him. Every time I brought up the subject, Angus would say that I was his sister, the sister he never had. Laughed at me, that last time, when I told him about my feelings for him, that I still cared,' Deb said.

'When? Just before the accident?'

'Two months before. I was up there for a few days, the two of them planning the trip.'

'And then, after your brother accused Angus of letting him fall, the pieces fell into place. The rejection, the accident, the hatred your brother had for Angus, the anger you couldn't help, reciprocating emotions with your brother.'

'Alright, I did hate him. Not at first when Mike came back in an air ambulance, not when he was in that hospital, but in time, I could see it. Angus, charming, loved by everyone, an optimistic outlook on life, and my brother, sullen, unloved, loved by me, fleetingly by Kate. I understood my brother; you wouldn't.'

'It was you, wasn't it? It was you that took that shot?'

'DCI!' Wendy exclaimed. She was shocked by his accusation.

'How dare you?' Deb said.

'You knew of the unresolved issues with your brother, remembered that last rejection. You decided to act,' Isaac said. 'You had spent time with a bikers' gang. You would have witnessed violence, received it more than once. No doubt the occasional ritual, the slaying of other gangs' members. Death didn't concern you.'

'You can't prove that.'

'Wendy, phone for a couple of uniforms from the local police station, cordon this place off.'

'Gordon Windsor?' Wendy said.

'They can come down as soon as possible. For now, take hold of that rifle leaning up against the wall in the other room, put it into an evidence bag. We found the bullet, didn't we?'

'They did at the Shard. Are you saying…?'

'That rifle fired the shot at Angus Simmons. That's what I'm saying. Deborah Hampton, what about you?'

'Mike wasn't responsible for that woman's death; you do know that? He never killed anyone.'

'I do now.'

Wendy went out to the car, took an evidence bag from the boot. In the house, on her return, Deb looked at Wendy. 'I did it for Mike, don't you see?'

'The uniforms?' Isaac said.

'Five minutes. I'm not pleased with this,' Wendy said.

'Nor am I.'

After another two hours, with Deb Hampton locked in a cell in Dorset and with Gordon Windsor and his team on their way down to check the house, Isaac and

Wendy drove back to London. The arrested woman would be transferred to London the next day.

Jock, unable to comprehend the situation, returned to his farm, promising to come over the next day and check on the place.

***

Jerome Jaden did not appreciate the chief inspector's attitude, and he wasn't slow to let him know.

'What are you accusing me of, Cook?'

'I'm accusing you of duplicity. Of letting Tricia Warburton believe she was to be the star of a new show, even going so far as to present her with a contract, knowing full well that you had no intention of honouring the agreement.'

'I didn't kill her, did I?'

'Indirectly, you did. Not that you'll let your conscience get in the way. How much did you gain from her death? How much from Simmons's?'

'Nothing. They both hurt ratings.'

'But now you're running documentaries on the two of them, making out that your station stands for law and order, new programmes focussed on crime and the breakdown of society. Are more people watching your station? Is the advertising revenue up?' Isaac asked.

'I admit that I took the opportunity to bolster the revenue, lift the stock price in this company, and cover further losses. That's not deceitful or malicious; that's good business practice.'

'When were you going to tell her that the programme wasn't going to happen?'

'She would still have had a programme, but it would be based in this country, and she'd have to do her bit. No more every man's fancy, but someone who'd be willing to get dirty, to take a risk.'

'To jump off a bridge,' Larry said.

'As you say. How was I to know that the cord was going to break?'

'You weren't. What had you told McAlister? Offered him her job? No doubt he was a lot cheaper than her, and you only needed to fill the time slot. You've just admitted that financially you're covered.'

'It's still the company I set up. I don't want it to fold.'

'No doubt you don't, but you're a pragmatist, not an ideological fool. If it's over, then you'll walk away with your money and your reputation intact.'

'You're right, Chief Inspector. How did you figure this out?'

'It was obvious. Once I had proved that Hampton's sister shot Angus Simmons, the pieces fell into place, and as Breslaw had said, with the number of cameras focussed on the bridge, there was no way that Mike Hampton could have cut that cord.'

'And now?' Jaden said.

'Are you about to tell your people that you're financially secure, but they're not?'

'That's for me to decide, not for me to answer. I've broken no law.'

'Breslaw reckoned he got out at the right time. It seems that man knows you better than anyone else.'

'He should. We set this station up together. He is, regardless of what he may say about me, the only person I owe any allegiance to. As to you, Chief Inspector, I would appreciate it if you and your inspector leave my office.'

'With pleasure,' Isaac said.

***

Otto McAlister sat in the interview room. He listened to the facts as they were laid out. He was told that Deb Hampton had taken the shot at Angus Simmons and subsequently confessed. And that he had been right, in that Mike Hampton was capable of walking, and there was the possibility of a full recovery.

Jerome Jaden confirmed that Tricia Warburton would never get the programme she had signed a contract for. And he had inferred that Otto McAlister was a possible replacement host and that he had covered his losses and didn't care either way.

'I still don't understand,' McAlister said. A legal aid sat to one side, not saying much, unlikely to get a chance. Detective Chief Inspector Isaac Cook of the Challis Street Police Station, Homicide, was on a roll. He wasn't about to be stopped by anyone.

'Then let me spell it out in simple terms that you'll understand,' Isaac said. 'Otto McAlister, you murdered Tricia Warburton, not through neglect, but because you saw Mike Hampton standing near you. How did you expect to get away with it?'

'I saw him there. I assumed he wanted to talk to me, to have it out with me, and pressure me not to tell Ashley Otway any more. And hasn't he confessed to both murders?'

'He has, but Mike Hampton's no fool. He had suspected his sister, not because he wanted to, but because he had told Deb that he wanted Simmons dead, to pay him back for what he had done to him. Deb Hampton had a rough life as a child and then as an adult,

295

and she has admitted that madness ran in the family. She killed Simmons for her brother, for herself.

'Mike Hampton confessed to two murders, not because he had committed either, but his confession of Tricia Warburton's death would not be easy to disprove. After all, he had been there, and if he had confessed to one murder, then the other one wouldn't be doubted, not if his condition continued to improve. He saw a solution on how to protect his sister, not that she had ever admitted it to him, but the bond between Mike and Deb is deep, deeper than any of us would understand. And you, Otto McAlister, would have got away with murder.'

'If he thought all that up, he's as mad as his sister,' McAlister said.

'He might be, but that's not why we're here. When did you decide to kill Tricia Warburton?'

'I didn't. Why should I?'

'Here's what I reckon,' Isaac said. 'You're up there. You've checked the cord, taken a jump. It's safe for Tricia Warburton, and you know that if she's successful, your chance of a job with Jaden is slim. You're enamoured of fame, of being recognised as someone important, a better class of women. After all, you had Ashley Otway, and you want more women like her, not the usual easy lays, but you can't see a way around it.

'You're committed to making sure Tricia's safe, but there's Hampton. He's disguised, but you know the man well, can see that it's him standing there. You're on the bridge, a split-second decision, knowing that we will recognise Hampton in time and he'll get the blame.'

'I deny it.'

'I've not finished. It's a decision you could make on a mountain, whether to cut the climber's rope below to save your skin and that of others. Have you ever made such a decision?'

'No.'

'Has Mike Hampton or Angus Simmons? Was it Simmons who caused Hampton to fall, or was it the other way around? Or was it an accident?'

'Who knows?'

'Precisely. It might have been Simmons for all we know, but that's unimportant. The bridge, a split-second. You kneel, we've got that on camera, the bungee jump crew jostling to get their faces on the television. You can see that Hampton had walked away, probably decided it wasn't worth it. Is that how it was?'

'You can't prove it.'

'Can't we? What if I told you there was another camera focussed on that bridge, a keen amateur making home videos?'

'Okay, it was me. I wasn't sure if it would break, but I reacted impulsively, saw a way out of the malaise of my life.'

'So, you destroy a life for selfish reasons.'

'If you led my life, you'd understand.'

'I wouldn't. A full confession?'

'Prison can't be much worse.'

'You had Ashley Otway. That was a benefit,' Isaac said.

'A highlight, but what does it matter?'

Isaac could have told the man that prison would be a lot worse. He had killed a beautiful and popular television personality, the type of woman that men in prison lust after. His life would be hell. It was what he deserved.

In the corridor outside, Larry spoke. 'I don't remember an amateur photographer.'

'Nor do I. Go through the footage we have, check McAlister's house, conduct an extensive search under the bridge, look for a knife. We'll find it. I'm sure of that.'

Two days later, Maddox Timberley left for the Caribbean. One week after Jerome Jaden resigned as his company's chief executive officer, Tom Taylor met with Ashley Otway.

The End

ALSO BY THE AUTHOR

DI Tremayne Thriller Series

Death Unholy – A DI Tremayne Thriller – Book 1

All that remained were the man's two legs and a chair full of greasy and fetid ash. Little did DI Keith Tremayne know that it was the beginning of a journey into the murky world of paganism and its ancient rituals. And it was going to get very dangerous.

'Do you believe in spontaneous human combustion?' Detective Inspector Keith Tremayne asked.

'Not me. I've read about it. Who hasn't?' Sergeant Clare Yarwood answered.

'I haven't,' Tremayne replied, which did not surprise his young sergeant. In the months they had been working together, she had come to realise that he was a man who had little interest in the world. When he had a cigarette in his mouth, a beer in his hand, and a murder to solve he was about the happiest she ever saw him, but even then he could hardly be regarded as one of life's most sociable people. And as for reading? The most he managed was an occasional police report, an early-morning newspaper, turning first to the back pages for the racing results.

Death and the Assassin's Blade – A DI Tremayne Thriller – Book 2

It was meant to be high drama, not murder, but someone's switched the daggers. The man's death took place in plain view of two serving police officers.

He was not meant to die; the daggers were only theatrical props, plastic and harmless. A summer's night, a production of Julius Caesar amongst the ruins of an Anglo-Saxon fort. Detective Inspector Tremayne is there with his sergeant, Clare Yarwood. In the assassination scene, Caesar collapses to the ground. Brutus defends his actions; Mark Antony rebukes him.

They're a disparate group, the amateur actors. One's an estate agent, another an accountant. And then there is the teenage school student, the gay man, the funeral director. And what about the women? They could be involved.

They've each got a secret, but which of those on the stage wanted Gordon Mason, the actor who had portrayed Caesar, dead?

Death and the Lucky Man – A DI Tremayne Thriller – Book 3

Sixty-eight million pounds and dead. Hardly the outcome expected for the luckiest man in England the day his lottery ticket was drawn out of the barrel. But then, Alan Winters' rags-to-riches story had never been conventional, and some had benefited, but others hadn't.

Death at Coombe Farm – A DI Tremayne Thriller – Book 4

A warring family. A disputed inheritance. A recipe for death.

If it hadn't been for the circumstances, Detective Inspector Keith Tremayne would have said the view was outstanding. Up high, overlooking the farmhouse in the valley below, the panoramic vista of Salisbury Plain stretching out beyond. The only problem was that near where he stood with his sergeant, Clare Yarwood, there was a body, and it wasn't a pleasant sight.

Death by a Dead Man's Hand – A DI Tremayne Thriller – Book 5

A flawed heist of forty gold bars from a security van late at night. One of the perpetrators is killed by his brother as they argue over what they have stolen.

Eighteen years later, the murderer, released after serving his sentence for his brother's murder, waits in a church for a man purporting to be the brother he killed. And then he too is killed.

The threads stretch back a long way, and now more people are dying in the search for the missing gold bars.

Detective Inspector Tremayne, his health causing him concern, and Sergeant Clare Yarwood, still seeking romance, are pushed to the limit solving the murder, attempting to prevent any more.

Death in the Village – A DI Tremayne Thriller – Book 6

Phillip Strang

Nobody liked Gloria Wiggins, a woman who regarded anyone who did not acquiesce to her jaundiced view of the world with disdain. James Baxter, the previous vicar, had been one of those, and her scurrilous outburst in the church one Sunday had hastened his death.

And now, years later, the woman was dead, hanging from a beam in her garage. Detective Inspector Tremayne and Sergeant Clare Yarwood had seen the body, interviewed the woman's acquaintances, and those who had hated her.

Burial Mound – A DI Tremayne Thriller – Book 7

A Bronze-Age burial mound close to Stonehenge. An archaeological excavation. What they were looking for was an ancient body and historical artefacts. They found the ancient body, but then they found a modern-day body too. And then the police became interested.

It's another case for Detective Inspector Tremayne and Sergeant Yarwood. The more recent body was the brother of the mayor of Salisbury.

Everything seems to point to the victim's brother, the mayor, the upright and serious-minded Clive Grantley. Tremayne's sure that it's him, but Clare Yarwood's not so sure.

But is her belief based on evidence or personal hope?

The Body in the Ditch – A DI Tremayne Thriller – Book 8

A group of children play. Not far away, in the ditch on the other side of the farmyard, the body of a troubled young woman.

The nearby village hides as many secrets as the community at the farm, a disparate group of people looking for an alternative to their previous torturous lives. Their leader, idealistic and benevolent, espouses love and kindness, and clearly, somebody's not following his dictate.

The second death, an old woman, seems unrelated to the first, but is it? Is it part of the tangled web that connects the farm to the village?

The village, Detective Inspector Tremayne and Sergeant Clare Yarwood find out soon enough, is anything, but charming and picturesque. It's an incestuous hotbed of intrigue and wrongdoing, and what of the farm and those who live there. None of them can be ruled out, not yet.

The Horse's Mouth – A DI Tremayne Thriller – Book 9

A day at the races for Detective Inspector Tremayne, idyllic at the outset, soon changes. A horse is dead, and then the owner's daughter is found murdered, and Tremayne's there when the body is discovered.

The question is, was Tremayne set up, in the wrong place at the right time? He's the cast-iron alibi for one of the suspects, and he knows that one murder leads to two, and more often than not, to three.

The dead woman had a chequered history, not as much as her father, and then a man commits suicide. Is he the murderer, or was he the unfortunate consequence of a tragic love affair? And who was it in the stable with the woman just before she died? There is more than one person who could have killed her, and all of them have secrets they would rather not be known.

Tremayne's health is troubling him. Is what they are saying correct? Is it time for him to retire, to take it easy and to put his feet up? But that's not his style, and he'll not give up on solving the murder.

DCI Isaac Cook Thriller Series

Murder is a Tricky Business – A DCI Cook Thriller – Book 1

A television actress is missing, and DCI Isaac Cook, the Senior Investigation Officer of the Murder Investigation Team at Challis Street Police Station in London, is searching for her.

Why has he been taken away from more important crimes to search for the woman? It's not the first time she's gone missing, so why does everyone assume she's been murdered?

There's a secret, that much is certain, but who knows it? The missing woman? The executive producer? His eavesdropping assistant? Or the actor who portrayed her fictional brother in the TV soap opera?

Murder House – A DCI Cook Thriller – Book 2

A corpse in the fireplace of an old house. It's been there for thirty years, but who is it?

It's murder, but who is the victim and what connection does the body have to the previous owners of the house. What is the motive? And why is the body in a fireplace? It was bound to be discovered eventually but was that what the murderer wanted? The main suspects are all old and dying, or already dead.

Isaac Cook and his team have their work cut out, trying to put the pieces together. Those who know are not talking because of an old-fashioned belief that a family's dirty laundry should not be aired in public, and never to a policeman – even if that means the murderer is never brought to justice!

Murder is Only a Number – A DCI Cook Thriller – Book 3

Before she left, she carved a number in blood on his chest. But why the number 2, if this was her first murder?

The woman prowls the streets of London. Her targets are men who have wronged her. Or have they? And why is she keeping count?

DCI Cook and his team finally know who she is, but not before she's murdered four men. The whole team are looking for her, but the woman keeps disappearing in plain sight. The pressure's on to stop her, but she's always one step ahead.

And this time, DCS Goddard can't protect his protégé, Isaac Cook, from the wrath of the new commissioner at the Met.

Murder in Little Venice – A DCI Cook Thriller – Book 4

A dismembered corpse floats in the canal in Little Venice, an upmarket tourist haven in London. Its identity is unknown, but what is its significance?

DCI Isaac Cook is baffled about why it's there. Is it gang-related, or is it something more?

Whatever the reason, it's clearly a warning, and Isaac and his team are sure it's not the last body that they'll have to deal with.

Murder is the Only Option – A DCI Cook Thriller – Book 5

A man thought to be long dead returns to exact revenge against those who had blighted his life. His only concern is to protect his wife and daughter. He will stop at nothing to achieve his aim.

'Big Greg, I never expected to see you around here at this time of night.'

'I've told you enough times.'

'I've no idea what you're talking about,' Robertson replied. He looked up at the man, only to see a metal pole coming down at him. Robertson fell down, cracking his head against a concrete kerb.

Two vagrants, no more than twenty feet away, did not stir and did not even look in the direction of the noise. If they had, they would have seen a dead body, another man walking away.

Murder in Notting Hill – A DCI Cook Thriller – Book 6

One murderer, two bodies, two locations, and the murders have been committed within an hour of each other.

They're separated by a couple of miles, and neither woman has anything in common with the other. One is young and wealthy, the daughter of a famous man; the other is poor, hardworking and unknown.

Isaac Cook and his team at Challis Street Police Station are baffled about why they've been killed. There must be a connection, but what is it?

Murder in Room 346 – A DCI Cook Thriller – Book 7

'Coitus interruptus, that's what it is,' Detective Chief Inspector Isaac Cook said. On the bed, in a downmarket hotel in Bayswater, lay the naked bodies of a man and a woman.

'Bullet in the head's not the way to go,' Larry Hill, Isaac Cook's detective inspector, said. He had not expected such a flippant comment from his senior, not when they were standing near to two people who had, apparently in the final throes of passion, succumbed to what appeared to be a professional assassination.

'You know this will be all over the media within the hour,' Isaac said.

'James Holden, moral crusader, a proponent of the sanctity of the marital bed, man and wife. It's bound to be.'

Murder of a Silent Man – A DCI Cook Thriller – Book 8

A murdered recluse. A property empire. A disinherited family. All the ingredients for murder.

No one gave much credence to the man when he was alive. In fact, most people never knew who he was, although those who had lived in the area for many years recognised the tired-looking and shabbily-dressed man as he shuffled along, regular as clockwork on a Thursday afternoon at seven in the evening to the local off-licence.

It was always the same: a bottle of whisky, premium brand, and a packet of cigarettes. He paid his money over the counter, took hold of his plastic bag containing his purchases, and then walked back down the road with the same rhythmic shuffle. He said not one word to anyone on the street or in the shop.

Murder has no Guilt – A DCI Cook Thriller – Book 9

No one knows who the target was or why, but there are eight dead. The men seem the most likely perpetrators, or could have it been one of the two women, the attractive Gillian Dickenson, or even the celebrity-obsessed Sal Maynard?

There's a gang war brewing, and if there are deaths, it doesn't matter to them as long as it's not their death. But to Detective Chief Inspector Isaac Cook, it's his area of London, and it does matter.

It's dirty and unpredictable. Initially it had been the West Indian gangs, but then a more vicious Romanian gangster had usurped them. And now he's being marginalised by the Russians. And the leader of the most vicious Russian mafia organisation is in London, and he's got money and influence, the ear of those in power.

Murder in Hyde Park – A DCI Cook Thriller – Book 10

An early morning jogger is murdered in Hyde Park. It's the centre of London, but no one saw him enter the park, no one saw him die.

He carries no identification, only a water-logged phone. As the pieces unravel, it's clear that the dead man had a history of deception.

Is the murderer one of those that loved him? Or was it someone with a vengeance?

It's proving difficult for DCI Isaac Cook and his team at Challis Street Homicide to find the guilty person – not that they'll cease to search for the truth, not even after one suspect confesses.

Six Years Too Late – A DCI Cook Thriller – Book 11

Always the same questions for Detective Chief Inspector Isaac Cook — Why was Marcus Matthews in that room? And why did he share a bottle of wine with his killer?

It wasn't as if the man had amounted to much in life, apart from the fact that he was the son-in-law of a notorious gangster, the father of the man's grandchildren. Yet, one thing that Hamish McIntyre, feared in London for his violence, rated above anything else, it was his family, especially Samantha, his daughter; although he had never cared for Marcus, her husband.

And then Marcus disappears, only for his body to be found six years later by a couple of young boys who decide that exploring an abandoned house is preferable to school.

Grave Passion – A DCI Cook Thriller – Book 12

Two young lovers out for a night of romance. A short cut through a cemetery. They witness a murder, but there has been no struggle, only a knife to the heart.

It has all the hallmarks of an assassination, but who is the woman? And why was she alongside a grave at night? Did she know the person who killed her?

Soon after, other deaths, seemingly unconnected, but tied to the family of one of the young lovers.

It's a case for Detective Chief Inspector Cook and his team, and they're baffled on this one.

The Slaying of Joe Foster – A DCI Cook Thriller – Book 13

No one challenged Joe Foster in life, not if they valued theirs. And then, the gangster is slain, his criminal empire up for grabs.

A power vacuum; the Foster family is fighting for control, the other gangs in the area aiming to poach the trade in illegal drugs, to carve up the empire that the father had created.

It has all the makings of a war on the streets, something nobody wants, not even the other gangs.

Terry Foster, the eldest son of Joe, the man who should take control, doesn't have the temperament of his father, nor the wisdom. His solution is slash and burn, and it's not going to work, and people are going to get hurt, some of them are going to die.

Murder Without Reason – A DCI Cook Thriller – Book 15

DCI Cook faces his greatest challenge. The Islamic State is waging war in England, and they are winning.

Not only does Isaac Cook have to contend with finding the perpetrators, but he is also being forced to commit actions contrary to his mandate as a police officer.

And then there is Anne Argento, the prime minister's deputy. The prime minister has shown himself to be a pacifist and is not up to the task. She needs to take his job if the country is to fight back against the Islamists.

Vane and Martin have provided the solution. Will DCI Cook and Anne Argento be willing to follow it through? Are they able to act for the good of England, knowing that a criminal and murderous action is about to take place? Do they have an option?

Standalone Novels

The Haberman Virus

A remote and isolated village in the Hindu Kush mountain range in North Eastern Afghanistan is wiped out by a virus unlike any seen before.

A mysterious visitor clad in a spacesuit checks his handiwork, a female American doctor succumbs to the disease, and the woman sent to trap the person responsible falls in love with him – the man who would cause the deaths of millions.

Hostage of Islam

Three are to die at the Mission in Nigeria: the pastor and his wife in a blazing chapel; another gunned down while trying to defend them from the Islamist fighters.

Kate McDonald, an American, grieving over her boyfriend's death and Helen Campbell, whose life had been troubled by drugs and prostitution, are taken by the attackers.

Kate is sold to a slave trader who intends to sell her virginity to an Arab Prince. Helen, to ensure their survival, gives herself to the murderer of her friends.

Malika's Revenge

Malika, a drug-addicted prostitute, waits in a smugglers' village for the next Afghan tribesman or Tajik gangster to pay her price, a few scraps of heroin.

Yusup Baroyev, a drug lord, enjoys a lifestyle many would envy. An Afghan warlord sees the resurgence of the Taliban. A Russian white-collar criminal portrays himself as a good and honest citizen in Moscow.

All of them are linked to an audacious plan to increase the quantity of heroin shipped out of Afghanistan and into Russia and ultimately the West.

Some will succeed, some will die, some will be rescued from their plight and others will rue the day they became involved.

Prelude to War

Russia and America face each other across the northern border of Afghanistan. World War 3 is about to break out and no one is backing off.

And all because a team of academics in New York postulated how to extract the vast untapped mineral wealth of Afghanistan.

Steve Case is in the middle of it, and his position is looking very precarious. Will the Taliban find him before the Americans get him out? Or is he doomed, as is the rest of the world?

ABOUT THE AUTHOR

Phillip Strang was born in England in the late forties. He was an avid reader of science fiction in his teenage years: Isaac Asimov, Frank Herbert, the masters of the genre. Still an avid reader, the author now mainly reads thrillers.

In his early twenties, the author, with a degree in electronics engineering and a desire to see the world, left England for Sydney, Australia. Now, forty years later, he still resides in Australia, although many intervening years were spent in a myriad of countries, some calm and safe, others no more than war zones.

Printed in Great Britain
by Amazon

75446563R00189